dead air

a savannah shadows thriller
book three

L.T. Ryan

with
Laura Chase

Copyright © 2025 by L.T. Ryan, Liquid Mind Media, LLC, & Laura Chase. All rights reserved. No part of this publication may be copied, reproduced in any format, by any means, electronic or otherwise, without prior consent from the copyright owner and publisher of this book. This is a work of fiction. All characters, names, places and events are the product of the author's imagination or used fictitiously.

For information contact:

contact@ltryan.com

http://LTRyan.com

https://www.facebook.com/JackNobleBooks

savannah shadows series

Echos of Guilt
The Silence Before
Dead Air

chapter one

THE NIGHT WAS OPPRESSIVELY humid with clouds gathering overhead, typical for Savannah in August. Detective Erin Lawson leaned against her unmarked car, the metal still warm beneath her palm despite the late hour. She wiped sweat from her forehead with the back of her hand and checked her watch for the third time in as many minutes. Monica was late.

They had agreed to meet at the abandoned warehouse at 11:00 p.m. sharp. Monica had called earlier, her voice tight with excitement. "I've got something big on the Rafferty case. Meet me at the old paper mill warehouse tonight. Come alone."

That last part had raised flags, but Lawson trusted her partner's judgment. Monica Landry had been with Savannah PD for eight years, two years longer than Lawson herself. They'd been partners for the last three years, and during the past eleven months, their relationship had evolved beyond the professional boundaries of the force—a fact they kept carefully hidden.

Lawson's phone buzzed. A text from Monica: *Two minutes away. Get ready.*

Lawson shoved her phone back into her pocket and drew her service weapon, checking it before returning it to her holster. The Rafferty investigation had been consuming their lives for months now—a drug trafficking operation that reached into the highest echelons of Savannah society. They were close to a breakthrough. Monica had been working her connections, and it seemed she'd finally hit pay dirt.

She took a long drag from her cigarette, the ember glowing orange in the darkness. The nicotine did little to calm her frayed nerves. The distant thrum of an engine broke the night's stillness. Headlights flashed once, briefly illuminating the crumbling brick facade of the warehouse. Lawson recognized Monica's silver sedan as it pulled alongside her own unmarked cruiser.

"Thought you'd quit," Monica said, nodding at the cigarette as she opened the door.

Lawson flicked ash onto the pavement. "I quit quitting. What took you so long?" Lawson asked as Monica stepped out.

"Had to shake a tail," Monica replied, glancing nervously over her shoulder. Stray tufts of her usually immaculate dark hair jutted out at wild angles, and her olive complexion looked pale even in the moonlight.

"A tail? What's going on? Why are we meeting here, anyway?" Lawson asked.

"I think someone at the precinct is compromised."

Lawson frowned. "That's a serious accusation."

"I know it is." Monica's eyes darted around the darkness surrounding them. "I've been following the money on the Rafferty case. The deeper I dig, the more convinced I am that someone's protecting their operation from the inside."

"You have proof?" Lawson asked, her pulse quickening.

Monica shook her head. "Not yet. But I have a source meeting me tonight. Says they have evidence—bank records, offshore accounts, the whole nine yards."

"Jesus," Lawson whispered. "When's this meeting?"

"Twenty minutes from now."

"Here? This place is—"

"Neutral ground," Monica interrupted. "My source picked it. Said it would be safe."

A flicker of unease crawled up Lawson's spine. "I don't like this, Mon. It feels off."

Monica reached out, her fingertips brushing against Lawson's wrist—the closest thing to public affection they ever allowed themselves. "Trust me, Erin. This is our chance to break this case wide open."

Lawson checked her watch again. "Fine. Twenty minutes. Then we take what we have to Internal Affairs, with or without your source."

Monica nodded, then tensed suddenly, her eyes fixed on something behind Lawson. "Did you hear that?"

Lawson turned, her hand moving to her holster. The warehouse loomed like a hulking beast, its windows black and empty. "Hear what?"

"I thought I heard—" Monica stopped, shaking her head. "Never mind. Probably just rats."

Lawson wasn't convinced. "Let's wait in my car."

They started toward the car when a sharp crack split the air. Lawson felt something whiz past her ear, followed by the metallic ping of a bullet striking her car door.

"Get down!" she yelled, drawing her weapon and pushing Monica toward the ground. They scrambled behind the cruiser as two more shots rang out, shattering the driver's side window.

"My source," Monica gasped. "It must be a setup."

Lawson peered around the car's bumper, trying to locate the shooter in the darkness. Another shot, this one closer, struck the pavement inches from her foot. The muzzle flash gave away the position—second-floor window of the warehouse.

"I'm calling for backup," Lawson said, reaching for her radio.

"No time," Monica replied, her own weapon drawn now. "We need to move. That car won't shield us for long."

Lawson nodded grimly. "On three, we make for the loading dock entrance. One ... two ..."

Before she could say "three," Monica was on her feet, sprinting toward the warehouse. Lawson cursed under her breath and followed, keeping low as another shot kicked up dirt at her heels. The loading dock was thirty yards away, exposed ground with no cover.

Lawson stood but a brilliant white floodlight suddenly blazed to life, mounted on the corner of the warehouse. The harsh beam swept across the lot, blinding her. She threw up her arm to shield her eyes, spots dancing in her vision.

In that blinding moment of vulnerability, a shot cracked through the night.

Lawson blinked to clear her vision. As the world came back into focus, she saw Monica standing exposed in the floodlight's merciless glare, her body jerking backward. A dark stain blossomed across her white blouse, spreading with terrifying speed.

"Monica!" Lawson screamed, lunging forward as her partner crumpled to the ground.

A figure emerged from the shadows at the edge of the light—just a silhouette, featureless and dark. Before Lawson could aim, the shooter melted back into the darkness, footsteps fading as they fled into the night.

Lawson reached Monica's side and dropped to her knees beside her fallen partner. Blood soaked Monica's clothes, hot and slick against Lawson's hands as she pressed down on the wound. Monica's eyes were wide with shock, her breathing already shallow and labored.

"I've got a 10-999! Officer down! Send help immediately!" Lawson shouted into her radio. "Warehouse district, old paper mill. Shots fired, officer down. Need immediate medical assistance!"

Monica's eyes fluttered weakly, her breathing shallow and rapid. Lawson pressed her hand against the wound in Monica's chest, feeling warm blood seep between her fingers.

"Stay with me, Mon," Lawson pleaded, tears blurring her vision. "Help is coming. Just stay with me."

"Monica?" Lawson's voice broke. "Monica!"

No response.

Lawson barely registered the approaching sirens, or the shouts of officers securing the perimeter. She remained kneeling beside Monica's body, her hand still futilely trying to stem the flow of blood from a heart that had already stopped beating.

Later, she would remember fragments of the aftermath. Someone pulling her away. The paramedics working frantically. The pronouncement of death at 11:47 p.m. Her supervisor, Captain Richardson, arriving on scene, his face a mask of professional concern as he put a comforting hand on her shoulder.

"We'll find who did this," he promised.

Lawson said nothing. Because she knew how corruption worked. It devoured everything, even the truth. Especially the truth.

Monica's source would never be found. The investigation would hit dead end after dead end until investigators eventually shelved it as an unsolved tragedy.

As the ambulance doors closed on Monica's body, Lawson made a silent vow. She would find justice for Monica, even if it took the rest of her life. Even if it meant becoming someone she barely recognized.

Even if it meant becoming someone Monica would have hated.

The first drops of rain began to fall, washing away the blood on the loading dock. But nothing would ever wash away Lawson's memory of this night.

Nor the guilt that would haunt her for years to come.

dead air episode 1:

"Silence in Savannah"

[Soft electronic theme music fades in, builds slightly, then quiets under narration]

LEAH BLACKWELL: Welcome to Dead Air. I'm Leah Blackwell, and this is the first episode of our new season: "Silence in Savannah."

Five years ago, Detective Monica Landry was murdered at the old paper mill warehouse on the eastern edge of Savannah. The case remains officially unsolved. No arrests. No suspects named publicly. But tonight, we're going to hear something that's never been released.

[Brief pause]

LEAH: This is the emergency radio call made by Detective Erin Lawson, Monica Landry's partner, moments after the shooting:

[Audio clip plays] "I've got a 10-999! Officer down! Send help immediately! Warehouse district, old paper mill. Shots fired, officer down. Need medical help now!"

[More distressed sounds, emotional breathing] "Stay with me, Mon. Help is coming. Just stay with me!"

LEAH: That was Detective Erin Lawson, Monica Landry's partner, calling for help that would arrive too late. This recording has never been released to the public until now. Multiple sources within the Savannah PD have confirmed it's authentic.

[Music shifts to a more somber tone]

LEAH: The official investigation concluded that an unknown attacker shot Detective Landry in the chest and escaped into the night without being identified. But there are troubling problems with this story.

Why were two detectives meeting at an abandoned warehouse after hours? Why was Detective Lawson, the only witness, unable to identify the shooter? And why, despite an extensive investigation, was no evidence ever found to identify who lured Detective Landry to her death that night?

[Brief pause]

LEAH: I've spent the last eight months investigating what really happened on August 17th, five years ago. What began as an examination of one detective's murder has uncovered something far more disturbing—a pattern of sealed evidence, redirected investigations, and questions that powerful people don't want answered.

LEAH: Let's start with the basics. Monica Landry was a rising star in the Savannah Police Department. Thirty-six years old. Eight years on the force. Three years in Homicide. Her personnel file, which we obtained through public records requests, shows consistent commendations and rapid advancement.

LEAH: Her former captain, now retired, Thomas Richardson, declined our request for an interview, but provided this statement:

[Reading from statement] "Detective Landry was an exemplary officer whose loss continues to impact us all. The investigation into her murder remains active, though no suspects have been identified at this time."

LEAH: Active investigation. That's the official line. Yet department sources tell a different story.

SPD SOURCE (voice disguised): Nobody's actively working Landry's case. Hasn't been touched in years. After the initial push, everything just ... stopped. Orders from above. Focus on active cases, they said. Not cold ones.

LEAH: This source, who requested anonymity due to fear of professional repercussions, described how the investigation stalled within months of the murder.

SPD SOURCE: The case got reassigned three times in six months. Evidence disappeared from the file. Witness statements that didn't match the official narrative were buried. Anyone who pushed too hard got transferred or shut down.

[Music intensifies]

LEAH: In the weeks before her death, Detective Landry was working a major drug trafficking case involving a dealer named James Rafferty. According to case notes, she believed the operation extended beyond street-level distribution into money laundering through legitimate Savannah businesses.

LEAH: Her partner, Detective Erin Lawson, continued the investigation after Landry's death. But within six months, the Rafferty case was quietly closed due to "insufficient evidence."

LEAH: Detective Lawson declined multiple requests for an interview. Her only public statements about her partner's death came during a brief press conference five years ago:

[Archive audio clip] "Detective Landry was not only my partner but my friend. I will not rest until her killer is brought to justice. That's all I have to say at this time."

LEAH: Sources close to Detective Lawson describe how the case consumed her in the years that followed.

FORMER COLLEAGUE (voice disguised): Lawson became obsessed. Kept copies of everything. Worked the case on her own time. Her performance suffered. Started drinking. The department tried to get her help, but she pushed everyone away.

[Music shifts, becomes more investigative]

LEAH: What drove this obsession? What did Detective Lawson believe the department was missing—or hiding?

LEAH: We obtained the original crime scene photographs through a Freedom of Information request. They show the warehouse where Monica Landry died. Blood pool beneath a loading dock. Shell casings marked with evidence tags. And something peculiar—a mounted floodlight positioned to illuminate the exact spot where Landry was standing when shot.

LEAH: According to Detective Lawson's statement, this floodlight suddenly activated moments before the shooting, temporarily blinding both officers. When her vision cleared, Landry was already down.

LEAH: But here's the problem: that warehouse had no electricity. It had been abandoned for seven years. Power had been disconnected long before the shooting.

LEAH: So how did the floodlight work? Who installed it? And why wasn't this discrepancy highlighted in the investigation?

[Brief pause]

LEAH: The questions only multiply from here. Surveillance footage from a nearby business shows multiple vehicles near the warehouse that night, vehicles never mentioned in police reports. Witness statements from homeless individuals who frequented the area describe seeing a man in a suit entering the warehouse hours before the meeting, statements later removed from the case file.

[Music softens]

LEAH: In the coming episodes, we'll explore these inconsistencies and more. We'll examine Detective Landry's relationship with her partner, which sources suggest went beyond professional boundaries. We'll investigate the Rafferty case and why it was so quickly abandoned after her death.

LEAH: And we'll reveal new evidence about a detective from the Narcotics division who had his own relationship with Monica Landry, a relationship that ended just days before her murder.

[Music builds]

LEAH: Someone knows the truth about what happened to Detective Monica Landry. Someone has kept that truth buried for five years.

LEAH: I'm heading to Savannah next week to continue this investigation in person. To walk the scene where Detective Landry died. To speak with those who knew her. To find the answers that have remained hidden for too long.

LEAH: This is Dead Air. The truth doesn't stay buried forever.

[Theme music plays out]

chapter two

LAWSON JOLTED AWAKE, sheets soaked with sweat and twisted around her legs. Her heart pounded as the nightmare faded. The taste of copper filled her mouth. The clock read 3:17 a.m. Another sleepless night.

She rubbed her face and tried to slow her breathing. Five years since Monica's murder, but in her dreams, it happened yesterday. The floodlight, the gunshot, Monica falling. The blood spreading across her white shirt. The details never faded.

Her bedroom felt like an oven. The old air conditioner wheezed against Savannah's August heat. She kicked off the sheets and stared at the half-empty whiskey bottle on her nightstand. Six months ago, she would have poured a glass. A year ago, she would have skipped the glass. Tonight, she just traced the label with her finger.

Four months, two weeks, and three days sober. Her longest stretch since Monica died. The craving gnawed at her stomach like hunger, but something stopped her from opening the bottle. Maybe it was Richardson's warning after she'd shown up hungover the last time.

"You're more useful to the victims sober," he'd said.

She put the bottle back. Tomorrow meant another day of pretending she had her life together.

Her phone buzzed on the nightstand, lighting up the dark room. Who texted at this hour? She grabbed it and squinted at the screen.

A message from Claire Stevens: *I think you're going to want to listen to this.*

Claire was complicated. They'd started on opposite sides of the courtroom. Claire the defense attorney who'd overturned Anthony Bates' conviction, Lawson, the detective whose bad work had made it possible. That case should have made them enemies. Instead, it created an alliance built on respect. Lawson had pushed Claire to take a job with the DA's office after everything settled. Claire still thought about it, and they'd maintained a careful professional relationship.

Below Claire's text sat a link to something called "Dead Air" with the subtitle: The 10-999 Tape.

Lawson's blood turned cold. 10-999. Officer down.

Her finger hovered over the link. This wouldn't be good. She took a deep breath and tapped the screen.

The podcast loaded. A black and white logo appeared before a woman's voice filled the room.

"Welcome to Dead Air. I'm Leah Blackwell, and this is the first episode of our new season: 'Silence in Savannah.'"

Lawson sat up straight, every muscle tight.

"Five years ago, Detective Monica Landry was murdered at the old paper mill warehouse on the eastern edge of Savannah. The case remains officially unsolved. No arrests. No suspects named publicly. But tonight, we're going to hear something that's never been released."

A pause, then audio that made Lawson's stomach drop.

"I've got a 10-999! Officer down! Send help immediately!" Her own voice, raw with panic. "Warehouse district, old paper mill. Shots fired, officer down. Need medical help now!"

The sound of her ragged breathing, muffled sobs as she tried to stop Monica's bleeding.

"Stay with me, Mon. Help is coming. Just stay with me!"

Lawson's chest tightened. That call had never been released. It was sealed as part of an active investigation. How did this podcaster get it?

"That was Detective Erin Lawson," the woman continued, "Monica Landry's partner, calling for help that would arrive too late. This recording has never been released to the public until now. Multiple sources within the Savannah PD have confirmed it's real."

The room spun. Lawson's breathing became quick and shallow. Panic squeezed her lungs. She fumbled for the whiskey bottle, her hand shaking as it closed around the smooth glass. Four months, two weeks, three days of sobriety hung in the balance as she unscrewed the cap. The sharp scent of bourbon filled her nose.

She held the bottle inches from her lips. The amber liquid promised to make the memories stop. Monica's blood on her hands. The light fading from her eyes. The sound of her own voice, broken and desperate, begging for help that came too late.

Lawson slammed the cap back on and threw the bottle across the room. It rolled across the hardwood floor and stopped against the wall.

She bent forward, head between her knees, forcing deeper breaths as her heart hammered. Her hands balled into fists, nails digging into her palms until the pain brought her back to reality.

"The official investigation concluded that an unknown attacker shot Detective Landry in the chest and escaped into the night without being identified. But there are troubling problems with this story."

The podcaster's voice sharpened.

"Why were two detectives meeting at an abandoned warehouse after hours? Why was Detective Lawson, the only witness, unable to identify the shooter? And why, despite an extensive investigation, was no evidence ever found to identify who lured Detective Landry to her death that night?"

Lawson's breathing quickened.

"I'm heading to Savannah next week to investigate these questions and more. Someone knows the truth about what happened to Detective Monica Landry, and I intend to find it. Stay tuned to Dead Air, because this story is just getting started."

The podcast ended. Lawson sat in silence, listening to her harsh breathing. She grabbed her phone and typed "Leah Blackwell Dead Air podcast" into the search bar.

Results flooded her screen. The podcast had over three million subscribers. Blackwell had started it while in law school at Columbia, focusing on cold cases and wrongful convictions. Her investigations had reopened three cases and freed one innocent person. She'd won multiple awards and recently signed a deal with Netflix.

Lawson clicked on an image. Leah Blackwell looked younger than expected. Early thirties, with sharp features and intense eyes that seemed to see through the camera. She looked like someone who wouldn't back down.

Lawson scrolled through previous episodes. Blackwell had covered cases from across the country, but none from Savannah. So why Monica's case? Why now?

She found the answer in a recent interview with Blackwell in a digital media magazine. The reporter had asked why she'd chosen Monica's case.

"I never choose my cases; they choose me," Blackwell had said. "Someone reached out with compelling information suggesting Detective Landry's murder wasn't random violence, but a targeted hit to silence her. When they sent me that radio call, I knew I had to look deeper."

Someone reached out? Someone with access to sealed evidence and a grudge? Someone who wanted the past dug up?

Lawson hurled her phone across the room. It hit the wall with a crack before dropping to the hardwood. She stood and paced like a caged animal, her breathing ragged.

Five years. Five damn years she'd spent trying to find Monica's killer. Hitting wall after wall, dead end after dead end. Running up against the blue line that appeared whenever she got close to something important. Richardson's warnings still echoed in her ears. "Let it go, Lawson. For your own good."

She'd never let it go, not really, but she'd learned to live with the open wound. To function despite it. To do her job while carrying the weight of that failure. The wound festered just under the surface.

Now, this Blackwell woman would rip it all open again, probing and digging. And the worst part? She seemed to be suggesting Lawson had something to do with it.

Lawson picked up her phone. The screen now sported a web of cracks. She pulled up Claire's number and typed a response.

Where did you find this?

The reply came immediately: *It's everywhere. Viral on TikTok.*

Of course it was. The public loved a juicy conspiracy, especially one involving corrupt cops. They'd eat this up, regardless of the damage it might do to the department or to the people who still mourned Monica.

You need to hear the rest of it, Claire texted. *She mentions files that went missing after Monica's death.*

The Rafferty case files. Monica had been certain someone inside the department was protecting the operation. She'd been killed before she could prove it. After her death, key documents had disappeared, including Monica's personal notes.

Lawson had tried to pursue it, convinced Monica's murder was connected, but the case got reassigned. Six months later, the Rafferty investigation was quietly closed due to "insufficient evidence." Whenever Lawson brought it up, she was reminded that she was too close, too emotional. Eventually, she'd been given a choice: drop it or turn in her badge.

She'd chosen to keep her badge, convinced she could do more good inside the system than out. But the guilt had eaten away at her, driving her deeper into the bottle each year.

Now Blackwell was coming to town, ready to expose everything, with no idea of the danger she was putting herself in.

If someone had killed Monica to protect a secret, they wouldn't hesitate to kill again.

Lawson grabbed her gym bag from the closet and stuffed in a change of clothes. She needed to clear her head, and sitting in her apartment staring at the whiskey bottle wouldn't help. The twenty-four-hour gym downtown was usually empty this time of night. She could pound out her frustration on a punching bag, then shower and head straight to the precinct.

She had one week to prepare for Blackwell's arrival. One week to decide whether to help her uncover the truth or warn her away from a grave she was about to dig.

Neither option would bring Monica back. But at least one of them might keep this podcaster from joining her.

chapter
three

LAWSON BENT OVER HER DESK, pressing her fingertips into her temples. Case files spread across the surface in messy stacks. Two hours at the gym hadn't helped. Punching bags and treadmills couldn't silence the voices from that podcast. Monica's blood. The accusations. They clung to her thoughts like smoke.

Her partner's desk sat empty. Four different partners in five years. None stuck around longer than twelve months. The department stopped trying to assign her anyone new. She worked better alone anyway. The precinct moved around her like water around a stone. Officers found reasons to bypass her office. Conversations died when she entered the break room.

The coffee in her mug had turned cold hours ago. Black sludge with a film on top. She drank it anyway, needing the caffeine more than the taste. Her computer screen showed seventeen unread emails. Internal memos about policy changes. Training updates. A reminder about the department picnic next month. All the normal business of police work felt surreal after listening to herself beg for Monica's life on a podcast.

"Detective Lawson?"

A woman filled her doorway. Small frame, sharp haircut that made her face look like it could cut glass. Navy blazer, white shirt, jeans that cost more than Lawson made in a week. Designer boots. But her eyes grabbed Lawson's attention first. They moved constantly, taking in everything, filing it away.

"Leah Blackwell." The woman stepped inside without an invitation. "Dead Air podcast."

Lawson's back teeth ground together. "I know who you are."

"Good. Saves us both time." Blackwell settled into the visitor's chair like she owned it, one leg crossed over the other. "Wasn't sure you followed my work."

"Make yourself at home," Lawson muttered. "Who signed you in?"

Leah's smile never wavered. Either deaf to sarcasm or immune to it. She pulled a small notebook from her bag, flipped through several pages covered in neat handwriting. Phone numbers. Names. Questions written in blue ink.

"You're early," Lawson said. "Thought Savannah wouldn't see you until next week."

"I scout locations first. Get the lay of the land before I start digging." Blackwell's shoulders lifted in a careless shrug. "Meet the key players."

"I'm a key player?"

"You're the star." A digital recorder appeared from Blackwell's bag. Sleek black plastic that she placed between them like a chess piece. "I want your version of Monica Landry's murder. Your truth."

Lawson leaned back in her chair. The leather creaked under her weight. Five years of sitting in this same spot, working cases, avoiding the one case that mattered most. The Monica Landry file sat in her bottom drawer, an unofficial copy she'd made before the case got reassigned. She'd read it so many times the pages were soft from handling.

"My truth. Right."

"Facts matter to me." Blackwell's voice stayed level despite Lawson's tone. "I investigate. I don't make things up for entertainment."

"By stealing sealed evidence? Broadcasting private radio calls?"

"Nobody stole anything. Someone gave me that recording because they think people deserve to know what really happened."

The radio call. Lawson's voice pleading for Monica's life while blood pooled on concrete. She'd never heard the recording before now. Police radio calls were archived, stored on servers most people forgot existed.

Someone with access had pulled that file. Someone who wanted the world to hear Lawson's desperation.

"What really happened?" Lawson leaned forward. "I couldn't save my partner. The shooter escaped. I live with that every day."

Blackwell watched her for several heartbeats. "You're smarter than that. This case has layers you haven't talked about."

"This case has a podcaster trying to make money off a dead cop."

"Listen to my previous episodes before you judge my motives." Blackwell pulled out her phone. A sleek device in a leather case. Everything about her screamed expensive. Money from podcast success or family wealth. Either way, she'd never understand what it meant to work cases where every mistake could cost lives.

"Here's a sample from episode two. Maybe it'll change your perspective."

The screen lit up before Lawson could protest. Blackwell's recorded voice filled the office, crisp and professional.

"Detective Landry's death marked the beginning of her partner's downward spiral. Erin Lawson received three excessive force citations in the following five years. Two insubordination charges. Multiple incidents involving alcohol during work hours. Department sources describe increasing isolation, obsessive behavior around cold cases, and open defiance toward supervisors."

Lawson knew exactly what each citation represented. The excessive force reports came from suspects who resisted arrest—suspects in whose faces she saw Monica's killer. The insubordination charges stemmed from refusing to let cold cases die. The alcohol incidents were Wednesday mornings when bourbon seemed more manageable than facing another day of unsolved mysteries.

Blackwell paused the playback. Her eyes never left Lawson's face.

"You missed the public indecency charge," Lawson said. Her voice came out flat, emotionless. Inside, her blood turned cold. Those records weren't public. Personnel files lived in locked cabinets behind access-controlled doors.

"That charge got dropped." Blackwell didn't hesitate. "The night in lockup didn't."

The night in lockup. Lawson remembered fragments. A bar fight that started when someone made a joke about dead cops. Waking up in a cell with bruised knuckles and a split lip. Richardson bailing her out at dawn, his face a mask of professional disappointment.

Heat flooded Lawson's chest, rising into her throat. "Where did you get this information?"

Blackwell's smile widened just enough to show teeth. "Multiple sources. People who think it's time for transparency."

Multiple sources meant a conspiracy. Someone wanted Lawson destroyed. The question was who and why. Richardson had protected her career despite her mistakes. Other officers avoided her but didn't actively work against her. The leak came from someone with access and motivation.

"I also know about the prescription medications," Blackwell said. "Anxiety. Depression. Sleep aids. All prescribed after Detective Landry's death."

The prescription history was protected medical information. Someone had violated federal privacy laws to give Blackwell ammunition. This wasn't journalism anymore. This was warfare.

She stood and gathered her equipment. "I'll contact you again soon. When you're ready for that interview, you have my contact information."

"You didn't give me a card."

Blackwell paused, genuine surprise crossing her features. Then she laughed. "You're right." Her hand disappeared into her blazer and emerged with crisp white cardstock. "Oversight on my part."

The card was heavy stock paper with raised lettering. Leah Blackwell, Investigative Journalist. Dead Air Podcast. An email address and a New York phone number.

She left without another word. Expensive perfume lingered in the air along with the taste of dread.

Lawson grabbed her phone the second the door closed. Claire's number was already highlighted. The call connected on the second ring.

"This can't be legal," she said instead of hello. "She has my disciplinary file, Claire. My complete disciplinary file."

"Take a breath." Claire's voice carried that lawyer calm that made everything worse. "What exactly happened?"

"Blackwell ambushed me at work. Played audio from her next episode. Every mistake I've made since Monica died. The drunk tank, the write-ups, all of it. Tell me she broke some law."

Papers shuffled in the background. Claire was probably reviewing case files while they talked. Always multitasking, always thinking three steps ahead. It made her a great lawyer but a frustrating friend.

Silence stretched across the connection. "Depends how she obtained the information," Claire finally said. "If department personnel leaked it ..."

"Of course someone leaked it! Personnel files aren't public record!"

"Then the leaker might face consequences. But she's protected as a journalist. First Amendment covers reporting information she receives, even if the source obtained it improperly."

Lawson's fist hit the desk hard enough to rattle her coffee mug. Cold liquid sloshed over the rim, spreading across case files. She grabbed tissues from her drawer and dabbed at the spill, watching ink blur on witness statements.

"So she broadcasts my failures to millions of people? Paints me as a suspect?"

"You don't have to cooperate. Refuse interviews. But stopping the podcast requires proving malice. That she's knowingly spreading lies to damage you."

"She is damaging me." The anger drained away, leaving something rawer behind. "She's building a case that I killed Monica."

Another pause. Longer this time. "Actually, you might not have to do anything."

"What do you mean?"

"Judge Elizabeth Byrd called this morning. She's one of my private clients—I handle some personal legal matters for her occasionally. She's also a major donor to both the museum and the police benevolent fund." Claire's voice took on a cautious optimism. "She wants me to file for a temporary injunction against the podcast."

Lawson straightened in her chair. "On what grounds?"

"Interference with an ongoing investigation. The Monica Landry case was never officially closed, just went cold. Judge Byrd argues that broadcasting sealed evidence and encouraging amateur investigation could compromise any future prosecution."

"That would work?"

"It's a valid legal argument. A temporary injunction could halt publication while the court reviews whether the podcast materially interferes with law enforcement. Could buy us weeks, maybe months."

"Good." The word came out harder than Lawson intended. "Do it."

"Erin, there's something else. If she's this thorough, she's not chasing viral content. She has specific goals."

"To destroy me."

"Or to solve a five-year-old murder." Claire's tone softened around the edges. "Antagonizing her makes you look guilty. If you're worried about her narrative, maybe control it yourself. Talk to her."

"Not if Byrd can shut her down first."

"The injunction isn't guaranteed. And even if we get it, Blackwell can appeal. She has resources and a legal team."

Lawson stared at the business card on her desk. "Let me worry about Blackwell. You just file that paperwork."

The business card lay on her desk. The raised lettering caught the fluorescent light from overhead.

"I have to go."

"Erin ..."

She killed the call and shoved the phone away. Her bottom desk drawer called to her. The bourbon bottle waited inside, amber liquid promising temporary peace. Her hand moved toward the handle, fingers brushing the cold metal.

No. Blackwell wouldn't drive her back to drinking. Four months sober meant something. Monica would have wanted her to stay clean, to keep fighting for justice. The bottle could wait.

Lawson snatched her jacket and keys. The Rafferty files would be archived in the county records basement by now. Boxes of evidence and witness statements gathering dust in climate-controlled storage. If Blackwell was investigating Monica's death, she'd start there too. The drug trafficking case had consumed Monica's final months. She'd been convinced someone inside the department was protecting the operation.

Time to discover how much the podcaster already knew. And maybe find out who wanted Lawson destroyed badly enough to feed sealed records to a journalist.

dead air episode 2:

"The Partner"

[Electronic theme music fades in, then quiets under narration]

LEAH BLACKWELL: Welcome back to Dead Air. I'm Leah Blackwell.

In our first episode, we introduced Detective Monica Landry's unsolved murder and the questions surrounding that night at the old paper mill warehouse. Today, we turn our focus to Detective Erin Lawson—Monica's partner and the only witness to her death.

[Brief pause]

LEAH: When investigating an officer's murder, the partner is always scrutinized closely. Not necessarily as a suspect, but as the person who knew the victim best professionally. Detective Lawson worked alongside Monica Landry for three years before her death. Their partnership was, by all accounts, successful, with an impressive case clearance rate and multiple commendations.

[Sound of pages turning]

LEAH: Department records show they were assigned as partners in 2016 under then-Captain Thomas Richardson. Monica had been with the Savannah PD for eight years, two years longer than Lawson herself. They quickly established themselves as one of the precinct's most effective teams, specializing in homicide cases with organized crime connections.

SPD SOURCE (voice disguised): Lawson and Landry were the go-to team for complex cases. Different styles that complemented each other. Monica was methodical, detail-oriented. Lawson was more intuitive, good with witnesses. Together, they closed cases others couldn't touch.

[Music shifts to a more intense investigative tone]

LEAH: Yet something changed in the weeks before Detective Landry's death. Multiple sources within the department describe growing tension between the partners.

FORMER COLLEAGUE (voice disguised): Everyone noticed it. They'd been inseparable for years, then suddenly they barely spoke. Different lunch breaks. No more car-pooling. Cold professionalism instead of their usual rapport.

LEAH: This professional distance coincided with their assignment to the Rafferty investigation—a complex drug trafficking operation with connections to Savannah's business community. According to case notes we've obtained, Detective Landry believed the operation extended beyond street-level distribution into money laundering and political protection.

[Brief pause]

LEAH: Yesterday, I visited the Savannah Police Department to speak directly with Detective Lawson about these tensions and her recollections of the night Monica died. What happened during that interview raises even more questions.

LEAH: Initially, Detective Lawson refused to discuss her partner's case, citing an ongoing investigation. When pressed about the night at the warehouse, her responses became defensive and evasive.

[Audio clip from interview] **LAWSON:** The radio call. Lawson's voice pleading for Monica's life while blood pooled on concrete. She'd never heard the recording before last night.

LEAH: That statement is troubling. Detective Lawson claims she never heard her own emergency call until our podcast released it. Yet department procedure requires officers to review all evidence from incidents they're involved in, especially officer-involved shootings or deaths.

LEAH: Why wouldn't Detective Lawson have heard this recording during the initial investigation? Who made the decision to keep it from her? And why?

[Music intensifies]

LEAH: Detective Lawson's personnel file, which we obtained through public records requests, shows a concerning pattern following her partner's death.

[Audio clip plays] **LEAH:** Detective Landry's death marked the beginning of her partner's downward spiral. Erin Lawson received three excessive force citations in the following five years. Two insubordination charges. Multiple incidents involving alcohol during work hours. Department sources describe increasing isolation, obsessive behavior around cold cases, and open defiance toward supervisors.

LEAH: These behavioral changes suggest deep trauma, understandable after witnessing a partner's murder. But they also raise questions about Detective Lawson's state of mind both before and after that night.

FORMER COLLEAGUE (voice disguised): She became a different person after Monica died. Obsessed with the case. Confrontational with supervisors. Started drinking heavily. The department tried to get her help, but she refused counseling, refused to take leave. Just kept working, kept digging.

[Brief pause]

LEAH: Perhaps most concerning is what happened to the Rafferty investigation after Detective Landry's death. Detective Lawson continued working the case for six months before it was reassigned – against her vocal objections. Three months later, the case was closed due to "insufficient evidence."

LEAH: Internal memos show Detective Lawson filed formal protests about evidence that disappeared from the Rafferty case file. Evidence that might have been connected to her partner's murder.

[Music shifts]

LEAH: So what do we know about Detective Lawson's actions the night her partner died?

LEAH: According to her official statement, she arrived at the warehouse at approximately 11:00 p.m. after receiving a text from Detective Landry requesting the meeting. She parked her vehicle and approached the loading dock area, where she observed her partner standing alone.

LEAH: Detective Lawson stated that before they could speak, a floodlight suddenly activated, temporarily blinding them both. When her vision cleared, Detective Landry had been shot. She claimed she saw no shooter and could provide no description of potential suspects.

LEAH: But surveillance footage from a nearby business shows a different timeline. Detective Lawson's vehicle arrived at 10:47 PM, thirteen minutes earlier than her statement claims. The footage also shows a third vehicle leaving the scene shortly after her arrival.

[Music becomes more pointed]

LEAH: More concerning is what witnesses at the Driftwood Tavern told us about Detective Lawson's activities earlier that evening.

BARTENDER: She was here from about 6:30 till maybe 10:30, 11:00. Had several whiskeys. Seemed upset about something. Checking her phone a lot. Left in a hurry after getting some kind of message.

LEAH: Multiple witnesses confirm Detective Lawson consumed alcohol in the hours before meeting her partner at the warehouse—a detail never mentioned in her official statement or the subsequent investigation.

LEAH: When asked about this discrepancy, Detective Lawson abruptly ended our interview. Her final statement was telling:

[Audio clip from interview] **LAWSON:** You weren't there. You don't know what happened that night.

[Brief pause]

LEAH: I don't know what happened that night. But I do know the official investigation contains significant inconsistencies. I know evidence disappeared. I know the Rafferty case Detective Landry was working on was suddenly abandoned after her death.

LEAH: And I know Detective Erin Lawson carries information she hasn't shared, information that might explain why her partner was murdered and why no one has been held accountable.

[Music softens]

LEAH: This isn't just about exposing failures in an investigation. It's about understanding the complex relationship between two detectives and how that relationship might have influenced the events of that night.

LEAH: In our next episode, we'll explore another relationship in Detective Landry's life—one that adds yet another layer of complexity to this case. Detective Ray Hutchinson of the Narcotics Division claims he and Monica Landry were romantically involved in the months before her death. His story contradicts much of what we've been told about Monica's final days.

[Music builds]

LEAH: This is Dead Air. The truth doesn't stay buried forever.

[Theme music plays out]

chapter
four

FIVE YEARS *Ago*

Monica's bare feet whispered across Lawson's hardwood floor. Window to couch. Couch to window. Endless pacing while two coffee mugs grew cold on the counter.

"I'm done hiding." Monica stopped at the window. Afternoon sun turned her dark hair copper at the edges. "Tired of pretending we're just partners. Tired of lying to everyone at work."

Lawson wore yesterday's jeans and a wrinkled t-shirt. The apartment smelled like weekend—coffee grounds scattered around the sink, Monica's body wash ghosting out from the bathroom. Evidence of their time together that suddenly felt incriminating.

"You know how the department works."

"I know how you think it works." Monica spun from the window. Those brown eyes carried the same stubborn fire that cracked suspects during interrogations. "Tell me one person who got fired for being gay. One."

"Richardson barely tolerates having women on the force."

"Richardson tolerates whoever brings in arrests and keeps his clearance rates up. He doesn't care what we do off the clock."

Lawson needed distance. She grabbed one of the mugs from the counter—still warm, bitter as motor oil the way Monica liked it.

"Gossip travels fast in the department."

"So let it travel." Monica followed her into the tiny kitchen. "I'd rather deal with whispers than pretend you don't matter when other people are watching."

The mug slipped in Lawson's hands. She caught it, set it down harder than necessary. Her knuckles went white against the fake granite.

"You think I don't care?"

"I think you care more about your reputation." Monica moved closer, bringing warmth and the faint scent of her perfume. "This is about holding hands at the department barbecue. Not pretending you're just my work friend."

"We agreed to keep quiet."

"Eleven months ago. Things change."

Hope and frustration battled across Monica's features. The same look she got working cold cases—patient but relentless.

"What if Richardson splits us up? Partners aren't supposed to be involved."

"Then we request different shifts. Different divisions." Monica reached for Lawson's hands. "Better to be together somewhere else than work side-by-side pretending we're strangers."

Monica's touch sent sparks racing up Lawson's arms. Those palms carried years of calluses from handling weapons, cuffs, steering wheels. Rough hands that knew exactly how to be gentle.

"Erin." Monica's voice dropped into that low register she used in bed. "I love you. I want people to know I love you."

The words should have been perfect. Instead, they lodged in Lawson's throat like stones. Love meant vulnerability. Love meant having something that could be taken away.

"I can't. Not yet."

Monica yanked her hands back like she'd grabbed hot metal. "When? After you make sergeant? Lieutenant? When Richardson retires and someone else takes over?"

"I don't know."

"You don't know." Monica's voice flattened out. "Three years as partners. Eleven months in the same bed. And you don't know when you'll be ready to admit I exist."

"That's not what I meant."

"Isn't it?" Monica snatched her jacket from the chair. "You flirted with that prosecutor last week. Played it up for the whole squad. Made jokes about my nonexistent dating life."

The blood drained from Lawson's cheeks. "Those were just jokes."

"To you." Monica jammed her arms through the jacket sleeves. "To me they felt like you were erasing us."

"Monica, wait."

But Monica was already at the door, hand on the knob. She didn't look back.

"Your badge means more to you than we do. When you figure out which one matters, call me."

The door clicked shut. Monica's engine turned over outside. Lawson stood surrounded by cooling coffee and lingering perfume, listening to tires disappear into traffic noise.

She didn't move until the silence became unbearable.

The Driftwood Tavern squatted three blocks from the precinct—close enough to walk, far enough to avoid most cops. Lawson claimed a corner stool and ordered whiskey straight. The bartender looked about twenty-two, young enough to card everyone regardless of obvious age.

Grease hung in the air mixed with stale beer. Rock music pounded from overhead speakers just loud enough to drown conversation without completely killing it. Saturday drinkers filled the other stools—construction workers with concrete dust under their fingernails, retirees stretching out errands, office types drowning whatever had driven them here.

Lawson fit right in.

Her phone buzzed against the scarred bar top. Monica's name on the screen: *We need to talk.*

Lawson stared at the message for maybe thirty seconds before flipping the phone face down. The whiskey burned going down her throat, promising to make everything simpler. Another buzz against the wood. She didn't look.

"Want another?" The bartender looked like he'd rather be anywhere else.

"Yeah."

The second shot went down easier. The third, easier than that. By the fourth, her phone had gone quiet. Evening drinkers started filtering in, voices getting louder as alcohol loosened tongues and good judgment.

Lawson checked her phone. Three missed calls. Four unread texts. Her finger hovered over Monica's contact for a long moment before sliding toward the bartender instead.

"One more."

Two weeks later

Work became arctic. Monica answered direct questions with yes or no. Filed reports without looking up. Took lunch breaks at different times. The partnership that had felt natural for three years turned mechanical overnight.

Lawson retreated to the Driftwood every evening after shift. Same corner stool, same whiskey order, same bartender who'd stopped asking questions. The routine numbed the sharp edges of regret.

"Rough day?" Tommy, the construction worker two stools down, always showed up around six. Concrete dust permanently embedded under his nails, thermos of coffee that smelled like motor oil.

"They're all rough days." Lawson signaled for another round.

"Tell me about it. My foreman's been riding us about the Henderson project. Three weeks behind schedule, but it ain't our fault the permits got held up." Tommy drained his beer and ordered another. "You in construction?"

"Cop."

"No shit. My brother-in-law's a cop up in Atlanta. Says the job'll eat you alive if you let it."

Lawson nodded and focused on her drink. Small talk felt impossible when every conversation reminded her of Monica's laugh, Monica's stories about her crazy family, Monica's theories about human nature gleaned from years of questioning suspects.

The bar filled with its usual evening crowd. Office workers loosening ties, service industry folks still wearing name tags, retirees who treated the place like their personal club. Everyone had reasons for being there. Most didn't ask about anyone else's.

"You married?" Tommy persisted despite Lawson's obvious disinterest in conversation.

"No."

"Smart. Marriage is complicated enough without throwing a badge into the mix. My ex-wife used to say I loved concrete more than her. Wasn't true, but I couldn't prove it working sixty-hour weeks."

Lawson's phone buzzed against the bar. She glanced at the screen out of habit—probably Richardson with some administrative bullshit that couldn't wait until morning.

Monica's name appeared instead.

Meet me at the old paper mill warehouse. 11 PM. Come alone.

Lawson stared at the message. Two weeks of silence and now this. The paper mill sat in the warehouse district, where drug deals went bad and bodies turned up in dumpsters. Not the kind of place for reconciliation conversations.

Another text followed: *I have something on the Rafferty case. Big enough to break it open.*

The Rafferty investigation. They'd been working it for months before their fight, following money trails and offshore accounts that led to dead ends. Monica had been convinced someone inside the department was protecting the operation.

Lawson's finger hovered over the reply button. Two weeks of hurt and anger and wounded pride battled against curiosity and something deeper—the hope that maybe Monica had found a reason to reach out beyond work. Or maybe it was the chance Erin needed to make amends herself.

"Another round?" The bartender appeared without being summoned.

Lawson looked at her phone again. 10:15 PM. Forty-five minutes to decide whether to show up or let Monica wait alone in that warehouse district wasteland.

"Yeah. Make it a double."

The whiskey burned going down. Tommy was still talking about construction schedules and permit delays, but his voice faded into background noise. Lawson focused on the phone screen and the messages that might represent an olive branch or just another professional obligation.

10:30 PM. Monica would be getting ready to leave, checking her weapon, grabbing keys. The same pre-operation routine they'd developed over three years of partnership.

Lawson ordered another drink.

10:45 PM. Monica's car would be pulling out of her apartment complex, heading toward the warehouse district and whatever information she'd uncovered about Rafferty.

The bar spun slightly when Lawson turned her head. Four whiskeys on an empty stomach—dinner had been a bag of pretzels and professional guilt.

"You okay there?" Tommy squinted at her with the concern of someone who'd watched too many people drink themselves stupid.

"Have to go." Lawson dropped cash on the bar and grabbed her keys. The parking lot tilted under her feet, but she managed to find her car without falling over. Four drinks wasn't blackout territory. She'd driven in worse condition.

The warehouse district looked different through whiskey-tinted vision. Darker. More threatening. But Monica was there somewhere, waiting with information that could break the Rafferty case wide open.

Lawson checked her weapon and headed into the darkness.

Lawson jerked awake, sheets soaked and wrapped around her legs. Her hand swept across the mattress to empty space where Monica used to sleep. Cool fabric that hadn't held another person's warmth in five years.

The nightmare ended. The guilt didn't.

That fight played on repeat—Monica begging for honesty while

Lawson chose career safety over love. Two weeks of silence broken only by Monica's final text message and eventual death.

She'd arrived buzzed, reaction time dulled by whiskey and wounded pride. Four drinks slowing her reflexes when Monica needed her partner at full capacity.

Maybe sober Lawson would have spotted the muzzle flash sooner. Maybe she'd have tackled Monica to the ground before that first shot rang out. Maybe those four whiskeys had cost Monica her life.

Five years of carrying this weight. Five years of letting everyone think Monica's death was random violence when the truth cut deeper: Monica died because Lawson had chosen liquid courage over clear thinking.

She'd never told anyone about their relationship. Not Richardson, not Internal Affairs, not the detectives who caught Monica's case. Let them investigate a stranger's murder instead of her girlfriend's execution. Never mentioned the drinking either—how she'd stumbled through that warehouse lot with whiskey on her breath while Monica bled out on concrete. She passed off her subsequent alcoholism as grief, and everyone around her had bought it. They just didn't know that her grief had started two weeks before Monica's death.

Now Blackwell was excavating everything, asking questions that would lead to answers Lawson couldn't afford to give. How long before she found out about Monica and Lawson? How long before someone discovered that she had been impaired when her partner died?

The bedside clock read 4:23 a.m.. Too late for sleep, too early for anything else. Lawson got up and walked to the kitchen, stepping around the bourbon bottle she'd thrown the night before. It sat against the wall, amber liquid catching light from the hallway.

She picked it up and carried it to the sink. The cap came off easily. The alcohol smell rose up, promising to make the memories stop hurting, to dull the sharp edges of what-if and maybe-if.

For maybe ten seconds, she wavered. Four months, two weeks, and four days sober versus the weight of secrets she'd been carrying alone. The bottle trembled in her hands, amber liquid sloshing against glass.

The bourbon spiraled down the drain, disappearing into darkness below.

chapter five

LAWSON KILLED her headlights as she turned onto Magnolia Way. Richardson's house sat three doors down, with white columns and green shutters. A home where a retired police captain could pretend he'd left the job behind.

The porch light threw shadows across a row of manicured azaleas. Nine thirty on a Tuesday night, and every window glowed yellow against the darkness. She parked across the street and watched the house for two full minutes. A silhouette moved past the front window. Richardson's wife, Amy, smaller than her husband but just as formidable.

Lawson's knuckles rapped against the door before she could reconsider. The sound echoed across the porch, disturbing a pair of cardinals nesting in the eaves.

The door swung open. Richardson filled the frame. Six foot two of hard angles softened by retirement. The badge was gone, but the posture remained. His eyes narrowed at the sight of her.

"Lawson." He didn't sound surprised. "Figured you'd show up eventually."

"Captain." She couldn't break the habit of using his rank, even three years after his retirement party.

"Just Tom now." He stepped back, opening the door wider. "Come in before the neighbors start talking."

The foyer smelled of lemon polish and old books. Photos lined the walls. Richardson in uniform, Richardson shaking hands with the mayor, Richardson fishing with two grown sons who'd moved away years ago.

Amy appeared from the kitchen, drying her hands on a blue dish towel. "Detective Lawson. What a surprise." Her tone made clear it wasn't a pleasant one.

"Honey, would you mind giving us a few minutes?" Richardson's voice carried the gentle authority that had managed three decades of crisis situations.

Amy's mouth tightened at the corners. "I'll be upstairs." She disappeared up the staircase.

Richardson led Lawson to his study. A room that belonged in a different century. Leather-bound books filled oak shelves. A globe stood in one corner, tilted at an angle that put Savannah at its center. The desk dominated everything. Solid mahogany with brass fittings, scarred from years of use.

"Bourbon?" Richardson pulled a crystal decanter from a side cabinet.

"I'm four months sober." The words came out sharper than intended.

"Water, then." He poured himself two fingers of amber liquid without adding ice. "Why are you here, Lawson?"

She remained standing while he settled into the leather chair behind his desk. "You've heard the podcast."

"Everyone's heard it." He took a measured sip. "Judge Byrd called me this afternoon. Said she's filing an injunction."

"The tape shouldn't exist outside the department." Lawson's hands clenched at her sides. "Someone pulled it from archives."

"And you think I know who."

"You were captain when Monica died. You controlled access to evidence."

Richardson set his glass down with careful precision. "Five years since Landry's murder, and this is the first time you've darkened my doorstep. Now a podcast airs your radio call, and suddenly you need answers from me?"

The room temperature seemed to drop ten degrees. "I need to know how Blackwell got that recording."

"So do I." Richardson leaned forward, elbows on the desk. "I had nothing to do with this, Erin."

Her first name hung between them. A rarity from a man who called everyone by their last name regardless of rank or relationship.

"Then who did?" Lawson moved closer to the desk. "Only senior officers have access to sealed evidence. You, Walsh, Diaz, maybe Freeman."

"And two dozen clerks, IT specialists, and administrators." Richardson's jaw tightened. "Digital archives aren't my specialty. I retired, remember?"

"Convenient timing. Right after the Rafferty case closed due to 'insufficient evidence.'"

He didn't flinch. "My retirement had nothing to do with Rafferty or Landry."

"Monica thought someone inside was protecting Rafferty's operation. She was killed before she could prove it."

"And you've spent five years trying to prove the conspiracy theory of a dead cop." The edge in Richardson's voice could have cut glass. "How's that working out for you?"

Richardson paused, swirling the bourbon in his glass. "Monica was ... complicated in those final weeks. Started asking questions about overtime pay structures. Whether officers could legitimately supplement their income through consulting work. It made me wonder what kind of financial pressure she was under."

Lawson's nails dug into her palms hard enough to leave marks. "You reassigned the case after she died. Buried it under administrative transfer orders. Why?"

"Because you were too close." Richardson stood, his height advantage forcing Lawson to look up. "Your partner was murdered, and you wanted blood. That's not investigating. That's revenge."

"I wanted justice."

"You wanted someone to pay for your guilt." His voice dropped lower. "I know what happened that night, Lawson. The real story."

Ice formed in her veins. "What are you talking about?"

"You think I didn't know you were drinking before you met Landry at that warehouse?" Richardson's eyes never left hers. "The responding officers smelled it on your breath. Patrol sergeant noted it in his initial report."

The room tilted sideways. Lawson steadied herself against the bookshelf. "That's not in the official file."

"Because I removed it." Richardson circled the desk, closing the distance between them. "I protected you. Kept your career intact when half the force wanted you suspended or worse."

"Why?"

"Because losing your partner was punishment enough." A shadow crossed his features. "And because the department couldn't afford the scandal of a detective showing up drunk to a meet that got her partner killed."

All these years, she'd carried her secret alone, and Richardson had known from the beginning.

"You buried evidence." The accusation scraped her throat raw.

"I made a judgment call." Richardson returned to his desk, picking up his bourbon. "One that saved your badge and probably your life."

Five years of self-destruction flashed through her mind. The drinking, the fights, the recklessness that had become her trademark. Richardson hadn't saved her. He'd only prolonged the inevitable fall.

"Did you know about us?" The question escaped before she could stop it.

His expression shifted, confusion replacing anger. "Know what?"

"Monica and me. That we were ..." She couldn't finish the sentence.

Understanding dawned in his eyes. "No. That I didn't know."

Lawson's legs suddenly felt unsteady. She sank into the visitor's chair, the leather cool against her back. "We kept it quiet. Department policy against partners being involved."

Richardson ran a hand across his face. "Jesus, Lawson. That would have changed everything about the investigation."

"I know." Her voice sounded distant, even to her own ears. "That's why I never told anyone."

Silence stretched between them, broken only by the ticking of an antique clock on the mantel. Richardson finished his bourbon in one swallow.

"This Blackwell woman," he finally said. "She's dangerous."

"Because she's asking questions or because she might find answers?"

"Both." He set the empty glass down. "She's not just after a story. Someone's feeding her information. Specific information designed to implicate you."

The thought had occurred to Lawson, but hearing Richardson say it made it real. "Who benefits from destroying my reputation now? Monica's been dead five years."

"The Rafferty case touched powerful people. Money laundering operations with political connections. Maybe someone's worried you're still digging."

"I am."

Richardson's expression hardened. "Then maybe this podcast is a warning. Back off or get buried."

"I don't respond well to threats."

"No, you respond with a bottle and self-destruction." The words came out tired rather than accusatory. "You're four months sober, Erin. Don't let this drag you back."

His concern felt genuine, and that somehow made it worse. Lawson stood, needing to escape the suffocating walls of his study. "I need a name. Someone who could access that recording."

"I've been retired three years. The department's changed."

"Your connections haven't." Lawson moved toward the door. "You still play golf with the chief and Judge Byrd. You still have breakfast with Walsh every Wednesday at Martin's Diner."

Richardson's eyebrows rose slightly. "You keeping tabs on me?"

"Old habits." She paused at the threshold. "Find out who leaked that tape. I'll handle Blackwell."

"How exactly will you handle her?"

"By giving her what she wants. An exclusive interview with Monica's partner."

Alarm flashed across Richardson's face. "That's playing with fire."

"Fire's all I've got left." Lawson turned to leave. "Someone's using this podcast to come after me. I'm going to find out who. Even if I have to burn down everything to do it."

Richardson moved with surprising speed for his age, blocking the doorway. "Listen to me. This isn't just about you anymore. If what Landry suspected was true, if someone inside the department was protecting Rafferty, then they're still there. Still powerful enough to silence threats."

"Like Monica."

"Like Monica," he agreed. "And maybe like you, if you push too hard."

"I'm already a target." Lawson stepped around him. "Difference is, now I know it."

Richardson followed her to the front door. "Be careful who you trust, Lawson. Even people who seem like allies might have their own agendas."

She stopped with her hand on the doorknob. "Including you?"

His expression gave nothing away. "I'll make some calls about the leak. But whatever you're planning with Blackwell, think it through. Once you start talking, you can't control where the story goes."

chapter six

RIVER STREET BUSTLED with Tuesday afternoon tourists. Sunburned families strolled between gift shops. College students clustered on benches with iced coffee cups sweating in the heat. The Savannah River stretched dark and wide beyond the cobblestones, cargo ships sliding past like floating buildings.

Lawson arrived fifteen minutes early. Force of habit from years of stakeouts. The River Café occupied prime real estate with outdoor tables shaded by striped umbrellas. She claimed the corner table with her back to the wall. Her gaze swept across every entry point, every shadow, every stranger who lingered too long.

Her phone buzzed. Text from Claire: *Careful with Fiona. She's my sister, and I love her, but she usually has an angle.*

Fiona Stevens appeared right on time. Navy linen pantsuit despite the August heat. Hair pulled into a loose knot that somehow looked both effortless and expensive. The Savannah Chronicle's star investigative reporter moved with the practiced confidence of someone accustomed to walking into rooms where she wasn't welcome.

"Detective." Fiona slid into the chair opposite Lawson. Her smile revealed teeth whitened beyond nature. "Thanks for meeting me."

"Your message suggested urgency." Lawson kept her voice neutral. "You wanted to talk about Leah Blackwell."

Fiona waved to a server before answering. "Iced tea, please. Unsweetened with lemon." Her gaze returned to Lawson. "Claire mentioned you heard the podcast."

"All of Savannah heard it." Lawson studied Fiona's face. Looking for tells. The slight eye movements that betrayed lies during interrogations. "Your text implied you had information."

The server delivered Fiona's tea and refilled Lawson's water glass. Fiona stirred three sweetener packets into her drink. A contradiction of her unsweetened order.

"Information might be too strong." Fiona took a careful sip. "Context might be more accurate."

"Context."

"Leah Blackwell and I attended a journalism conference in Atlanta last year. She presented on ethics in true crime reporting." Fiona's fingers traced patterns in the condensation on her glass. "Brilliant speaker. Law degree from Columbia. Turned down offers from top firms to chase cold cases."

"You sound impressed."

"Professional respect." Fiona leaned forward. "What she did with the Wallace case in Detroit was impressive. State reopened a twenty-year murder based on her investigation."

Lawson had researched Blackwell's work. The Wallace case had freed a man wrongfully convicted of killing his business partner. But Blackwell's methods had involved questionable source cultivation. Paying witnesses. Promising story control to families.

"She gets results." Lawson conceded this much.

"At any cost." Fiona's voice dropped lower. "Her legal background gives her an edge most crime reporters lack. She knows exactly how far she can push before crossing lines."

"Why are you telling me this?"

"Because your partner deserves justice." Fiona held Lawson's gaze. "But Blackwell cares about stories more than justice. You should know who you're dealing with."

Lawson thought about the Richardson conversation last night. His warning about being careful with Blackwell. Now, Fiona appeared with similar cautions. Coincidence seemed unlikely.

"The Dolores Bates story at the regatta last year." Lawson changed direction. "That was your story, right?"

Fiona straightened, pride flickering across her features. "I uncovered the connection between Dolores and her late husband's mistress. Proved her self-defense claim when nobody believed her."

"I remember." Lawson recalled the night everything unraveled. Claire had called her to help get a recorded confession. The mistress's son lured Fiona onto a boat after dark at gunpoint. Lawson had called in backup on short notice.

"You saved me trouble that night." Fiona's voice softened with what might have been genuine gratitude. "I never properly thanked you."

"No need. I was helping Claire."

"Still." Fiona leaned forward. "I know what it means to chase justice when others want to let sleeping dogs lie. Your partner deserves resolution." Her eyes brightened with familiar ambition. "Cold cases require fresh perspectives sometimes."

Lawson caught the subtext. Fiona was positioning herself as a potential ally. Or perhaps seeing another career-making story. "Is that why you wanted to meet? Professional interest in Monica's case?"

"I help people find truth. You help people find justice." Fiona spread her hands. "Our methods differ, but our goals align."

"Methods like obtaining sealed evidence?" Lawson held Fiona's gaze. "Radio calls from active investigations?"

Fiona's fingers stopped moving on her glass. "I didn't provide Blackwell with that recording."

"But you know who did."

"I have theories." Fiona sipped her tea. "Disgruntled officers. Administrative staff with access. Maybe someone with a grudge against you."

"Or a journalist looking for column inches."

Fiona set her glass down with careful precision. "That recording helps no one at the Chronicle. We focus on local politics. Business development. Community issues."

"Monica was local." Lawson kept her voice steady despite the surge of anger. "Her murder was a community issue."

"Which we covered extensively five years ago." Fiona folded her napkin into perfect quarters. "This podcast does nothing but reopen wounds for ratings."

"Unless it solves her murder."

"Is that what you think will happen?" Fiona leaned forward. "Blackwell finds what the entire Savannah PD couldn't?"

The question carried loaded implications. Either the department was incompetent or deliberately obstructive. Neither option reflected well on Lawson nor on her colleagues.

"You reached out to me." Lawson redirected. "Said it was important. Yet you haven't told me anything I don't already know about Blackwell."

Fiona glanced at her watch. "I thought you deserved a warning from someone who understands her methods."

"Methods like what?"

"She left law practice under unusual circumstances." Fiona's tone shifted. More casual. Too casual. "Makes you wonder why she really left law."

There it was. The real purpose of this meeting. Classic journalist technique that Lawson had encountered during dozens of investigations. Probe for information while pretending to provide it.

"Why did you really ask me here?" Lawson kept her gaze fixed on Fiona. "Claire already warned me about Blackwell. You have nothing new to add."

Fiona's smile tightened at the corners. "Professional courtesy. One woman looking out for another."

"We worked together once on the Dolores Bates situation." Lawson leaned forward. "Now suddenly we're girlfriends sharing warnings?"

"I thought after what happened at the regatta ..." Fiona let the sentence trail off. "You helped me when things went sideways with that man. I wanted to return the favor."

"Again, that was a favor for Claire." Lawson watched Fiona's reaction. "This feels different."

"Different how?"

"Like you're fishing for something. A story angle. Your own cold case breakthrough."

Fiona gathered her purse. "This conversation has taken an unexpected turn."

"Has it?" Lawson remained seated. "You contacted me about a podcast that uses leaked evidence. Evidence only someone with department access could provide."

"I protect my sources." Fiona stood. "Always."

"Even when they break the law? Compromise investigations?"

"Especially then." Fiona adjusted her blazer. "The public deserves truth. Sometimes accessing that truth requires... flexibility."

"Flexibility." Lawson looked up at her. "Like paying for sealed evidence? Trading favors for confidential files?"

"I never said that." Fiona's voice hardened. "And you should be careful making accusations without proof."

"Not accusations. Questions." Lawson remained seated. Deliberate power move, letting Fiona stand alone. "Same questions I asked during the regatta case. Same questions I'm asking about Blackwell's podcast."

Fiona glanced around the café. Checking who might overhear. "This meeting was a mistake."

"Was it?" Lawson finally stood. "Or did you get exactly what you came for? Reaction quotes from Monica Landry's partner about the podcast? Background for your next front-page story?"

The flicker in Fiona's eyes confirmed it. This meeting had never been about warning Lawson. It had been reconnaissance. Information gathering disguised as friendly concern.

"The Chronicle will cover the podcast." Fiona admitted this much. "Public interest is too high to ignore it."

"And you wanted exclusive comments." Lawson nodded slowly. "Lead reporter angle while Blackwell gets national attention."

"I thought you might prefer speaking with someone who understands Savannah." Fiona's tone shifted to professional reporter mode. "Someone who remembers Monica."

"You didn't know her."

"I covered her funeral." Fiona's expression softened with practiced sympathy. "Three hundred officers in dress blues. Your eulogy moved many to tears."

The memory of that day sliced through Lawson. Standing at the podium while rows of uniforms blurred through tears. Reading words that could never capture who Monica had been. What they had meant to each other.

"Don't use her name to manipulate me." Lawson kept her voice low. "We're done here."

"When you're ready to tell your side, call me. Before Blackwell shapes the narrative beyond your control."

"Goodbye, Fiona."

chapter seven

LAWSON SAT cross-legged on her living room floor, laptop balanced on the coffee table. Three empty coffee mugs formed a semicircle around her. The room had grown dark while she worked, but she hadn't bothered with lights. Only the glow of the screen illuminated her face.

She pressed play for the forty-seventh time.

"I've got a 10-999! Officer down! Send help immediately!" Her own voice, frantic and raw. "Warehouse district, old paper mill. Shots fired, officer down. Need medical assistance!"

Five years since she'd made that call. Five years of avoiding the sound of her own desperation. Now she couldn't stop listening. Each replay exposed new layers of her panic, her breathing ragged between words, her voice breaking on "officer down."

Her fingers moved across the keyboard, adjusting parameters on the audio software she'd downloaded three hours ago. Increased gain. Reduced background noise. Isolated frequency ranges. The audio engineering terms blurred together as she pushed buttons based on YouTube tutorials rather than expertise.

She pressed play again.

Something lurked beneath her voice. Something she'd missed during previous listens. A shadow in the audio. She increased the volume until her eardrums protested, focusing on the space between her pleas for help.

There. A voice. Not hers. Not Monica's. Male. Low. Almost lost beneath the sound of her own ragged breathing.

She repeated the segment, isolating just those three seconds. Stripped away her voice, enhanced what remained.

"Erin."

Her name. Whispered or spoken softly. Not shouted. Not panicked. Just stated. Matter of fact.

Cold spread through her chest. She sat motionless, fingers hovering above the keyboard. Someone else had been there that night. Someone who knew her name.

The official report listed only two people at the scene when shots were fired. Lawson and Monica. Backup arrived four minutes after her radio call. By then, Monica lay dead on concrete, and Lawson knelt beside her, hands pressed to the wound, blood soaking through her clothes.

She played it again. *"Erin."*

Who said her name? The voice triggered something deep in memory. Familiar but impossible to place. She closed her eyes, trying to remember faces from that night. The responding officers. Paramedics who pronounced Monica dead. Richardson arriving later, face grim in the flashing lights.

The bedroom clock read 2:17 a.m. when she started comparing audio samples. She'd recorded statements from dozens of officers over the years. Witness interviews. Suspect interrogations. She dug through her digital archives, pulling male voices, converting formats to match the podcast audio.

Nothing matched. Either the voice belonged to someone whose statement she'd never recorded, or the audio quality was too poor for accurate comparison.

She opened a new browser tab. Searched for audio forensics software. Professional versions cost thousands. Trial versions offered limited functionality. She downloaded three different programs, installing each before moving to the next.

Her fingers cramped from hours at the keyboard. Her eyes burned from staring at sound wave patterns. Still, she persisted, the voice haunting her like a ghost.

"*Erin.*"

Not Monica calling out. Someone else. Someone who shouldn't have been there.

She played the full podcast segment again, focusing on Blackwell's commentary after the radio call. "That was Detective Erin Lawson, Monica Landry's partner, calling for help that would arrive too late."

Did Blackwell know about the male voice? Had she heard it during her investigation? The thought sent Lawson digging through the podcast website, searching for contact information, production credits, anything that might reveal Blackwell's audio engineer.

The website listed sound editing by Adam Hughes, audio restoration specialist. His profile mentioned work on historical recordings and forensic audio analysis. Professional equipment. Expert ear. If there was a voice on that recording, Hughes had heard it.

Which meant Blackwell knew someone else had been at the scene.

Lawson leaned back against the couch, her spine protesting the hours hunched over the laptop. The living room looked alien in the blue screen light. Shadow furniture. Empty coffee mugs. The framed photo of her academy graduation, face down on the side table where she'd knocked it during her search for headphones.

She played the isolated audio once more. "*Erin.*"

The voice scratched at her memory. Someone she knew. Someone who had no business being at that warehouse the night Monica died. Someone who had never appeared in any official report.

Had she heard it that night? Five years of replaying those moments in nightmares, and she'd never remembered another voice. The floodlight blinding her. The gunshot. Monica falling. Blood spreading across her white shirt. Those memories remained vivid, technicolor trauma that visited her sleep.

But the voice? Nothing. A blank space where recognition should be.

Unless she'd blocked it out. Trauma did strange things to memory. Created gaps. Rearranged timelines. The department psychologist had explained this during mandatory sessions after the shooting. Parts of that night might never return clearly.

Or perhaps she'd been too focused on Monica to register someone else speaking. The human brain filtered sensory input during a crisis.

Prioritized immediate threats. Maybe she'd heard her name but categorized it as unimportant compared to Monica bleeding out under her hands.

She opened another audio program. This one promised enhanced pattern recognition. Military grade algorithms. She highlighted the voice segment and initiated analysis. The software searched for matching patterns in her sample library. Names and faces scrolled past as it compared waveforms and frequency distributions.

No match found.

She tried again. Different parameters. Different voice samples. Same result.

Her fingers hovered over the keyboard. She could enhance the audio further. Clean it more aggressively. Risk distorting it beyond recognition while hunting for clarity. Or she could find someone with professional equipment. Someone like Adam Hughes.

The wall clock ticked toward morning. Tomorrow's interview with Blackwell loomed closer with each passing minute. Questions multiplied faster than answers. Did Blackwell know about the voice? Was she withholding it for a dramatic reveal in a future episode? Or had she missed it completely?

Lawson typed a search string into the audio software. Male voices, age thirty-five to fifty-five, within specific frequency ranges. Narrowed the parameters to match what she heard on the recording.

The computer churned through possibilities. She stared at the progress bar, counting seconds with each blink.

A fragment of memory surfaced. Standing over Monica's body while paramedics worked. The warehouse lot filled with police cars, lights painting everything red and blue. Richardson's hand on her shoulder. His voice in her ear. "We'll find who did this."

She tensed. Richardson.

The software beeped its completion. Still no definitive match. Maybe these damn things were all a hoax.

Lawson reached for her phone. Recorded herself saying "Richardson." Processed the audio. Compared it to the mystery voice. Not close enough for the software to flag as a match, but the timbre and resonance shared qualities.

She tried another name. Recorded "Walsh." Processed it. The software registered higher similarity, but still below the threshold for confirmation.

Her eyes burned from screen glare and lack of sleep. Her shoulders ached from tension. The coffee had worn off hours ago, leaving jittery exhaustion in its wake.

She needed better equipment. Professional software. Clean reference recordings of potential matches. Without those, she chased digital ghosts through distorted audio.

The voice had said her name. Just her name. No context. No explanation for why someone else had been present at a scene officially documented as having only two people before backup arrived.

Lawson saved her work to a flash drive. Backed it up to cloud storage. Documented every step of her analysis in case the original files became compromised.

She closed the laptop. The sudden darkness left afterimages floating across her vision. Her apartment returned to formless shadows. She didn't move, letting her eyes adjust while her mind raced.

Leah Blackwell must have heard that voice too.

chapter
eight

LAWSON FOLLOWED Claire into a second-floor office overlooking Forsyth Park. The space wasn't flashy, more lived-in than swank, but sunlight from tall windows gave it a genteel Savannah charm. A row of desks and battered bookcases suggested this was a shared arrangement, not the kind of corner suite high-priced firms flaunted downtown. Claire's desk sat nearest the window, papers stacked in two uneven piles. From Lawson's angle, she could only make out the museum letterhead peeking from one, and the legal-size formatting of the other.

"The Savannah Historical Society still gets most of my hours," Claire said, catching Lawson's glance. "But I've taken on three cases in the last month. Testing the waters."

Lawson nodded. Claire's gradual return to law after the Anthony Bates case made sense. The museum provided stability while she rebuilt her practice and herself. "Looks like you're getting busy."

Lawson paced between bookshelves while Claire typed. The oak floorboards creaked under her boots. Three hours of sleep left her running on caffeine and adrenaline.

"Sit down before you wear a path in my floor." Claire never looked up from her keyboard. Her fingers moved with mechanical precision, tapping out search queries. "Legal databases aren't designed for speed."

Lawson dropped into the visitor chair. "What do we have so far?"

"Leah Blackwell. Columbia Law. Top ten percent of her class."

Claire scrolled through search results. "Started her podcast during her final year of law school. It gained traction while she clerked for Judge Markinson in the Second Circuit."

"After her clerkship, she joined Hutchinson and Associates as an associate in their white collar criminal defense division." Claire's eyes narrowed at something on the screen. "Only stayed a year before leaving when the podcast took off."

"Corporate law?"

"White collar criminal defense. Interesting."

Lawson leaned forward. "What?"

"Hutchinson specialized in high profile clients." Claire turned the monitor so Lawson could see. "Politicians. CEOs. Celebrities with legal problems."

The firm's website displayed marble columns and mahogany paneling. Partners posed in tailored suits with practiced smiles. Power disguised as professionalism.

"Why leave that for podcasting?" Lawson asked.

"Money." Claire continued typing. "True crime exploded after the Serial podcast went viral. Corporate sponsors. Book deals. Netflix adaptations. Top podcasters earn seven figures."

"Not idealism then."

"I never said that." Claire pulled up another screen. "Looks like Blackwell was working on the Wallace case for a while before publishing the first season."

Lawson knew about the Wallace case. Business partners in real estate development. One murdered, the other convicted on circumstantial evidence. Blackwell's investigation had exposed prosecutorial misconduct. Wallace walked free after twenty years in prison.

"She got results," Lawson admitted.

"She got attention." Claire continued searching. "The Wallace case went viral. Five million downloads. New York Times coverage. Speaking engagements."

"You sound skeptical."

"I'm a defense attorney who overturned a conviction." Claire finally looked up. "I believe in justice for the wrongfully convicted. I also understand career advancement disguised as moral crusading."

Lawson circled back to the earlier point. "Hutchinson and Associates. Any connection to Savannah?"

Claire returned to her search. "Checking court records now. Their client list is mostly New York based, but larger firms often have satellite offices or take cases with national implications."

Lawson stared out the window while Claire worked. Forsyth Park stretched green and manicured below. Joggers circled the fountain. A yoga class formed geometric patterns on the grass. Normal life continued while she hunted ghosts through computer records.

"Found something." Claire's voice sharpened. "Hutchinson briefly represented Victor Mendez in 2020."

"Mendez." The name clicked immediately. "The mechanic."

"First suspect in Monica's murder." Claire pushed a printed file across the desk. "Picked up two days after the shooting. Released three weeks later when charges were dropped due to insufficient evidence."

Lawson flipped through the file. Victor Mendez. Thirty-eight at time of arrest. Auto mechanic with connections to the Rafferty operation. Allegedly serviced vehicles used for drug transport. His garage sat four blocks from the warehouse where Monica died.

"We could never connect him directly to the shooting." Lawson scanned the case notes. "Anonymous tip placed him near the scene that night. His alibi had holes. But forensics found nothing definitive."

"According to this, Hutchinson sent a junior attorney for his bail hearing." Claire pointed to a notation. "Charges dropped before they got further involved."

Lawson frowned. "Why would a Manhattan law firm represent a Savannah mechanic on murder charges?"

"Exactly." Claire leaned back in her chair. "Small time mechanic gets a white shoe New York firm for representation? Someone with money or influence arranged it."

"Someone connected to Rafferty."

"Likely."

Lawson turned to the final page. Case closure form signed by the district attorney. Reason for dismissal: Insufficient evidence to proceed.

"This was Blackwell's firm." Lawson looked up from the file. "She would have had access to case details. Witness statements. Police reports."

"Not necessarily." Claire raised a finger. "Large firms compartmentalize. Associates work on assigned cases only. Client confidentiality is sacred."

"But she might have seen something. Heard something in office conversation."

"Possible." Claire turned back to her computer. "Let me check if she was directly involved."

Lawson resumed pacing. Victor Mendez. The name brought back memories of interrogation rooms. Mendez sitting stone-faced across the table while she fired questions. His calm denial of involvement. The frustration when forensics failed to place him at the scene.

"No direct connection." Claire pushed away from her desk. "Blackwell worked in corporate liability during that period. Different department from criminal defense."

"Still the same firm." Lawson stopped at the window. "Might explain her interest in Monica's case."

"Or complete coincidence." Claire closed her laptop. "Thousands of cases pass through firms like Hutchinson. Most associates never see files outside their department."

"I don't believe in coincidences."

"You believe in conspiracies." Claire stood and stretched. Hours at the computer left creases in her silk blouse. "Which reminds me. Judge Byrd filed the temporary restraining order against the podcast."

Lawson turned from the window. "When will it take effect?"

"These things take time." Claire poured water from a crystal decanter. "Legal proceedings move at their own pace."

"Even with an active judge filing it?"

"Especially then." Claire handed Lawson a glass. "No one wants accusations of bending rules for a colleague."

Lawson set the untouched water on a side table. "What's the point then?"

Claire paused with her own glass halfway to her lips. "Wow. Never thought I'd hear Erin Lawson question legal procedure."

"Four months sober." Lawson pinched the bridge of her nose.

"Sleepless nights. Voice recordings saying my name at a murder scene. Now, learning the podcaster digging through my past worked for the firm that represented our prime suspect."

"The firm represented him." Claire emphasized the distinction. "Not Blackwell personally."

"Still." Lawson sank back into the chair. "This whole thing ..."

"Is getting to you." Claire sat on the edge of her desk. The informal position contrasted with her courtroom demeanor. "I understand what it feels like when cases hit too close to home."

Lawson nodded. Claire had faced her own demons two years ago with the Anthony Bates case. A wrongful conviction she'd overturned that had dredged up personal history. Old wounds reopened in public view.

"How did you handle it?" Lawson asked.

"Well, as you know, poorly at first." Claire smiled without humor. "Stopped sleeping. Stopped eating properly. Became the case instead of working it."

"Sounds familiar."

"We're similar that way." Claire's gaze held steady. "Too invested. Too willing to burn ourselves down to find the truth."

"Monica deserves justice."

"You deserve peace." Claire set her glass down. "Those two things might not arrive simultaneously."

Lawson considered this. Five years pursuing justice while peace remained elusive. Now Blackwell threatened what little stability she'd managed to construct.

"An interview with Blackwell ..." Claire began.

"Is necessary." Lawson stood. "I need to know what she knows. What she suspects."

"Be careful. She's built a career extracting information from reluctant sources."

"So have I." Lawson gathered her notes. "Thanks for this. I owe you."

"Professional courtesy." Claire returned to her desk. "Besides, I never trusted Hutchinson and Associates. Too polished. Too connected. Their attorneys always acted like they knew judges personally."

Lawson paused at the door. "You think Blackwell maintains those connections?"

"Worth considering." Claire reopened her laptop. "Legal networks run deep. Former colleagues become valuable sources."

"I'll keep that in mind."

Lawson left Claire's office and stepped out into the midday heat. Savannah in August felt like walking through soup. The humidity pressed against her skin, immediately dampening her shirt between her shoulder blades.

Her phone chimed with an email notification as she reached her car. Department address, marked urgent. She opened it while starting the engine and cranking the air conditioning.

FROM: Chief Wallace

TO: All Personnel

SUBJECT: Internal Affairs Liaison Assignment

In light of recent public scrutiny regarding the Monica Landry investigation, the department has assigned Lieutenant Eli Park as temporary Internal Affairs liaison to the precinct. Lieutenant Park will review case materials and coordinate departmental response to media inquiries.

All personnel involved in the original investigation are directed to cooperate fully while maintaining standard protocols regarding active cases.

Chief Wallace

Lawson stared at the screen. Internal Affairs. The department rats who investigated other cops. Bringing one in meant trouble. Bringing one in with explicit orders to review Monica's case meant serious trouble.

A second email arrived before she could process the first.

FROM: Lt. Eli Park

TO: Det. Erin Lawson

SUBJECT: Meeting Request

Detective Lawson,

I've been assigned to review the Monica Landry case in light of recent public attention. Please plan to meet with me tomorrow at 10:00 a.m. in Conference Room B.

Bring all notes, files, and materials related to the original investigation in your possession.
This is a formal inquiry. You may bring representation if desired.
Lt. Eli Park
Internal Affairs Division

The car's air conditioning blasted cold air against her face, yet sweat still beaded along her hairline. Internal Affairs. Formal inquiry. Representation. Language designed to intimidate officers into compliance.

Lawson closed the email and put the car in drive. Five years of carrying an unofficial copy of Monica's case. Five years of quiet investigation outside official channels. All potentially exposed by an Internal Affairs review.

Blackwell's podcast had achieved its first victory. The department now investigated its own. And Lawson stood directly in the crosshairs.

chapter nine

CONFERENCE ROOM B sat at the far end of the precinct. Glass walls afforded no privacy, turning interviews into aquarium exhibits for passing officers. Lawson arrived fifteen minutes early, coffee in hand.

The room stood empty. She claimed the chair facing the door and spread her files across the table. Official copies only. The unauthorized material remained locked in her apartment.

Precinct activity continued outside. Officers processed morning arrests. Phones rang. Keyboards clicked. Life moved forward despite the sword hanging over her career.

Ten minutes passed before the door opened. A man entered carrying a leather messenger bag and a coffee mug with the Marine Corps emblem. His gray suit looked military in its precision. No wrinkles, perfect creases. His haircut matched—high and tight, revealing a scar that curved behind his right ear.

"Detective Lawson." His voice carried the clipped cadence of someone accustomed to giving orders. "Lieutenant Eli Parks. Internal Affairs."

She stood and offered her hand. "Lieutenant."

His grip proved firm without domineering pressure. A handshake that communicated competence rather than intimidation.

He glanced around the conference room with obvious distaste, then took a sip from his mug. The grimace that followed seemed involuntary.

"Your coffee tastes like battery acid filtered through a sweaty sock." He set the mug down. "Perimeter Coffee Shop two blocks south makes something resembling actual coffee. Care to continue this there?"

Lawson blinked. "You arranged this meeting here."

"That was before I tasted your coffee." Parks gestured toward the hallway. "Important conversations deserve adequate caffeine. My treat."

His casual tone contrasted with IAB's reputation for rigid formality. "Won't your superiors expect an official setting?"

"My superiors expect results, not location reports." Parks checked his watch. "Fifteen minutes walking and ordering still puts us within our scheduled window."

The unexpected suggestion threw her. Conference Room B offered controlled conditions, even witnesses if Parks became adversarial. Recording equipment if needed. The coffee shop meant civilians, background noise, unpredictable variables.

It also meant Parks couldn't secretly record their conversation using precinct equipment.

"Let me grab my jacket." She gathered her files while weighing possibilities. Either Parks genuinely preferred honest conversation in neutral territory, or this represented a calculated tactic to lower her defenses.

They walked in professional silence. Parks matched his stride to hers without apparent effort. His gaze swept the street with military vigilance—corners, rooflines, vehicles. The habit of a man who'd spent time in combat zones.

Perimeter Coffee occupied a narrow storefront between a bookshop and a vintage clothing store. Edison bulbs hung from exposed ceiling beams. The espresso machine hissed and gurgled behind a copper counter. College students hunched over laptops while professionals conducted quiet meetings at corner tables.

Parks claimed a booth near the back exit. "Ethiopian dark roast, black. Detective?"

"Americano, room for cream." She slid into the booth opposite him, arranging her files as a barrier between them.

He returned minutes later with steaming mugs and a small plate with two chocolate croissants. "Owner adds cocoa to the pastry dough. Worth the calories."

The casual approach continued to unbalance her expectations. Internal Affairs typically maintained a formal distance. Parks behaved more like a colleague than an investigator.

"Your file says eight years with SPD." Parks opened the top folder after settling in. "Last five in homicide after your partner's death. Three commendations. Four citations for excessive force. Two for insubordination."

"My greatest hits." She sipped her coffee—significantly better than precinct sludge. "I expected more formality from Internal Affairs."

"Formality serves paperwork, not truth." Parks studied her over his mug. "This situation needs careful handling."

"Which situation? A podcast airing sealed evidence or the department's panic response?"

He almost smiled. "Both qualify." He pulled several papers from his folder. "You understand why I've been assigned?"

"Department needs someone to control the narrative before Blackwell does."

"Close." Parks laid out documents in a neat row. "I need to determine if Blackwell possesses evidence that will embarrass the department, or merely speculation that can be dismissed."

His honesty startled her. IAB usually cloaked objectives behind procedure.

"My assignment includes reviewing the original investigation." Parks tapped the file. "Determining if proper protocols were followed."

"They weren't." The words escaped before she could filter them.

His eyebrows rose. "Explain."

Lawson considered her options. Parks offered either a genuine ally or a sophisticated trap. Either way, playing defense would accomplish nothing.

"Monica believed someone inside the department protected the Rafferty operation." She kept her voice low despite no one seeming to be paying any attention to them. "Before she could prove it, she was murdered. Afterward, the case went cold with remarkable speed."

Parks nodded but offered no immediate reaction. "When was the last time you reviewed the complete case file?"

"Five years ago. Before it went to storage." This much remained true while concealing her unauthorized copy.

"I pulled it yesterday." Parks extracted a page from his folder. "Evidence log shows forty-three items collected from the scene. Only twenty-seven received complete processing."

Lawson leaned forward. "Which sixteen items didn't?"

"Soil samples from around the body. Partial shoe impressions from the loading dock. Paint chips from the floodlight housing. Shell casings found twenty yards from the primary scene." Parks slid the paper toward her. "All logged but never analyzed."

Her stomach tightened. She'd never seen this discrepancy. The case file copy she'd secretly maintained ended with a different evidence log—one showing all items processed.

"Someone altered my copy." The realization escaped aloud.

"Your copy?"

She recovered quickly. "The copy I reviewed before the case transferred."

Parks studied her with unnerving intensity. "Evidence gaps represent only part of the problem. Witness canvass shows eight interviews conducted on the night of the shooting. Three witness statements reference a vehicle leaving the scene."

"Black sedan. No plates visible. Driver description varied." She remembered those details clearly.

"Correct." Parks nodded. "Follow up interviews never occurred. No vehicle matching partial descriptions appeared in subsequent reports."

Lawson fought to maintain a neutral expression. This information contradicted everything she knew about the investigation. "That makes no sense. Standard procedure requires—"

"Follow up on all witness leads." Parks finished her sentence. "Yet the detective who took over your partner's case closed these avenues within forty-eight hours."

"Who reassigned the case?" She knew Richardson had orchestrated the transfer but wanted Parks' information.

"Orders came from Chief Mason through Captain Richardson." Parks slid another document across the table. "Detective Victor Walsh received primary."

Walsh. A twenty-year veteran who retired six months after the investigation closed. A man known for following orders without question.

"Walsh buried it." The pieces connected in her mind. "But why would Richardson allow that?"

"That question brought me to your doorstep." Parks gathered his papers back into a neat stack. "Richardson protected certain officers throughout his career. Protected you after your partner's death."

The shift in conversation chilled her. "Protected me how?"

"Your blood alcohol level the night of the shooting." Parks kept his voice clinical rather than accusatory. "The patrol sergeant noted alcohol on your breath. Standard procedure requires testing when officers discharge weapons."

"I didn't fire my weapon that night."

"No, but you witnessed another officer's death. Protocol still applied."

Lawson's hands tightened around her coffee mug. "No one ordered testing."

"Richardson arrived on scene and took command. Testing never occurred." Parks closed his folder. "First procedural irregularity in a case that accumulated many."

The shop suddenly felt airless.

"Am I under investigation?" She forced the question past dry lips.

"Everyone connected to the Landry case requires scrutiny. The podcast ensures public attention." Parks leaned back in his chair. "But my focus extends beyond individual officers."

"Department corruption."

"Systemic failures." He corrected gently. "Cases don't bury themselves. Evidence doesn't vanish without assistance."

Lawson considered her next words. Internal Affairs officers specialized in extracting information through false camaraderie. Yet Parks seemed genuinely troubled by what he'd found.

"Ever wonder why Monica's case went cold so fast?" Parks asked when she remained silent.

"Every day for five years."

"Someone wanted it buried." He tapped the folder. "The pattern appears throughout the file. Evidence logged but never processed.

Witnesses interviewed but never revisited. Leads documented then abandoned."

Parks paused, consulting his notes. "There's something else that bothers me. Financial records show regular cash deposits into Monica's account in her final months. Each one exactly five thousand dollars. No clear source documented in the investigation."

"You think Richardson directed this?"

"I think Richardson allowed it." Parks watched her closely. "Whether through active participation or deliberate oversight remains unclear."

His theory aligned with her private suspicions. Richardson had always maintained plausible deniability while enforcing department priorities. Budget constraints. Manpower allocation. Administrative necessities that somehow always benefited certain cases over others.

"This podcast creates opportunity." Parks continued when she didn't respond. "Public scrutiny forces thorough review where internal questions failed."

"You sound almost grateful to Blackwell."

"I appreciate catalysts regardless of motivation." He sipped his coffee. "This Blackwell woman serves her own agenda, but her spotlight might illuminate departmental shadows."

Lawson studied him with renewed interest. "Most Internal Affairs officers protect the department image above all else."

"Most Internal Affairs officers never worked military investigations." Parks smiled tightly. "Pentagon politics make police departments look transparent. I learned to follow evidence regardless of rank or consequence."

"That approach creates enemies."

"Already collected plenty." He shrugged. "Career advancement stopped mattering after my second tour in Afghanistan."

The comment landed differently than standard police bravado. Something genuine resided in his dismissal of politics. Maybe a man who'd faced actual war viewed departmental threats differently.

"What happens next?" She gestured toward his folder.

"I continue reviewing the original investigation. Interview all officers involved. Examine chain of custody for evidence." Parks recited procedures like someone who found comfort in protocol. "You continue your current duties while cooperating with my inquiries."

"And the podcast?"

"Remains problematic but potentially useful." He closed his messenger bag. "Blackwell possesses information someone leaked. That someone concerns me more than her journalistic methods."

Lawson nodded, still uncertain where Parks ultimately stood. Ally or adversary remained unclear, but his presence shifted the landscape. Someone besides her now questioned the official narrative.

"I need access to your notes from the original investigation." Parks stood, gathering his materials. "Your perspective as Landry's partner provides context the official file lacks."

"My notes became part of the case file." This lie flowed easily after years of repetition.

"Your official notes, yes." Parks slung his bag over his shoulder. "But detectives maintain personal observations. Theories. Connections that might seem insignificant until later."

Her unofficial case file flashed through her mind. Five years of private investigation compiled in notebooks and digital files. Revealing those materials could end her career—or provide the breakthrough Monica's case needed.

"I'll review what I have." This compromise bought time while she assessed Parks' trustworthiness.

"I appreciate your cooperation." He handed her a business card. "My direct line. Available anytime."

The card stock felt heavy between her fingers. Old school, like his paper files and precise handwriting. A man who left minimal digital footprints in a world of electronic surveillance.

"We'll speak again soon, Detective."

He departed with military efficiency, leaving Lawson alone with cooling coffee and unsettling revelations. The case file differences troubled her most. Someone had provided her with altered evidence logs after Monica's death. A deliberate attempt to conceal the incomplete processing.

Richardson's warnings echoed in her memory. Be careful who you trust. Even people who seem like allies might have their own agendas.

Did that warning now apply to Eli Parks? His forthright approach might represent genuine dedication to truth, or sophisticated manipulation designed to expose her unauthorized investigation.

Lawson gathered her materials and left the coffee shop. For the first time in five years, someone else questioned the official narrative surrounding Monica's death. The relief almost overwhelmed her suspicion.

Almost, but not quite.

chapter
ten

MAGNOLIA CEMETERY STRETCHED ACROSS forty acres of Savannah's east side; ancient live oaks draped in Spanish moss creating natural cathedrals above weathered headstones. Parks navigated the winding paths with practiced familiarity, a single white rose in his hand. Three years, two months, and sixteen days since he'd started making this weekly pilgrimage.

The headstone bore a simple inscription: Detective Bram Kowalski, Savannah Police Department, Beloved Partner and Friend. No mention of the circumstances that brought him here. No acknowledgment of the investigation that cost him his life.

Parks placed the rose beside the granite marker and settled onto the small bench he'd installed nearby. The cemetery maintenance crew had grown accustomed to his presence, leaving him undisturbed during these visits.

"Still working the corruption cases, Bram." His voice carried clearly in the morning stillness. "Found another one. Detective named Lawson, lost her partner five years ago. Same pattern as yours."

The memory surfaced unbidden—Kowalski's final phone call, voice tight with excitement and fear. *I found something, Eli. Evidence tampering going back years. Major cases thrown through deliberate mishandling. I'm taking it to Internal Affairs tomorrow.*

Tomorrow never came for Bram Kowalski. Single-car accident on Highway 17, vehicle leaving the roadway at high speed and striking a tree. Alcohol was found in his system despite Kowalski being a teetotaler. The investigation closed within forty-eight hours as driver error due to impairment.

Parks had known immediately something was wrong. Kowalski's methodical nature extended to every aspect of his life. The man who organized his sock drawer by color didn't suddenly develop reckless driving habits. But Parks had been a patrol sergeant then, lacking authority to challenge the official findings.

"The evidence you found disappeared from your apartment before I could retrieve it," Parks continued aloud, processing thoughts through familiar ritual. "But you were smart. Always backed up important files. I found your secondary storage three months after the funeral." Kowalski's hidden drive contained meticulous documentation of evidence tampering across multiple cases. Drugs that vanished from lock-up before trial. Weapons that developed chain-of-custody gaps. Financial records that became corrupted or misfiled at crucial moments. The systematic manipulation of physical evidence to ensure specific outcomes.

Every compromised case involved defendants who walked free on technicalities that shouldn't have existed.

Parks had spent three years expanding Kowalski's investigation, methodically documenting the evidence tampering network while building his own case. The Internal Affairs transfer hadn't been punishment—it had been strategy. Access to more cases, broader authority, ability to examine patterns across multiple precincts.

"Someone's been manipulating evidence for years," Parks said. "You found the pattern but not the people behind it. High-profile criminal cases systematically weakened through evidence problems, then dismissed on technicalities."

The scope remained unclear, but the methodology was consistent. Cases that should have resulted in convictions instead ended in acquittals or plea bargains that kept dangerous criminals on the streets. The pattern suggested coordination rather than random corruption.

Parks opened his notebook, reviewing details he'd committed to memory years ago. "You identified the tampering but didn't live long enough to discover who was orchestrating it. You thought it was just a few dirty cops taking bribes. Didn't realize how deep it went."

A jogger passed on the nearby path, earbuds blocking out the world. Normal morning routine for someone whose partner hadn't been murdered for pursuing justice. Parks envied the simplicity while recognizing his own path had been chosen deliberately.

"Monica Landry discovered something similar." Parks turned to a fresh page, documenting new connections. "But she had resources you lacked. Should have made her safer."

Instead, it had made her a larger threat. Whatever she'd uncovered had escalated the stakes beyond local corruption into something worth killing to protect.

Parks stood, brushing cemetery dirt from his pants. "Lawson doesn't know about you yet. Doesn't realize her partner's death fits a pattern. When she's ready, I'll show her everything."

The decision felt inevitable. Kowalski's evidence provided historical context for the current investigation. Proof that Monica Landry's murder wasn't an isolated incident but part of a systematic elimination of threats to whatever network operated in Savannah's shadows.

"Your work mattered, Bram. Still matters." Parks touched the headstone once more before walking toward his car. "Going to finish what you started."

The morning had grown warmer, humidity building toward another sweltering Savannah day. Parks drove toward the precinct, Kowalski's evidence secure in his messenger bag alongside current case files. Past and present investigations converging toward a resolution that had been three years in development.

Kowalski's ghost could finally rest. After the corruption network fell and justice emerged from the wreckage, the debt to his murdered partner would be paid in full.

But first, there was work to do. Evidence to secure. Testimonies to gather. Cases to build that could survive legal challenges and political interference.

Parks merged into traffic, already planning his next conversation with Lawson. She needed to understand the scope of what they faced—

not just Monica's individual murder, but systematic corruption that had been killing good cops for years.

The time for subtle investigation was ending. Someone had grown too bold, too confident in their protection. Kowalski's death had taught Parks patience. Monica's murder demanded action.

chapter eleven

LAWSON'S PHONE chimed as she walked back toward the precinct. New email from an address she didn't recognize: L.Blackwell@DeadAirPodcast.com.

Subject line: I Know Why She Was Killed

Her thumb hovered over the notification. Opening it meant engaging with Blackwell on the podcaster's terms. Ignoring it meant wondering what evidence might exist.

She deleted it without reading.

The walk back to the precinct took twelve minutes. She appreciated the solitude, needing space to process Parks' revelations about evidence never analyzed and witnesses never re-interviewed.

Noon sun baked the pavement. Her blouse stuck to her back when she reached the precinct parking lot. The day stretched endlessly ahead—reports to file, witness statements to review for current cases, the looming shadow of Blackwell's podcast hanging over everything.

Instead, she drove toward Ardsley Park. Tree-lined streets with craftsman bungalows and renovated colonials. Upper middle-class families who maintained pristine yards and voted in local elections. Monica's sister Rachel had moved there after the funeral, using life insurance money for the down payment.

Rachel Banks née Landry lived in a pale-yellow house with white trim and a wraparound porch. Ceramic pots overflowed with ferns and flowering plants. A child's bicycle lay abandoned on the lawn beside a soccer ball. Signs of normal life continuing despite tragedy.

Lawson parked across the street and checked her appearance in the rearview mirror. Dark circles marked her eyes like bruises. Her shirt collar looked rumpled from the day's meetings. She straightened it before stepping out into the heat.

The doorbell echoed inside. Footsteps approached, followed by the rattle of a security chain.

Rachel Banks opened the door halfway. Five years had carved subtle changes into features that still resembled Monica's. Same dark hair and olive complexion, but different eyes. Where Monica's had sparkled with determination, Rachel's carried wariness.

"Detective Lawson." Rachel didn't sound surprised. "Figured you'd show up eventually."

"Hello Rachel. May I come in?"

Rachel hesitated before stepping back. "Twenty minutes. I need to pick up Ellie from summer camp at three."

The interior carried a faint trace of lavender detergent and yesterday's coffee. Bright crayon drawings, taped unevenly to the walls, outnumbered the framed photos. In the pictures that did hang, Rachel grinned at the camera—on a roller coaster with James and Ellie, clutching a Mickey Mouse balloon; James beaming in his MBA robes; Ellie gap-toothed, clutching a backpack nearly half her size. Monica appeared in several frames. Monica at Rachel's wedding. Monica holding newborn Ellie. Monica in her dress blues at academy graduation. A life preserved in frozen moments.

"Coffee?" Rachel asked without enthusiasm.

"No thanks."

"Then stop staring at my walls and tell me why you're here."

The kitchen reflected Rachel's personality. Organized but lived-in. Copper pots hung above the center island. A bowl of fruit sat beside math worksheets and colored pencils. The refrigerator displayed Ellie's artwork alongside a family calendar.

Rachel leaned against the counter, arms crossed. "This about the podcast?"

Lawson nodded. "You've heard it."

"First episode aired two days ago. Three million downloads already." Rachel's tone carried accusation. "Five years of silence, then suddenly everyone cares who killed my sister."

"I never stopped caring."

"You stopped visiting." Rachel gestured toward a chair but remained standing herself. "First year after Monica died, you came for dinner every month. Second year, three visits total. Then nothing."

Lawson sat despite Rachel's refusal to join her. "I never stopped investigating."

"Yet here we are. No arrests. No suspects." Rachel grabbed a dish towel and twisted it between her hands. "Now some New York podcaster digs up the 10-999 call, and suddenly the case matters again."

"The case always mattered."

"To who?" Rachel slapped the towel against the counter. "Not to your department. Not to the prosecutors. Not to anyone with power to do something."

The accusation stung because it contained truth. The department had buried Monica's case with procedural efficiency. Only Lawson maintained vigil over the investigation, and even she had failed to notice the discrepancies Parks revealed.

"I'm here because I need to know if Blackwell contacted you."

Rachel laughed without humor. "So that's it. You're not here for me. You're chasing the podcaster."

"Rachel—"

"She contacted me last month." Rachel moved to the refrigerator and extracted a business card from beneath a butterfly magnet. "Very professional. Asked permission to cover Monica's case. Said she believes the official investigation missed crucial evidence."

Lawson swallowed her surprise. "And you agreed?"

"I gave her Monica's personal effects." Rachel's gaze turned challenging. "Journals. Planner. Personal laptop. Items the department returned after closing the investigation."

Cold spread through Lawson's chest. Monica's personal effects might contain references to their relationship. Notes about the Rafferty case that never entered official records. Private thoughts that could reshape the entire narrative.

"Those items could compromise—"

"What?" Rachel interrupted. "The investigation you claim never stopped? The justice you promised five years ago?"

The kitchen fell silent except for the soft hum of the refrigerator. A clock ticked from the adjacent living room. Somewhere upstairs, pipes knocked as water moved through old plumbing.

"You promised to find who killed her." Rachel's voice dropped lower. "You stood at her funeral and told me you wouldn't rest until someone paid. Yet here we are."

"The evidence—"

"Maybe this podcaster will succeed where you failed." Rachel turned away, staring out the kitchen window at her backyard. "Maybe she actually cares about truth more than protecting fellow officers."

"That's not fair."

"Fair?" Rachel spun back, color rising in her cheeks. "Fair would be my sister attending Ellie's birthday parties. Fair would be Monica walking her niece to school. Fair would be growing old together instead of visiting a granite headstone."

Lawson absorbed the anger without defense. Rachel deserved her rage after five years of unanswered questions.

"Monica changed before she died." Rachel continued into the silence. "Last few weeks, she barely called. Missed Sunday dinner twice. Seemed distracted when she did visit."

"The Rafferty case consumed her." Lawson offered the explanation she'd accepted years ago.

"More than that." Rachel shook her head. "She seemed paranoid. Checked her car before driving. Kept the blinds closed at her apartment. Jumped when her phone rang."

Rachel paused, a puzzled expression crossing her face. "It was strange though—Monica had always struggled with money, student loans and mom's medical bills, but those last few months she seemed more relaxed about finances. Even mentioned taking a vacation once everything settled down. I never understood where that confidence came from."

"Did she explain why?"

"She said she couldn't trust anyone." Rachel met Lawson's gaze directly. "Not even you."

Lawson shook her head in shock. Monica's lack of trust contradicted everything Lawson believed about their relationship—professional and personal. Despite their fight, despite the distance during those final weeks, she'd never doubted their fundamental connection.

"That doesn't make sense." Lawson stood, needing movement to process this revelation. "We were partners for three years. We trusted each other with our lives."

Rachel opened a drawer and removed a small notebook bound in blue leather. "Found this after the funeral. Her personal journal. Most entries discuss cases or department politics."

She slid it across the counter. Lawson recognized it immediately. Monica carried it everywhere, jotting observations or questions that occurred during investigations. Private thoughts that never entered official reports.

"Read the last entry." Rachel nodded toward the notebook. "Three days before she died."

Lawson opened the journal with unsteady hands. Monica's handwriting filled the final pages—tight, precise letters that slanted slightly right. Lawson found the date Rachel indicated and began reading.

Meeting Ray Hutchinson tonight. Claims high-level connection to Rafferty operation. Something about him makes me uneasy. Too smooth. Too eager to help. But his information checks out so far. Money trail through offshore accounts matches what I already found. Haven't told E. We're still not talking. Better this way if things go sideways.

The entry stopped there. No elaboration on Hutchinsons' identity. No explanation about why he made her uncomfortable. No details about what information he'd already provided.

"She never mentioned Ray Hutchinson." Lawson looked up from the journal. "Never told me about these meetings."

"Because you two weren't speaking." Rachel's words carried finality rather than accusation now. "She said you had some kind of falling out. Wouldn't tell me details, but she was upset about it."

Lawson closed the journal. Guilt twisted her insides. Their fight about going public with their relationship had created the distance that ultimately left Monica vulnerable. "May I borrow this?"

"Keep it." Rachel glanced at the clock above the stove. "I gave Blackwell copies of everything except that. Couldn't part with Monica's actual handwriting."

"Thank you."

"Don't thank me." Rachel gathered her purse and keys from a hook by the door. "Just find who killed her. Five years is long enough to wait for justice."

Lawson followed her to the entryway. Family photos watched their passage—frozen smiles from happier times when Monica still breathed and laughed and planned her future.

"She loved you." Rachel paused at the front door. "Whatever happened between you those final weeks, she never stopped caring."

The comment sparked alarm. "What do you mean 'between us'?"

Rachel's expression shifted to something unreadable. "Sisters know things, Detective. Even when they're not explicitly told."

"Rachel—"

"I need to get Ellie." Rachel opened the door, ending the conversation. "Let yourself out."

Lawson stood alone in the entryway after Rachel departed. Monica smiled from every wall—immortalized in moments of joy now overshadowed by her violent end. The weight of broken promises pressed down on Lawson's shoulders.

She'd failed both sisters. Failed to protect Monica. Failed to deliver justice to Rachel. Failed to honor the vows made beside a flag-draped coffin.

The journal felt heavy in her pocket as she walked to her car. Monica's last written words revealed a partner who had deliberately excluded her from a crucial meeting. A partner who feared someone inside the department. A partner who died protecting secrets Lawson still couldn't access.

What hadn't Monica told her? What evidence had she uncovered that made isolation seem safer than partnership? What threat loomed so large that Monica would face it alone rather than endanger Lawson?

The car's interior had become an oven during her visit. She cranked the air conditioning and sat with the journal open on her lap. Reading each entry chronologically might reveal what Monica discovered in those final weeks. What connections she made that others missed.

Her phone chimed as she pulled away from the curb. Notification from Dead Air Podcast appearing on her screen: *New Episode Available: "Silence in Savannah - Episode Three: The Floodlight"*

dead air episode 3:

"The Floodlight"

[Electronic theme music fades in, then quiets under narration]

LEAH BLACKWELL: Welcome back to Dead Air. I'm Leah Blackwell.

In our previous episodes, we explored Detective Monica Landry's unsolved murder and the complex relationship with her partner, Detective Erin Lawson. Today, we focus on a crucial piece of physical evidence that raises troubling questions about what really happened that night: the floodlight.

[Brief pause]

LEAH: Let's revisit the scene. The old paper mill warehouse on Savannah's eastern industrial edge. Abandoned for seven years. No electricity. No security. The perfect location for a meeting that needed to remain off the record.

LEAH: According to Detective Lawson's statement, she arrived at the warehouse at approximately 11:00 p.m. to meet Detective Landry. They took cover behind her vehicle when shots were fired from the warehouse. As they attempted to reach the loading dock for better cover, a powerful industrial floodlight suddenly activated, momentarily blinding Detective Lawson. When her vision cleared, Detective Landry had already been shot.

LEAH: The floodlight detail appears in the initial police report, the medical examiner's findings, and Detective Lawson's formal statement. But here's the problem—that floodlight shouldn't have worked at all.

[Sound of rustling papers]

LEAH: I spoke with Rachel Banks, Detective Landry's sister, about this inconsistency:

[Audio clip from interview] **RACHEL:** The detectives never explained it. I specifically asked how a light could work in an abandoned building. They said it was probably battery-powered, brought by the shooter. But then why wasn't it taken as evidence? Why wasn't it fingerprinted? None of it made sense.

LEAH: Rachel's questions are valid. If the shooter brought the light, it would have been a crucial piece of evidence. Yet crime scene photographs show no light fixture entered into evidence, only mounting brackets where such a light would have been attached.

[Music intensifies]

LEAH: But the floodlight is just one of many pieces of evidence that mysteriously disappeared after Monica Landry's death. According to department sources, key files from the Rafferty case went missing within days of Detective Landry's murder.

SPD SOURCE (voice disguised): Monica kept detailed notes on the Rafferty investigation in a separate file. Personal observations, connections that weren't ready for the official record yet. That file vanished from her desk the day after she died. When Detective Lawson asked about it, she was told it never existed.

LEAH: Rachel Banks confirmed her sister maintained extensive personal records:

[Audio clip from interview] **RACHEL:** Monica documented everything. She had this blue notebook she carried everywhere. She would never go anywhere without it. Never.

LEAH: That notebook remains unaccounted for. Not listed in evidence. Not returned with her personal effects. Just gone—along with whatever information it contained about the Rafferty case and the corruption Monica believed she'd uncovered.

[Brief pause]

LEAH: We tracked down Carl Jensen, who worked security for the warehouse complex until its closure:

CARL JENSEN: Those old security floods pulled serious amperage. You'd need a dedicated setup to power one - generator, battery bank, something substantial. And they're heavy—maybe forty, fifty pounds. Not something you just happen to find working in an abandoned building.

LEAH: I asked Carl how long it would take to install such a system:

CARL JENSEN: With the right equipment and know-how, maybe an hour. You'd need mounting brackets, wiring, power source. And you'd need to test it to make sure the angle was right. This wasn't some spur-of-the-moment thing. Someone spent time setting this up.

[Music shifts]

LEAH: Six months after Detective Landry's death, the Rafferty investigation was quietly closed due to "insufficient evidence." Former colleagues tell us Detective Lawson fought the decision.

FORMER COLLEAGUE (voice disguised): Lawson went ballistic when they shelved the Rafferty case. Said evidence was being buried, witnesses intimidated. Filed formal complaints that went nowhere. She kept copies of everything, worked the case on her own time.

LEAH: Those complaints, which should be part of the departmental record, have also disappeared. When we filed public records requests for Detective Lawson's formal protests regarding the Rafferty case, we received this response:

[Reading from document] "No responsive documents exist matching your description. All case materials related to the referenced investigation have been properly archived according to department protocols."

LEAH: But multiple sources confirm these documents existed. Detective Lawson filed them. Captain Richardson acknowledged receiving them. Yet they've vanished from official records, just like the floodlight, just like Monica's notebook, just like crucial witness statements that didn't match the official narrative.

[Brief pause]

LEAH: The evidence points to careful planning and subsequent cover-up. Someone knew the meeting location in advance. Someone had access to the warehouse before the detectives arrived. Someone positioned that light to create momentary blindness at the critical moment.

LEAH: And after Detective Landry died, someone systematically removed evidence that might have revealed the truth about what she discovered in the Rafferty investigation.

[Music becomes more pointed]

LEAH: Cell tower data shows Detective Landry's phone in a different location when the meeting text was sent – near her apartment complex, not the police station where she was reportedly working late. Security footage from her building shows her car in the parking lot at 10:15 PM, but no sign of Detective Landry herself.

LEAH: We asked digital forensics expert Dr. Martin Chen about potential explanations:

DR. CHEN: Without examining the device, I can only speculate, but there are several possibilities. The phone could have been used by someone else. Text messages can be scheduled to send at specific times. Or, with the right expertise, texts can be spoofed to appear from a specific number.

LEAH: The Savannah Police Department's technical division should have analyzed these inconsistencies. Yet the case file shows no digital forensics performed on Detective Landry's phone beyond basic call and text logs.

LEAH: When we asked former Captain Thomas Richardson about this oversight, his office provided this statement:

[Reading from statement] "All investigative avenues were pursued according to department protocols. Technical limitations at the time prevented certain forensic analyses now considered standard."

LEAH: That explanation doesn't hold up. The FBI's Digital Evidence Laboratory offered assistance three days after the murder, standard procedure for officer killings. According to internal memos, that offer was declined by the Savannah PD.

[Brief pause]

LEAH: The floodlight. The suspicious text message. The missing files and notebook. The lack of digital forensics. Each detail points to the same troubling conclusion: Monica Landry's death wasn't random. It was planned, coordinated, and executed with insider knowledge.

LEAH: Someone knew exactly where she would be standing. Someone arranged for a momentary blindness that provided the perfect opportunity for a clean shot. Someone ensured the subsequent investigation would overlook crucial evidence.

[Music softens]

LEAH: In our next episode, we'll explore another piece of this puzzle – Detective Ray Hutchinson from Narcotics, who claims to have been romantically involved with Monica Landry in the months before her death. His story adds yet another layer to this already complex case.

[Music builds]

LEAH: This is Dead Air. The truth doesn't stay buried forever.

[Theme music plays out]

chapter twelve

THE MARRIOTT DOMINATED the riverfront skyline. Glass and steel reflected afternoon sunlight. Inside, marble floors and potted palms created artificial luxury. The lobby bar occupied a corner with views of cargo ships passing on the river.

Blackwell sat alone at a table near the windows. White blouse. Tailored black pants. Tablet propped against a water glass. Her gaze locked onto Lawson immediately, acknowledging her with a slight nod toward the empty chair.

Lawson paused in the doorway, studying her adversary. Blackwell's posture radiated controlled confidence—spine straight, shoulders squared, hands positioned precisely on the table. Everything calculated for maximum psychological impact. Even her choice of seating put the sun at her back, forcing anyone approaching to squint into the glare.

"Detective." No smile. No greeting beyond acknowledgment. "You listened to Episode Three."

"You know about Monica and me." Lawson remained standing, refusing to cede the tactical advantage of height. "How?"

"Sit down." Blackwell closed her tablet with deliberate precision. "This conversation requires privacy."

"Answer my question first."

Blackwell's expression didn't change, but something shifted in her eyes. A flicker of ... respect? Professional recognition? "I observed behavioral patterns. Micro-expressions during my interview attempts. Body language when Monica's name was mentioned. The way you positioned yourself protectively whenever her reputation was questioned."

Lawson claimed the chair, spine rigid. The leather squeaked beneath her weight. Around them, hotel guests conducted quiet business meetings and tourist families planned evening activities. Normal people living normal lives, unaware that two women were dissecting the anatomy of a five-year-old murder over afternoon drinks.

"You're very good at reading people," Lawson said.

"It's my job. Same as yours, Detective. We both study human behavior to uncover truth." Blackwell pulled her recorder out of her bag. "The difference is methodology."

"Your methodology includes stealing sealed evidence."

"My methodology includes following leads wherever they take me." Blackwell's fingers drummed a silent rhythm against the table surface. "Including uncomfortable places that official investigations avoid."

Lawson recognized the challenge—respond defensively and prove Blackwell's point about official obstruction or maintain professional distance and appear callously indifferent to justice.

"What do you want from me?" Lawson asked instead.

"Your version of Monica Landry's murder. Your truth." Blackwell leaned forward slightly, invasion disguised as intimacy. "Not the sanitized department statement. Not the careful legal language. What you saw. What you felt. What you've discovered during five years of private investigation."

"Private investigation?"

"Please." Blackwell's smile carried sharp edges. "Your unofficial pursuit of Monica's case is hardly a secret. Department sources describe your ... persistent interest in cold case files. Your tendency to work overtime on cases everyone else considers closed."

Heat spread across Lawson's neck. The surveillance extended beyond her recent activities into years of behavior patterns. "You've been watching me."

"I've been thorough." Blackwell activated the recorder. "Standard investigative practice. Background research on key figures ensures comprehensive understanding of their motivations and credibility."

"Credibility?"

"Your drinking problem, Detective. Your disciplinary citations. Your history of insubordination when cases don't proceed according to your expectations." Each point delivered with surgical precision. "These factors affect how audiences perceive your testimony."

Lawson's hands clenched beneath the table. "You're building a case against me."

"I'm examining all possibilities. Including the one where Monica's partner might have reasons to conceal the truth about that night." Blackwell's tone remained conversational despite the devastating implications. "Not necessarily malicious reasons. Guilt, perhaps. Shame about impairment during a critical moment. Fear of professional consequences."

The psychological pressure built with each exchange. Blackwell systematically dismantling Lawson's credibility while maintaining the facade of objective journalism. Professional assassination disguised as fact-finding.

"Listen for yourself." Blackwell pressed play on a second device.

A male voice emerged from the speaker. Deep with the slight drawl common to Savannah natives. Ray Hutchinson's distinctive cadence filled the space between them.

"Monica understood the Rafferty operation better than anyone. I provided background from Narcotics. She connected financial patterns." The voice paused. "Working together created a bond. Late nights. Shared purpose. It became more than professional."

Lawson's coffee cup trembled against the saucer as she set it down. Her chest tightened with each revelation. Monica's secret relationship playing out in clinical detail while tourists laughed at nearby tables.

"More how?" Blackwell's recorded voice asked.

"We started seeing each other. Nothing dramatic. Dinner after reviewing case files. Drinks when we made progress. My place or hers when we needed privacy."

The casual tone made it worse. Monica's intimate moments reduced to interview sound bites. Blackwell continued playing the recording, each detail another blade twisting in wounds Lawson thought had scarred over.

"When did this relationship begin?"

"Six months before she died. Monica suggested keeping it quiet. Department politics, you know. Partners dating other officers complicates things."

Lawson closed her eyes, absorbing the timeline. Six months of deception while she and Monica shared beds and secrets and quiet mornings over coffee. Monica's careful compartmentalization extending beyond work into the most intimate aspects of her life.

"Did anyone know about your relationship?"

"We were careful. Professional at work. No public displays. Separate cars to restaurants outside Savannah. Monica insisted on discretion."

Blackwell stopped the playback. Her gaze never left Lawson's face, cataloging every micro-expression of pain and recognition. "Quite the revelation, wouldn't you say?"

"She never mentioned him." The words escaped without conscious permission.

"Of course not. Monica kept multiple secrets, Detective. From everyone." Blackwell returned the recorder to her bag. "Including you."

The hotel bar continued its afternoon rhythm around them. Business travelers checked phones between meetings. A family with young children debated dinner reservations. Life proceeded normally while Lawson's understanding of the past five years crumbled.

"How much of the relationship was real?" Lawson asked, hating the vulnerability in her voice.

"That's not for me to determine." Blackwell's response carried unexpected gentleness. "Human relationships rarely fit into simple categories. Monica could have loved you both, for different reasons, at different times."

"Or she could have been using me as cover while conducting her real relationship with Hutchinson."

"Also possible." Blackwell didn't offer false comfort. "The question becomes: does it change what happened that night?"

Lawson considered this. Monica's deception stung, but murder remained murder regardless of personal betrayals. Justice didn't depend on the victim's honesty about her romantic entanglements.

"No," she said finally. "It doesn't change anything."

"Good answer." Blackwell's approval seemed genuine. "Victims deserve justice regardless of their personal choices or moral complexity."

"Yet you're using her secrets to build audience engagement."

"I'm using her secrets to build a complete picture of her final weeks." Blackwell leaned back, professional distance reasserting itself. "Monica withdrew from both relationships simultaneously. Hutchinson describes the same pattern you've mentioned—cancelled plans, avoided conversations, increasing isolation."

"Because she discovered something dangerous."

"Or because she was preparing to abandon both relationships for whatever came next." Blackwell opened her tablet, fingers moving across the screen. "Your theory assumes professional motivation for her withdrawal. Hutchinson's suggests personal."

"What's his theory?"

"That Monica planned to disappear. New identity, new location, new life. The federal investigation provided perfect cover for vanishing completely." Blackwell turned the screen toward Lawson. "Bank records show cash withdrawals totaling thirty thousand dollars in the weeks before her death. More than enough for initial relocation expenses."

The numbers blurred on the screen. Lawson blinked, forcing focus. "Monica didn't have that kind of money."

"Exactly. Which raises questions about income sources during her final weeks." Blackwell closed the tablet. "Questions your official investigation apparently didn't pursue."

Another indictment of departmental thoroughness. Or another piece of evidence supporting the cover-up theory. Lawson couldn't determine which interpretation served truth better.

"I need time to process this," she said.

"Of course." Blackwell gathered her materials with efficient movements. "I'll contact you again soon."

Lawson remained at the table, processing revelations that reframed five years of assumptions. Monica's secret relationship. Her unexplained financial resources. Her systematic withdrawal from everyone who cared about her.

The woman she'd loved had been a stranger. The case she'd pursued had been built on incomplete information. The justice she'd sought might have been chasing shadows of her own creation.

Around her, the hotel bar continued its anonymous rhythm. Strangers conducting business, making plans, living lives uncomplicated by murdered partners and buried secrets. Lawson envied their innocence while recognizing her own had died years ago in a warehouse parking lot.

She paid for a drink she hadn't finished and walked into Savannah's humid afternoon, carrying questions that multiplied faster than answers.

chapter
thirteen

THE SAVANNAH CONVENTION Center sprawled along the riverfront, glass walls reflecting morning sunlight across the water. Crowds moved through the main entrance, many wearing lanyards with the True Crime Collective logo—a microphone wrapped in crime scene tape.

Lawson parked three blocks away. The email announcing Blackwell's appearance had arrived late last night. An ethics panel titled "Truth at Any Cost?" Perfect platform for a podcaster building her career on Monica's murder.

Inside, the convention bustled with activity. Vendor booths lined the main hall—equipment suppliers, podcast networks, merchandise sellers. Enthusiastic twenty-somethings clustered around popular hosts, phones raised for selfies. Murder as entertainment.

The program guide directed her to Ballroom C. She slipped through the doors ten minutes before the panel began and found the room already filled to three-quarters capacity. Six hundred seats facing a raised stage with five chairs and table microphones.

Lawson claimed a spot in the back row. Perfect vantage point for watching without being watched. The audience skewed female, mid-twenties to forties. Many typed notes on tablets or laptops. Future podcasters studying the masters.

Four panelists entered from a side door. Three men in business casual attire. Then Blackwell, black blazer over a crimson blouse. Professional but camera-ready. Her hair caught the stage lights, gleaming under the spots.

The moderator introduced each speaker. Credentials flashed on the screen behind them. Blackwell's listed Columbia Law degree alongside podcast download statistics that dwarfed her fellow panelists.

"Today we examine the ethical considerations in true crime reporting," the moderator began. "Where does the pursuit of truth become exploitation? What responsibilities do creators bear toward victims, families, and the accused?"

Lawson tuned out the introductory remarks. Her focus remained on Blackwell, who sat with perfect posture, attentive but relaxed. A natural performer aware of every eye in the room.

Someone slid into the empty seat beside her. Fiona Stevens, press badge hanging around her neck. Navy pantsuit. Hair pulled back in a sleek ponytail. She smelled of Miss Dior and ambition.

"Didn't expect to see you here," Fiona whispered.

Lawson kept her gaze forward. "Professional interest."

"Aren't we all professionally interested?" Fiona positioned her recorder on her knee. "Though some more personally than others."

On stage, the discussion turned to victim privacy. A male panelist argued for restraint when discussing graphic details. Another countered that sanitizing truth undermined journalistic integrity.

Blackwell leaned toward her microphone. "Balance exists between exploitation and education. Our responsibility lies in determining which details serve the public interest versus personal curiosity."

The audience nodded along. Professional ethics delivered with practiced sincerity.

"She's good," Fiona murmured. "Columbia debate team champion before law school. Never loses an argument."

The moderator directed a question to Blackwell. "Your current season investigates an unsolved police shooting. How do you balance pursuing justice with respecting ongoing investigations?"

"Justice requires transparency." Blackwell's voice carried authority without arrogance. "When official channels fail victims, independent investigation becomes necessary. Five years without answers suggests institutional failure."

Lawson's fingers dug into her thigh. Monica reduced to a professional steppingstone. Her death repackaged as content.

"Law enforcement serves communities through accountability." Blackwell continued. "My work supplements rather than undermines their mission."

"Supplements." Lawson scoffed under her breath. "Like a bulldozer supplements a shovel."

A question from the audience. A young woman with purple-streaked hair. "How do you handle resistance from authorities when investigating cold cases?"

"Persistence." Blackwell smiled. "Truth exists whether institutions acknowledge it or not. Victims' families deserve answers regardless of who feels uncomfortable."

There. The micro-expression Lawson had been watching for. Satisfaction flickered across Blackwell's features. The slight curl of her lip. Momentary breaking of the professional mask to reveal something harder beneath. Not compassion but triumph.

"She believes her own mythology," Fiona whispered. "Crusader for justice rather than ratings chaser."

Another question. From an older man near the front. "Where's the line between investigation and interference?"

"No line exists when justice hangs in the balance." Blackwell leaned forward. "Cold cases require disruption. Comfortable narratives must be challenged. Institutional inertia broken."

The crowd absorbed her words with appreciative murmurs. True believers receiving gospel from their prophet.

"Notice anything?" Fiona nodded toward the third row.

Lawson scanned the audience. "What?"

"Man with the leather messenger bag. Recording everything. Not press. No badge."

Middle-aged man. Gray suit. Close-cropped hair. Focused intensity as he documented the panel with a professional camera.

"Private investigator hired by Dunwood Media," Fiona explained. "They're negotiating Netflix rights for Dead Air."

Lawson's jaw ticked in irritation. Beyond podcasts. Beyond Savannah. Monica's death—and by extension, Lawson's life—packaged for global streaming.

On stage, Blackwell fielded another question. "How do you respond to criticism that true crime exploits tragedy?"

"I pursue truth, not sensation." Her gaze swept the room with practiced sincerity. "Victims deserve voices. Families deserve closure. Communities deserve accountability. If my platform amplifies silenced stories, I accept that responsibility."

"God, she practices these lines in mirrors," Lawson muttered. "Polished but hollow."

The moderator announced the final question from a young man standing at the microphone. "Does success create pressure to find dramatic conclusions even when evidence might be inconclusive?"

Perfect question. Lawson leaned forward.

"Evidence speaks for itself." Blackwell's answer came without hesitation. "My responsibility lies in presenting facts without filtering them through predetermined narratives. If conclusions remain ambiguous, audiences deserve that honesty."

"Bullshit," Fiona whispered. "Her entire brand relies on satisfying conclusions. Open endings don't sell Netflix deals."

Lawson glanced sideways at Fiona. The journalist's cynicism struck a chord. Fiona recognized the performance behind Blackwell's polished answers. Maybe Lawson had misjudged her, categorizing her as just another reporter hunting for headline material. The woman beside her understood the business machinery beneath true crime's veneer of justice. Perhaps they shared more common ground than Lawson had admitted.

"You've studied her," Lawson murmured.

"Know your competition." Fiona tapped her pen against her notepad. "Blackwell frames herself as justice's champion while building a media empire on other people's tragedies. The righteousness is just marketing."

The panel concluded with polite applause. Audience members surged forward, seeking selfies and autographs. Networking opportunities with podcast royalty.

Blackwell stood to leave but paused. Her gaze traveled across the room, finding Lawson in the back row. Recognition flashed across her features, followed by something unreadable. She held eye contact for three seconds before mouthing words clearly enough for Lawson to read her lips.

Episode Four tomorrow.

The message delivered, Blackwell turned away, disappearing into the crowd of admirers.

"Well, that was pointed," Fiona said. "Wonder what bombshell drops next."

Lawson remained seated while the room emptied. Fiona gathered her recorder and notepad but lingered.

"You know she's creating a narrative, not reporting one." Fiona's voice lost its casual edge. "Blackwell built her reputation finding monsters lurking inside official stories. Every season needs its villain."

"You think I'm cast as the villain." The possibility had occurred to Lawson already.

"Or tragic hero. Depends on what serves her story better. I think that's why she's baiting you. Waiting to see how you write your own story." Fiona stood. "Either way, objectivity isn't her priority."

"What's yours?"

"Professional curiosity." Fiona adjusted her bag strap. "And maybe personal interest in watching a colleague face what I did last year."

Lawson recalled the Dolores Bates case. Fiona's reporting scrutinized by outside media. Her methods questioned. Her motives analyzed.

"The Chronicle runs my story on this convention tomorrow. Call if you want your perspective included."

The ballroom emptied completely. Lawson remained alone with the empty stage and lingering questions. Blackwell's silent message replayed in her mind.

Episode Four tomorrow.

chapter
fourteen

LAWSON'S CAR idled in the parking lot of Savannah Self Storage. Rain drummed against the roof, turning the world outside into watercolor smears. The digital clock on her dashboard read 9:47 PM. Two hours since Blackwell's podcast had ended. Two hours of driving aimlessly through Savannah's streets, processing revelations she couldn't unhear.

Monica had compiled a list of dirty cops. Officers on the Savannah force taking payoffs from local crime families. A parallel investigation she'd conducted alone, trusting no one with her findings.

Not even her partner.

Rachel's key sat heavy in Lawson's palm. Small brass, unremarkable except for what it unlocked.

The rain intensified. Water cascaded down the windshield faster than wipers could clear it. Lawson killed the engine and stepped out into the downpour. Cold water soaked through her shirt within seconds. The sensation matched her internal temperature—chilled from the inside out by Blackwell's methodical dismantling of everything she thought she knew.

The storage facility office stood empty. After-hours access required the gate code on Rachel's keychain. Metal gates rolled open with a mechanical groan. Security lights cast yellow pools across wet pavement as Lawson navigated the maze of identical metal doors.

Unit 147 occupied the back corner. Away from the main drive. Maximum privacy. The lock clicked open on the first try.

Lawson hesitated, hand on the pull-down door. Monica's possessions lay preserved inside like artifacts in a tomb. Untouched since Rachel packed them away after the funeral. Five years of dust settling over a life interrupted.

The door rolled upward with a metallic screech. Motion-activated lights flickered twice before stabilizing. Furniture was stacked against the back wall. Boxes labeled in Rachel's precise handwriting. KITCHEN. BOOKS. CLOTHES. PHOTOS.

Lawson stepped inside, pulling the door halfway down behind her. Rain pattered against the metal roof. Water dripped from her clothes onto the concrete floor. Where would Monica hide files too dangerous to keep at home or work? Not in obvious storage boxes. Somewhere overlooked. Somewhere disguised as ordinary.

Her gaze settled on a plastic bin labeled HOLIDAY DECORATIONS. Monica had hated seasonal decorating. Called it "commercial obligation disguised as tradition." Rachel wouldn't know that. Would assume the box contained Christmas lights or Halloween pumpkins.

The bin sat beneath two others. Lawson moved them aside, leaving wet handprints on the plastic lids. Holiday Decorations weighed more than tinsel and ornaments would justify. Inside, beneath a layer of tangled Christmas lights, she found a fireproof document box. Matte black metal with a combination lock.

Monica's academy graduation date opened it on the first attempt. The same combination she'd used for her gym locker. The same combination Lawson knew by heart, even five years later. The box held a single manila folder. Thick with documents. The tab labeled with a simple letter R.

Rafferty.

Lawson placed the box on a nearby dresser and opened the folder. The first page contained a handwritten list of names. Columns organized by department and suspected activity. Patrol officers facilitating drug shipments through traffic stops. Evidence technicians altering documentation. Detectives burying witness statements. Money amounts noted beside each name. Weekly payments. Monthly totals.

She recognized most names. Officers still working the streets. Detectives still closing cases. Sergeants promoted to lieutenants. The corruption extended beyond individuals into a systematic network.

Hutchinson's name appeared at the bottom, circled twice with a question mark beside it. No dollar amounts listed. No specific accusations. Just the question mark, suggesting Monica's uncertainty about his involvement.

The next set of documents detailed money transfers. Bank statements showing patterns. Cash deposits into accounts under false names. Property purchases through shell companies. Monica had mapped the financial architecture of corruption with meticulous precision.

Beneath the financial records lay photographs. Surveillance shots taken from a distance with a telephoto lens. Officers meeting with known criminals. Cash exchanging hands in parking lots. Conversations in cars with tinted windows.

The final section contained photos that stopped Lawson's breathing. Images of herself. Leaving her apartment. Walking to her car. Ordinary moments from the weeks before Monica died. The angles suggested someone watching from vehicles or adjacent buildings. Professional surveillance targeting both partners.

A handwritten note paper-clipped to the images: *They know about us. Not safe. Need leverage before moving forward.*

Monica's distinctive handwriting. The implication crashed through Lawson's careful compartmentalization. Monica hadn't kept her corruption investigation secret out of distrust. She'd done it for protection. Knowledge meant danger. Ignorance offered Lawson deniability if everything collapsed.

The rain intensified, drumming against the metal roof. Lawson sorted through more surveillance photos. The consistency suggested multiple photographers working in coordination. Resources beyond individual capacity. Organized surveillance authorized by someone with authority.

The final photo in the stack showed Monica and Lawson together. Standing in the threshold of Lawson's apartment door. Monica leaning in, their silhouettes merging in what was clearly an intimate moment. Proof of their relationship captured from across the street.

Lawson flipped the photo over. Monica's handwriting again: *Insurance policy in our place.*

Our place.

Three possible locations flashed through her mind. The bench at Forsyth Park fountain, where they'd first discussed moving beyond partnership. The waterfront bar where they'd celebrated their first year working together. The hotel room they'd booked for weekend getaways when they needed privacy from colleagues.

The fountain made the most sense. Public. Accessible 24/7. Unlikely to change or disappear over time. Monica would have chosen somewhere Lawson could access without drawing attention.

Lawson extracted several key folders, then she replaced the remaining documents in the lockbox. The combination clicked back into place. Everything returned to the plastic bin, Christmas lights arranged over the top exactly as she'd found them. The bin went back beneath the others, appearing undisturbed.

Outside, the rain had stopped. Wet pavement reflected security lights in fractured patterns. Lawson locked the storage unit and walked to her car. Water squelched in her shoes with each step, the weight of Monica's documents heavy against her chest.

Forsyth Park waited across town. The fountain. East side bench. Insurance policy hidden five years ago, undisturbed while Monica's murder went unsolved.

dead air episode 4:

"The Other Relationship"

[Electronic theme music fades in, then quiets under narration]
    LEAH BLACKWELL: Welcome back to Dead Air. I'm Leah Blackwell.
    In previous episodes, we explored Detective Monica Landry's murder, her partner Detective Erin Lawson's conflicting statements, and the mysteriously powered floodlight that shouldn't have worked. Today, we turn to a relationship that remained hidden until now—one that adds another layer to this increasingly complex case.
    [Brief pause]
    LEAH: I'm speaking with Detective Ray Hutchinson of the Savannah Police Department's Narcotics Division. Detective Hutchinson worked alongside Monica Landry on the Rafferty case in the months before her death. But according to multiple sources, their relationship extended beyond professional boundaries.
    [Audio clip from interview] **HUTCHINSON:** Monica understood the Rafferty operation better than anyone. I provided background from Narcotics. She connected financial patterns. Working together created a bond. Late nights. Shared purpose. It became more than professional.
    LEAH: Detective Hutchinson has agreed to speak publicly about their relationship for the first time:
    HUTCHINSON: We started seeing each other. Nothing dramatic.

Dinner after reviewing case files. Drinks when we made progress. My place or hers when we needed privacy.

LEAH: When did this relationship begin?

HUTCHINSON: Six months before she died. Monica suggested keeping it quiet. Department politics, you know. Partners dating other officers complicates things.

LEAH: Did anyone know about your relationship?

HUTCHINSON: We were careful. Professional at work. No public displays. Separate cars to restaurants outside Savannah. Monica insisted on discretion.

[Music shifts slightly]

LEAH: I asked Detective Hutchinson to describe the nature of their relationship:

HUTCHINSON: Intense. Intellectually and physically. She kept a toothbrush at my place. Left clothes in my drawer. We talked about vacation plans for when the Rafferty case closed.

LEAH: Did Detective Lawson know about this relationship?

HUTCHINSON: Monica said her partner wouldn't understand. Lawson was protective. Territorial about their partnership. Monica avoided the potential drama.

[Brief pause]

LEAH: Multiple colleagues corroborate Detective Hutchinson's account. Surveillance photos we obtained show Detective Landry entering his apartment building on numerous occasions during the time period he described. Credit card records reveal dinner purchases at restaurants outside Savannah city limits, exactly as he claimed.

LEAH: This relationship remained hidden during the official investigation into Monica Landry's death. No mention appears in case files. No witness statements reference it. Detective Hutchinson was never formally interviewed as someone with a close personal connection to the victim.

LEAH: When I asked why he didn't come forward at the time:

HUTCHINSON: I tried. Told my sergeant about our relationship the day after she died. He said it wasn't relevant to the investigation. When I pushed, he suggested keeping it quiet to "protect Monica's reputation."

[Music intensifies]

LEAH: What happened between Detective Landry and Detective Hutchinson in the weeks before her death adds another layer of complexity to this case:

HUTCHINSON: Something changed. Monica became secretive. Canceled plans. Stopped answering texts. Said she needed space to focus.

LEAH: How did you respond?

HUTCHINSON: Respected her wishes at first. Gave her time. But the distance grew. She started avoiding me at work. Taking files without consulting me. Making independent moves on our shared case.

LEAH: Did you confront her?

HUTCHINSON: I asked for an explanation, sure. Went to her apartment one night. Brought dinner as a peace offering. She wouldn't let me inside. Said we needed complete separation until the case closed.

[Brief pause]

LEAH: This timeline coincides precisely with the professional distance that developed between Monica Landry and her partner, Erin Lawson. According to department sources, both relationships deteriorated simultaneously – around three weeks before her death.

LEAH: What triggered this withdrawal? What did Detective Landry discover that caused her to isolate herself from both her professional partner and her romantic partner?

HUTCHINSON: Looking back, I believe she found something dangerous. Something that made her pull away from everyone. Not just me. Her sister mentioned she'd stopped Sunday dinners. Colleagues said she worked odd hours alone.

LEAH: When was the last time you saw her?

HUTCHINSON: Three days before she died. Passed her in the hallway at the station. She looked exhausted. Jumpy. Clutching that blue notebook she carried everywhere. She avoided eye contact. Took the stairs instead of sharing the elevator.

[Music shifts]

LEAH: That blue notebook, the same one her sister Rachel mentioned, the one missing from evidence, appears to be central to whatever Monica Landry discovered in her final weeks.

LEAH: Detective Hutchinson's Narcotics expertise gave him unique insight into the Rafferty operation:

HUTCHINSON: Rafferty wasn't just another dealer. His operation had protection from somewhere. Cases against his people kept falling apart. Evidence disappeared. Witnesses changed statements. Monica noticed the pattern first. Said it pointed to someone with authority manipulating outcomes.

LEAH: Did she name suspects?

HUTCHINSON: Never directly. But she focused on cases that passed through Judge Byrd's courtroom. Said the dismissal rate for Rafferty-connected cases was statistically impossible without intervention.

[Brief pause]

LEAH: Judge Elizabeth Byrd declined our request for an interview but provided this statement through her office:

[Reading from statement] "All judicial decisions in my courtroom follow strict adherence to legal standards and procedural requirements. Cases are dismissed when evidence fails to meet constitutional thresholds or when prosecutorial misconduct occurs."

[Music becomes more pointed]

LEAH: Detective Hutchinson's account adds crucial context to Monica Landry's final days. It suggests she was investigating not just street-level drug trafficking, but judicial corruption at the highest levels of Savannah's legal system.

LEAH: If true, this explains why evidence disappeared after her death. Why files went missing. Why the Rafferty investigation was abruptly closed. Someone with significant authority ensured that Monica Landry's discoveries remained buried, along with any chance of justice for her murder.

LEAH: I asked Detective Hutchinson directly if he believed Monica was killed because of what she discovered:

HUTCHINSON: Without question. Monica was methodical. Thorough. If she found a connection between Rafferty and people in the justice system, she documented it. That made her dangerous to someone with everything to lose.

[Brief pause]

LEAH: Detective Erin Lawson declined to comment when presented with Detective Hutchinson's account of his relationship with her partner. However, sources close to the investigation report Detective Lawson was unaware of the relationship at the time of Detective Landry's death.

LEAH: This creates a troubling scenario: Monica Landry keeping secrets from both her professional partner and her romantic partner in the weeks before her murder. Withdrawing from everyone close to her while pursuing evidence of corruption that potentially reached into the courthouse itself.

LEAH: The warehouse meeting where she died now appears increasingly like a trap, one set by someone who knew exactly where she would be standing. Someone with access to resources that could install an independently powered floodlight. Someone who could ensure evidence would disappear afterward.

[Music softens]

LEAH: Tomorrow, I'll be sitting down with forensic experts who've reviewed the available evidence from the crime scene. Their analysis reveals discrepancies in the official autopsy report that further challenge the narrative of a random shooting.

LEAH: In our next episode, we'll examine Detective Lawson's official statement about that night—and why key details contradict physical evidence from the scene.

[Music builds]

LEAH: This is Dead Air. The truth doesn't stay buried forever.

[Theme music plays out]

chapter fifteen

LAWSON SPREAD Monica's documents across her kitchen table. Bank statements from Monica's final six months, mixed in with utility bills and credit card receipts, all tucked away in a manila envelope that anyone else would have overlooked.

She organized the papers chronologically. Monica's regular paycheck deposits appeared every two weeks, matching department pay scales exactly. Rent payments on the fifteenth. Grocery purchases at the same three stores. The predictable financial rhythm of a working cop's life.

Then she found the irregularities.

Five deposits over Monica's final three months. Each for exactly $5,000. Each from a source listed only as "Private Transfer - Account #472891." No name. No institution identifier. Just numbers that provided no context.

Lawson checked the dates against her memory of Monica's investigation timeline. The first deposit coincided with Monica's assignment to the Rafferty case. The last appeared three days before her death. Thousands of dollars in unexplained income during the period when Monica was documenting departmental corruption.

Her phone buzzed. A text from Fiona: *Need comment on Blackwell's latest episode for Chronicle story. Coffee?*

Lawson stared at the bank statements, then at Fiona's message. She needed someone with investigative resources that wouldn't raise red flags.

Someone who might prove useful despite her reservations about trusting any journalist.

Perimeter Coffee. One hour.

The response came quickly: *I'll be there.*

Fiona had claimed the corner booth again, laptop open, notepad covered in her precise handwriting. She looked up as Lawson approached, closing the computer with care.

"Thanks for meeting."

Lawson slid into the opposite seat, placing the bank statements face-down on the table. "Need your help with something."

"What kind of something?"

Lawson flipped the documents over. Fiona's eyes immediately focused on the highlighted deposits, journalist instincts activated by the sight of potential evidence.

"Monica's financial records. Found them mixed in with her personal effects." Lawson pointed to the mysterious transfers. "Five payments over three months. Same amount each time."

Fiona leaned forward, scanning the numbers with practiced efficiency. She pulled out her phone, opening a note-taking app. "This account number provide any leads?"

"Private transfer requires court order for disclosure."

"Which you can't obtain without active case status." Fiona photographed the statements. "But I have other options."

"Banking sources?"

"I've got a friend who was a financial crimes reporter. Worked that beat for twelve years. Developed contacts throughout the industry." Fiona gave her a pointed look. "What's your theory about these deposits?"

"Either Monica was taking money from someone, or someone wanted it to look like she was."

"Payoffs from criminal informants?"

"Department protocol requires documentation of all informant payments. These don't appear in any official records." Lawson tapped the account number. "Someone went to considerable effort to keep these transfers invisible."

Fiona studied the timeline more carefully. "Rafferty case assignment here. First payment arrives. Investigation deepens, payments continue. She dies, payments stop. Perfect correlation between her progress and the money."

"Or a perfect setup if someone wanted to discredit her investigation," Lawson said defensively. "Plant evidence of corruption in the investigator's finances. Classic misdirection strategy."

Monica's reputation for integrity had been absolute within the department. Financial impropriety would have destroyed that reputation posthumously, undermining any evidence she'd gathered.

"I need to trace the source," Lawson said, trying to calm herself down. "Confirm whether Monica even knew about these deposits."

"My contact can help with technical tracking. But I need something from you." Fiona leaned back, switching to negotiation mode. "Background on Monica's investigation. Context for what these payments might represent."

"Most of her case materials were seized during the official investigation."

"But you maintained copies of key documents. Smart detectives always keep insurance files." Fiona's assessment carried certainty rather than speculation. "Especially when working corruption cases."

Lawson considered the request. Sharing Monica's materials violated department protocols and potentially compromised ongoing investigations.

"What I share stays confidential until we understand what we're dealing with."

"Agreed." Fiona extended her hand across the table. "Temporary partnership. Your police expertise, my financial resources."

They shook hands, and both stood simultaneously, business concluded. Fiona paused at the coffee shop exit.

"Why approach me with this? Could have taken it directly to federal investigators."

Lawson pushed through the door, the afternoon heat hitting her face as they emerged onto the sidewalk. "Because you understand how narratives get constructed around incomplete information. If someone planted this money trail, they built it knowing how investigators would interpret the evidence."

"You need someone who thinks like the people creating false stories."

"Exactly."

chapter sixteen

MORNING SUNLIGHT FILTERED through live oak branches, casting dappled shadows across Forsyth Park. The fountain sprayed water skyward in crystalline arcs. Joggers circled the perimeter while tourists posed for photos against the landmark.

Lawson sat on the east bench for the third time in twelve hours. Last night she'd searched by phone flashlight, fingers probing beneath the wooden slats, eyes scanning the fountain base for hiding spots. Rain-soaked and frustrated, she'd returned home past midnight only to arrive again at dawn.

The bench revealed nothing. No hidden compartment. No loose brick in the fountain wall. No insurance policy that Monica might have left five years ago.

She ran her hand along the bench underside again. Splinters snagged her fingertips. Birds scattered as a child raced past screaming with delight. Eight a.m. and already the park filled with activity, each passerby a potential witness to her increasingly desperate search.

Her phone vibrated. Claire's name on the screen. Lawson answered.

"Can you come to my office? Something you need to see."

"Now?"

"Five minutes ago, ideally." Keys jingled in the background. "Fiona brought information about your podcaster friend. Time-sensitive."

"On my way." Lawson stood, brushing bench dust from her jeans.

Lawson cut across the square, passing coffee shops open for morning business. Tourists consulted maps while locals moved with practiced efficiency toward workplaces.

The Victorian building that housed Claire's practice appeared unchanged from Lawson's previous visit. Inside, voices drifted from the second-floor conference room rather than Claire's private office. Lawson took the stairs two at a time.

Claire and Fiona hunched over a laptop, documents spread across the table between them. Both looked up as Lawson entered. Fiona wore yesterday's clothes with added wrinkles. Dark circles shadowed her eyes. Claire had managed business attire but left her hair loose instead of her usual courtroom-ready style.

"You look like you haven't slept," Lawson said.

"Kettle, pot." Fiona gestured to Lawson's rain-wrinkled shirt and muddied jeans.

Claire pushed a chair toward Lawson. "Sit. Coffee's fresh."

Lawson claimed the chair but ignored the offered mug. "What's this about?"

"Leah Blackwell's podcast metrics." Fiona turned her laptop screen. "Something felt off about her sudden success. Three million downloads for an inaugural episode? Unheard of without major platform backing."

The screen displayed analytics charts and social media metrics. Numbers and graphs that meant nothing to Lawson.

"In English."

"Her numbers are fake." Fiona tapped the screen. "Bot farms generating artificial downloads. Paid social media engagement. Coordinated amplification campaign across multiple platforms."

"Someone's inflating her popularity?"

"Someone with serious resources." Fiona clicked to another screen. "This level of manipulation costs six figures minimum. Professional services operating from overseas servers. Untraceable accounts. Corporate-level strategy."

Claire slid a document across the table. "Fiona traced financial transactions through three shell companies. The money trail ends here."

The paper showed incorporation documents for Equinox Media Solutions LLC. Lawson scanned the dense legal text until reaching the registration information. Principal address listed as 1440 Broadway, New York. Same building as Hutchinson & Associates."

"The law firm where Blackwell clerked." Lawson looked up from the paper. "This proves connection but not causation."

"There's more." Claire produced another document. "Fiona dug into the firm's senior partnership."

A professional biography filled the page. Thomas Hutchinson, founding partner. Harvard Law graduate. Twenty years specializing in corporate law and crisis management. The photograph showed an older version of a face Lawson recognized instantly.

"Ray Hutchinson's brother." The connection crystallized. "Thomas Hutchinson is funding Blackwell's podcast."

"Not directly." Fiona leaned forward. "The money flows through elaborate channels. Plausible deniability preserved. But the trail exists if you know where to look."

Lawson processed the implications. Ray Hutchinson had been involved with Monica. His brother ran the law firm where Blackwell clerked. Now, it seemed that firm funded Blackwell's investigation into Monica's murder through hidden channels.

"This isn't coincidence." The pieces aligned too perfectly. "Blackwell's entire investigation is orchestrated by Hutchinson."

"Which changes the fundamental nature of her podcast." Fiona closed her laptop. "This isn't ethical journalism."

Claire gathered the documents into a neat stack. "The question becomes why. What does Hutchinson gain from publicizing his brother's connection to a murdered detective?"

"Control of the narrative." Lawson stood, unable to remain seated. "Episode Three presented Ray as the heartbroken lover. Portrayed him sympathetically despite having a clear motive."

"Classic misdirection." Fiona nodded. "Focus audience attention on one story while obscuring another."

"But what story are they hiding?" Claire tapped her fingers against the table. "What's valuable enough to justify this elaborate scheme?"

Lawson thought of Monica's files. The list of corrupt officers. Hutchinson's name circled with a question mark. The surveillance photos proving someone had discovered their relationship.

"Reputation." Lawson paced along the windows. "Ray Hutchinson works Narcotics. Access to major cases. Connections to high-level investigations."

"And his brother represents clients who might benefit from such connections." Fiona completed the thought. "Corporate clients with potential legal exposure."

"Or clients looking to protect investments." Claire added another possibility. "Hutchinson & Associates specializes in crisis management for companies facing criminal investigation."

The implications expanded with each observation. Ray Hutchinson positioned inside law enforcement while Thomas Hutchinson managed damage control outside. Perfect symbiosis for clients needing protection from prosecution.

"I need to know which investigations Ray Hutchinson touched." Lawson pulled out her phone. "Which cases he might have influenced."

"That requires department access." Claire raised an eyebrow. "Records you don't officially have."

"I know someone who does." Lawson dialed Eli Parks' number. The call went to voicemail. She left a message requesting urgent contact.

"The temporary restraining order against Blackwell's podcast goes before Judge Werner this afternoon." Claire checked her watch. "Without evidence of direct harm to an ongoing investigation, he'll likely deny it."

"Even with proof she's funded by interested parties?"

"Legally irrelevant unless we can prove malicious intent." Claire shrugged. "Freedom of the press protects even financially motivated journalism."

Fiona gathered her materials. "I need to file my story before the Chronicle's deadline. This connection deserves public exposure even if courts won't intervene."

"Wait." Lawson placed her hand on Fiona's laptop. "Publishing now alerts Hutchinson that we've uncovered his involvement. We lose tactical advantage."

"My editor expects copy tomorrow by noon." Fiona checked her phone.

"Give me time." Lawson maintained eye contact. "Time to verify

Ray Hutchinson's case involvement. To strengthen the connection before exposing it."

Fiona hesitated. "Deadline journalism waits for no one."

"This isn't about journalism anymore." Lawson kept her voice level. "Monica died investigating corruption. Her files contained evidence that someone inside the department protected criminal interests. If Ray Hutchinson connects to those same cases—"

"You think he killed her." Fiona's expression sharpened. "That his brother is now using Blackwell to control the narrative around her death."

"I think a twenty-four-hour delay won't destroy your story but might help build mine."

The room fell silent except for the ticking wall clock. Claire watched the exchange without intervention. Fiona weighed professional opportunity against Lawson's request.

"Twenty-four hours." Fiona finally nodded. "Not one minute more."

Lawson released her hold on the laptop. "Thank you."

"Don't thank me yet." Fiona packed her bag. "This information becomes public tomorrow regardless of what you discover. The Hutchinson connection deserves exposure even if Ray's involvement remains unproven."

"Understood."

Fiona gathered her notes in a single, neat motion and was gone, the door sealing shut as neatly as she'd left the conversation.

"She'll wait exactly twenty-four hours." Claire gathered the remaining documents. "No journalistic courtesy beyond that."

"I need department access." Lawson checked her phone again. No response from Parks. "Ray Hutchinson's case history. Personnel file. Anything connecting him to Monica beyond his recorded statement."

"That requires a warrant or internal investigation." Claire organized file folders into her briefcase. "Neither of which you can initiate without evidence."

"Then I need to find evidence."

Claire studied her for a long moment. "What aren't you telling me?"

Lawson considered how much to reveal. The storage unit discovery remained too volatile to fully share. "Monica left files. Documentation of department corruption. Officers taking payoffs from criminal organizations."

"Where are these files now?"

"Secure location." The partial truth came easier than expected. "But they don't explicitly name Ray Hutchinson. I need departmental records to connect him to the cases Monica investigated."

Claire closed her briefcase with twin snaps. "If such evidence exists, Blackwell likely has it already. Her resources clearly exceed yours."

"But her motives don't align with justice." Lawson moved toward the door. "She's building a story that serves her backers, not the truth."

Her phone chimed with a notification. Dead Air Productions: *Episode Five: "The Officer's Statement" drops tomorrow at 9 AM. What Detective Lawson told authorities... and what she didn't.*

Lawson's stomach tightened. The episode title suggested Blackwell had obtained her official statement from the night Monica died. The statement where she'd omitted critical details—their relationship, her drinking before the meeting, the fight that had separated them those final weeks.

"Problem?" Claire asked, noting her expression.

"Tomorrow's episode." Lawson showed her the screen. "Blackwell's focusing on inconsistencies in my statement to authorities."

"Painting you as an unreliable witness or potential suspect?"

"Either of which destroys my credibility." Lawson pocketed her phone. "Twenty-four hours just became more urgent."

chapter
seventeen

LAWSON'S PHONE rang at 6:17 a.m., the shrill tone yanking her from the gray haze of restless sleep. Parks' number flashed on the screen. She swiped to answer, propping herself up on one elbow, voice rough from disuse.

"Parks, thanks for getting back to me so quick."

A heavy pause stretched across the line, thick with something unspoken, before his voice cut through, edged with gravel. "Sorry to say, Detective, it's not about that. And it's not good news. Ray Hutchinson is dead. Ridgewood Apartments. Unit 307."

She bolted upright, sheets tangling around her legs as the fog of exhaustion shattered. "What the hell? How?"

"Gunshot wound. Single bullet to the temple. Service weapon found in his hand."

"Suicide?"

"That's the official narrative." Something in Parks' tone suggested doubt. "Note left on the kitchen counter. Confession to Monica Landry's murder."

Lawson swung her feet to the floor, the phone pressed against her ear. "I'll be there in twenty."

"Make it fifteen. ME removes the body at seven."

The line went dead. Lawson dressed in yesterday's clothes, splashed water on her face, and grabbed her keys. The drive to Ridgewood Apartments took twelve minutes through empty early morning streets. The upscale complex near Forsyth Park housed several officers and city officials. Ray Hutchinson had lived well on a detective's salary.

Police vehicles lined the entrance. Curious neighbors clustered behind yellow tape, cell phones raised to capture the activity. Lawson badged the uniform at the perimeter, who checked her ID against the clearance list before lifting the tape.

The elevator smelled of artificial pine. The third floor hallway buzzed with activity. Crime scene techs moved between the apartment and their equipment cases. Uniformed officers kept curious residents back. Parks stood outside Unit 307, leather notebook open in his hands.

"His captain found him after he missed morning briefing and didn't respond to calls." Parks led her inside without preamble. "Hutchinson never failed to show up or call in before. Time of death between midnight and three a.m."

The apartment revealed expensive taste. Leather furniture. Original artwork. Hardwood floors with Persian rugs. A detective's salary stretched through outside income or family money.

The kitchen counter held an evidence marker beside a handwritten note secured in a plastic sleeve. Lawson read it without touching it.

I killed Monica Landry. The guilt has become unbearable. She threatened to expose our relationship and my connection to Rafferty. I arranged the meeting, set up the floodlight, and waited. I never meant for it to happen this way. I'm sorry.

"Ballistics processing the weapon?" Lawson asked.

"Standard protocol. Initial assessment matches his service weapon."

"Where's the body?"

"Bedroom. ME finishing the examination."

Lawson followed Parks through the apartment. Immaculate organization everywhere. Books alphabetized. Clothing arranged by color. Shoes in perfect pairs beneath hanging garments. It all felt at odds with how he'd chosen to die.

The medical examiner knelt beside the body sprawled across an unmade bed. Hutchinson wore boxers and a T-shirt. Blood soaked the pillow beneath his head. The entry wound created a small, neat hole at his right temple. The exit wound left a larger cavity on the opposite side.

"Detective Lawson." The ME nodded without looking up. "Interesting case."

"Suicide looks straightforward." Parks crossed his arms. "Except for inconsistencies."

"Such as?" Lawson asked.

The ME gestured toward Hutchinsons' arms. "Defensive wounds on forearms and hands. Bruising pattern indicates he shielded himself from attack. Occurred prior to death."

Lawson leaned closer. Purple bruises marked Hutchinson's forearms. Knuckles showed abrasions consistent with throwing punches.

"He fought someone before dying."

"Four to six hours before, based on bruise development." The ME stood. "Tox screen pending, but pupil dilation suggests potential sedative in his system."

"Someone subdued him." Lawson glanced at Parks. "Staged the suicide."

"Initial assessment supports that theory." The ME packed instruments into a black bag. "Gunshot residue pattern inconsistent with self-infliction. Angle suggests the shooter stood beside rather than in front of the victim."

"Murder disguised as suicide." Parks closed his notebook. "Complete with confession note."

"Handwriting analysis?" Lawson asked.

"Lab comparing it to known samples. Preliminary assessment suggests forgery." Parks checked his watch. "Body moves downstairs in ten minutes. Anything else you need to see?"

Lawson surveyed the bedroom again. Wallet and keys on the nightstand. Clothing draped over a chair. Nothing obviously disturbed or missing. "Security cameras in the building?"

"Lobby. Elevators. Parking garage." Parks nodded. "Footage already pulled. Tech is reviewing it now."

They returned to the living room, where crime scene technicians photographed blood spatter patterns. Hutchinson had died in the bedroom, but evidence suggested violence throughout the apartment. Overturned lamp. Scuff marks on hardwood.

"Timeline?" Lawson asked.

"Last seen leaving the precinct at eight last night." Parks consulted his notes. "No activity on his phone or credit cards after nine. Neighbor reported hearing a thump around midnight but attributed it to the upstairs tenant."

"The confession conveniently wraps up Monica's case." Lawson studied the note again through its plastic covering. "Too convenient."

"My assessment exactly." Parks tucked his notebook into his jacket pocket. "Especially twenty-four hours after Blackwell's podcast connected him to Monica."

Lawson turned toward him. "You listened to it?"

"Required monitoring as IA liaison." Parks maintained a neutral expression. "Recordings sent directly to my office for review."

The door opened as four morgue attendants entered with a gurney. The ME directed them toward the bedroom. Crime scene photographers completed final documentation before the body removal process began.

Parks led Lawson into the hallway. Fewer officers remained, the initial surge of activity tapering to methodical processing. The neighbors had retreated to their apartments, leaving the corridor empty except for a uniformed officer guarding the doorway.

"Someone wanted Hutchinson silenced." Lawson kept her voice low. "The suicide narrative provides closure to Monica's case without further investigation."

"Convenient for several parties." Parks maintained a professional distance. "Including Thomas Hutchinson. Family embarrassment contained. Firm reputation preserved."

"Blackwell loses her star interview subject."

"But gains a dramatic conclusion." Parks checked the hallway before continuing. "Nothing sells podcasts like unexpected death."

The elevator doors opened. The morgue attendants wheeled Hutchinson's sheet-covered body toward them. Lawson and Parks pressed against the wall to allow passage. The gurney wheels squeaked against the flooring. The officer held the elevator door as they loaded Hutchinson's final journey.

"Tech room downstairs has the security footage." Parks gestured toward the stairwell. "Worth reviewing before department politics intervene."

The basement tech room occupied former storage space. A young officer with thick glasses monitored multiple screens displaying security camera feeds. Two additional monitors showed footage from the previous night.

"Time index 23:40 through 01:15." Parks directed the technician. "External entrances and third floor corridors."

The screens displayed multiple angles. The lobby camera showed minimal activity after eleven. Delivery person. Late-night dog walker. Resident returning from evening shift work. The elevator camera captured similar routine movements.

"There." Lawson pointed at 00:17 timestamp. "Hoodie. Baseball cap. Face obscured."

The figure entered through a side door accessible only with a resident key fob. Medium height. Athletic build beneath loose clothing. Deliberate movements toward the elevator suggested familiarity with the building layout.

"Camera three shows them exiting on the third floor." The technician switched views. "Walking directly to Hutchinson's apartment."

The hallway camera captured the hooded figure knocking on Unit 307. Hutchinson answered, wearing the same T-shirt found on his body. No audio accompanied the footage, but body language suggested recognition. Hutchinson stepped back, allowing the visitor entry.

"Time stamp 00:21." Parks noted the information. "Next hallway activity?"

The technician fast-forwarded. "01:03. Same individual exits apartment. Note the different gait."

The hooded figure emerged from Hutchinson's unit. Head down. Shoulders hunched. The walking pattern changed from confident stride to cautious movement. Right hand remained inside the hoodie pocket. Left hand pulled the door closed.

"Forty-two minutes inside." Parks studied the retreating figure. "Enough time for confrontation, sedation, staging."

"Familiar." Lawson narrowed her eyes at the screen. "Something about that walk."

The footage continued. The elevator camera showed the hooded figure descending to the lobby. The lobby camera captured their exit through the same side door used for entry. No clear facial image appeared in any frame.

"Access requires a resident key fob." Parks turned to the technician. "Pull usage logs for that entrance between midnight and one AM."

The technician typed commands into his terminal. "System shows access at 00:14 and 01:05. Fob registered to Unit 307. Ray Hutchinson."

"They used his own key." Lawson processed the implication. "Had access to his fob before arriving."

"Seems like someone familiar with building security. Someone Hutchinson recognized and admitted into his apartment at midnight."

The elevator doors opened behind them. Chief Wallace entered with two suited men Lawson recognized from the district attorney's office. Their expressions suggested administrative intervention rather than investigative support.

"Lieutenant Parks." The Chief nodded curtly. "The DA's office assumes jurisdiction over Detective Hutchinson's death investigation. You'll transfer all materials to their team immediately."

Parks maintained a neutral expression. "Standard protocol places Internal Affairs as lead when officer deaths involve potential misconduct."

"Protocol adjusted given the circumstances." Chief Wallace's tone left no room for discussion. "The confession note provides clear resolution to the Landry case. Public interest requires expedited processing."

The suits flanked the tech officer, already collecting data drives. The Chief turned toward Lawson with barely concealed irritation.

"Detective Lawson. Your presence at this scene isn't necessary."

Lawson caught Parks' subtle head shake. Not the moment for confrontation. She nodded professionally. "Sir."

Outside, morning sunlight struck the parking lot with blinding intensity. News vans had arrived, reporters setting up for live segments. Lawson kept her head down, avoiding cameras as she reached her car.

Her phone chimed with a notification. Blackwell had posted on social media: *In light of Detective Hutchinson's tragic death, Episode 5 release postponed 24 hours. The investigation continues.*

The post had already accumulated thousands of shares and comments. Blackwell, already pivoting tragedy into promotion with practiced efficiency.

Parks appeared beside her car window. "Department channels compromised. Meet me at Riverfront Coffee. One hour."

He walked away without waiting for a response. Professional distance maintained for any watching eyes. Lawson started her engine and pulled away from the growing media circus.

Hutchinson's death changed everything. Apparent suicide with a convenient confession. The evidence left suggested a murder staged to close Monica's case permanently. The hooded figure, whose walking pattern nagged at Lawson's memory.

Her phone buzzed with an incoming call. Claire's number.

"Fiona canceled her story." Claire skipped greeting pleasantries. "Hutchinson's death created bigger headlines than podcast funding."

"Convenient timing."

"Too convenient." Claire's voice lowered. "Someone's coordinating this narrative, Erin. First Blackwell's podcast. Now, Hutchinson's confession. The story's being managed."

"By Thomas Hutchinson?"

"Possibly. Or someone with equal resources." Papers shuffled in the background. "Fiona's investigating the connection between Hutchinson & Associates and major Savannah business interests. Money trails between law firms and local power brokers."

"Keep me updated." Lawson checked her mirrors for potential surveillance; Parks' paranoia spreading to her actions. "I'm meeting Parks in an hour."

"Be careful. Hutchinson dying hours after Blackwell exposed him isn't coincidence."

The call ended. Lawson drove toward the riverfront, mind processing implications. Ray Hutchinson's death created perfect narrative closure. Confession without investigation. Case closed without exposing wider corruption.

Exactly what Monica's killers would want.

Her social media notification chimed again. Blackwell had posted another update with the security camera still image of the hooded figure leaving Hutchinsons' building. The caption read: *The real killer walks free. Justice demands truth. New episode reveals shocking connections.*

The media machine continued its inexorable operation. Tragedy transformed into content. Death repackaged as entertainment. All while the hooded figure disappeared into Savannah's morning crowds, mission accomplished.

For now.

chapter eighteen

RIVERFRONT COFFEE BUZZED with mid-morning activity. Tourists clustered near windows overlooking the Savannah River. Businesspeople tapped at laptops while nursing expensive espresso drinks. College students sprawled across corner sofas, textbooks open beside empty pastry plates.

Parks occupied a corner booth away from the windows. Back to the wall. Clear sightlines to both entrances. He wore civilian clothes—jeans and a button-down shirt beneath a lightweight jacket, despite the heat. The jacket concealed his shoulder holster.

Lawson slid into the booth opposite him. "Took precautions getting here?"

"Standard protocol when department channels are compromised." Parks pushed a coffee cup toward her. "Americano. Room for cream."

She accepted without comment. He'd remembered her order from their previous meeting. "Wallace shutting down the investigation?"

"Official statement calls it suicide with confession." Parks kept his voice low. "Case closed pending pro forma review."

"Convenient narrative."

"Too convenient." Parks glanced around before reaching into his messenger bag. "Which is why I secured this before the DA's team could misplace it."

He slid a clear evidence bag across the table. Inside lay a folded sheet of paper sealed in plastic. No official evidence tag. No chain of custody documentation.

"You took evidence from a crime scene." Lawson didn't touch the bag.

"Secured evidence that would otherwise disappear." Parks pushed it closer. "My authority as Internal Affairs investigator establishes legal chain of custody if needed."

"And if Wallace questions your authority?"

"I answer to Professional Standards Division, not the Chief." Parks tapped the bag. "Found this hidden inside an air vent in Hutchinson's bedroom. Taped behind the register cover."

Lawson opened the evidence bag carefully. The paper inside showed age—creases from multiple foldings, slight yellowing at the edges. She recognized the handwriting immediately. Monica's distinctive script. The same handwriting from the journal and storage unit documents.

She unfolded it carefully, preserving the plastic covering. Not a confession but a list of names. Department personnel organized by division. Patrol. Narcotics. Homicide. Vice. Her own name appeared at the top with a notation: "Can trust completely."

"This isn't what I expected." Lawson scanned the document. "These aren't dirty cops. These are the clean ones."

"Officers who refused bribes or participation in cover-ups." Parks nodded. "Landry documented the honest cops for protection."

Lawson examined the list more carefully. Most names had been crossed out. Some with dates noted beside them. Others with notations like "transferred" or "resigned." Only three names remained unmarked—her own, a patrol sergeant who'd retired last year, and a records clerk who'd moved to Atlanta.

"The pattern emerges when you check the dates." Parks sipped his coffee. "Five years of systematic removal. Every crossed-out officer was either dead, transferred, or forced out through manufactured complaints."

"Someone's been cleaning house." The realization crystallized. "Removing obstacles to department corruption."

"Exactly." Parks leaned forward. "Notice anything about Hutchinson's name?"

Dead Air

Lawson found it in the Narcotics section. Crossed out with different ink. More recent than the other markings. "Monica crossed him off the clean list."

"Changed her assessment at some point." Parks nodded. "Question becomes why."

"He turned. Started working with whoever was running the corruption." Lawson studied the document again. "But why would Hutchinson keep this? It implicates him."

"Leverage, perhaps. Protection against whoever runs the organization." Parks took the list back and returned it to his messenger bag. "Or evidence he planned to use for negotiation if caught."

"Or someone planted it for us to find." Lawson countered with another possibility. "Creating false connections."

"Unlikely given its location." Parks shook his head. "Hidden too carefully for planted evidence. Required specific knowledge of the apartment layout."

Lawson considered the implications. The list documented a systematic purge spanning five years. Clean officers removed through carefully orchestrated means. Monica tracking the pattern until her death. Hutchinson initially trusted, then marked untrustworthy.

"There's more." Parks extracted another evidence bag from his messenger bag. Smaller than the first. Single notecard inside. "Found this behind the same vent. Different paper. More recent."

Monica's handwriting again. A single line centered on the card: "He knows I know."

No name. No elaboration. Just four words documenting a fatal realization.

"She discovered who ran the corruption network." Lawson stared at the card. "Confronted Hutchinson about his involvement."

"Which gave him motive for her murder." Parks finished the thought. "Yet someone killed him to prevent that connection from emerging in Blackwell's podcast."

"Someone higher in the organization." Lawson remembered the hooded figure from the security footage. "Someone who couldn't risk Hutchinson talking if pressured."

"Exactly." Parks returned the notecard to his bag. "The confession note serves a dual purpose. Closes Monica's case while preventing further investigation into Hutchinson's connections."

The coffee shop filled with new customers. A tour group entered, chattering about riverboat cruises and historic homes. The noise provided additional privacy for their conversation.

"Department corruption explains the evidence gaps in Monica's case." Lawson kept her voice low. "The purposeful mishandling. The witnesses never re-interviewed."

"And why Internal Affairs received direct orders to stand down on certain investigations," Parks nodded. "Cases involving specific businesses or individuals quietly redirected despite clear evidence."

"Which businesses?"

"Construction companies. Import businesses. Entertainment venues." Parks recited from memory. "The pattern becomes visible only when examining five years of case assignments across divisions."

"Monica found the pattern." Lawson tapped her fingers against the table. "Started documenting the clean officers as potential allies."

"Then realized the corruption reached higher than she anticipated." Parks glanced toward the entrance as new customers arrived. "Became more cautious about who to trust."

Lawson thought about Monica's journal entry. The meeting with Hutchinson at the warehouse. Her uneasiness about him. The floodlight positioned for ambush. Pieces clicked into place.

"Hutchinson lured her to the warehouse." The scenario formed in her mind. "Set up the ambush on orders from whoever runs the organization."

"Then someone killed him to prevent that connection from becoming public." Parks nodded. "The question remains who benefits most from maintaining the corruption system."

The coffee shop television switched to breaking news. Camera footage showed the medical examiner's van outside Hutchinson's apartment building. The caption read: "Detective's Suicide Linked to Cold Case Murder."

Parks studied the screen with narrowed eyes. "Narrative control. Statement crafted to close both cases simultaneously."

"Wallace orchestrating the media response?"

"Or following instructions from above." Parks checked his watch. "The DA will announce case closure by noon. Department statement to follow confirming the confession matches evidence from Landry's murder."

"Except it doesn't." Lawson remembered Parks' earlier revelations about evidence never processed. "The forensics were deliberately mishandled."

"Which no one will ever investigate now that Hutchinson provided convenient closure."

Parks studied her for a long moment, seeming to weigh his words carefully. "There's something you should know about why I'm really here. Why I requested this case specifically."

Lawson set down her coffee, sensing the shift in his tone. "Go on."

"Three years ago, I lost my partner. Detective Bram Kowalski." Parks stared into his mug, voice taking on the careful cadence of someone who'd rehearsed this story many times. "Officially, it was a single-car accident. Bram supposedly drove off Highway 17 after drinking. Case closed in forty-eight hours."

"But you don't believe that."

"Bram was investigating evidence tampering. Had been for months. Found patterns in major drug cases—evidence disappearing, chain of custody problems, financial records becoming corrupted right before trial." Parks looked up, meeting her gaze. "He called me the night he died. Said he'd found something big. Was taking it to Internal Affairs the next morning."

The parallel struck Lawson immediately. "Like Monica."

"Exactly like Monica. Both discovered corruption. Both died before they could expose it. Both had their evidence disappear afterward." Parks pulled a small photograph from his wallet—two men in uniform, arms around each other's shoulders at what looked like a department barbecue. "Bram was methodical. Organized. The kind of guy who planned his grocery lists a week in advance. He didn't develop sudden drinking problems or reckless driving habits."

Lawson studied the photo. Kowalski had been younger than Parks, with the earnest expression of someone who still believed the system could be fixed from within.

"The alcohol in his system?"

"Blood draw showed point-one-two. Well over the limit. But I'd worked with Bram for four years. Never saw him drink more than a single beer, and that only at retirement parties." Parks returned the photo to his wallet. "Someone wanted him drunk when that car went off the road."

"Did you investigate?"

"Tried. But I was just a patrol sergeant then. No authority over traffic fatalities or Internal Affairs cases. By the time I got promoted and transferred to IA, most of the physical evidence had been destroyed according to standard retention schedules."

Parks leaned forward, voice dropping lower. "But Bram was smart. Paranoid, maybe, but smart. He kept backup copies of everything. It took me eight months after his funeral to find his secondary storage location."

"What did you find?"

"Documentation of evidence tampering going back at least five years. Systematic manipulation designed to ensure specific defendants walked free. The scope was staggering—dozens of cases, millions in seized assets that mysteriously disappeared, witnesses who changed their testimony after being 're-interviewed' by unknown parties.

"There's another pattern Bram documented. Financial irregularities among certain officers during that same period. We found irregular financial activity in several officers' accounts—including Detective Landry's. Pattern suggests systematic supplemental payments."

Lawson felt something cold settle in her stomach. "What kind of payments?"

"Regular deposits. Always the same amount. Same intervals. The kind of financial behavior that indicates someone was being compensated for services rendered." Parks's expression remained carefully neutral. "Could be overtime irregularities, consulting work, or ..."

He didn't finish the sentence, but he didn't need to. The implication was obvious.

"You've been building a case for three years."

"Building on Bram's foundation. Expanding his research. Documenting new instances of tampering while investigating the old ones."

Parks gestured toward his messenger bag. "Monica Landry's murder fits the pattern perfectly. She gets too close to the truth, ends up dead under suspicious circumstances, evidence disappears immediately afterward."

"Why tell me this now?"

"Because you're not the only one who's lost a partner to this network. Because you've been chasing the same corruption that killed Bram. And because I think together, we might actually be able to finish what they started."

The weight of shared loss settled between them. Lawson understood now why Parks had seemed genuinely invested in pursuing the truth rather than protecting departmental interests. His motivation ran deeper than professional duty.

"The people responsible for Bram's death," she said carefully, "are they still active?"

"Oh yes. More active than ever. The network will grow bolder now since they successfully eliminated two major threats. They'll think they're untouchable now." Parks finished his coffee, expression hardening. "Time to prove them wrong."

"What do you need from me?"

"Everything you've discovered about Monica's case. Official and unofficial. I'll share Bram's files in return. Two investigations that started separately but point toward the same conclusion." Parks stood and gathered his materials. "Corruption doesn't exist in isolation, Detective. It's systemic. Organized. And it's been operating in this city for years."

As they prepared to leave the coffee shop, Parks paused, "Bram used to say that good cops die when they forget they're outnumbered. But he also said that bad cops die when they forget good cops never stop hunting."

Lawson nodded, understanding the unspoken commitment they were making to each other. Two investigators bound by the ghosts of murdered partners, ready to finish what their friends had died trying to accomplish.

Parks gathered his belongings. "I need to return to the station before my absence raises questions."

"What about the evidence?" Lawson nodded toward his messenger bag.

"Secured in a location only I can access." Parks stood. "These documents don't officially exist until needed for prosecution."

"If prosecution ever becomes possible."

"When, not if." Parks maintained eye contact. "Monica Landry documented corruption that continues five years after her death. Officers who refused participation systematically removed. The organization remains active, Detective."

"With protection from the highest levels."

"Which makes our investigation extremely sensitive." Parks adjusted his jacket to better conceal his weapon. "Trust no one inside the department. Communication through personal channels only."

Lawson nodded. "Parks."

He paused, waiting.

"Why help me with this? Your job—"

"My job is to identify corruption within the department." Parks cut her off. "Our objectives temporarily align. Don't read anything more into it than that."

He zipped his messenger bag and prepared to leave, then hesitated. "By the way, where were you last night between midnight and three a.m.?"

Lawson maintained a neutral expression while her mind raced. Last night she'd been alone at Forsyth Park searching for the nonexistent insurance policy. Before that, she'd been at Monica's storage unit, which she didn't particularly want to share with Parks, especially in light of his recent pronouncement about their objectives. Hours spent in locations with no witnesses. No alibi during Hutchinson's murder window.

"Home." The lie came automatically. "Why?"

"Standard question for all officers connected to Hutchinson." Parks studied her face with professional detachment. "Eliminating variables."

"Am I a variable or a suspect?"

"Everyone's both until proven otherwise." Parks adjusted his jacket. "Stay reachable."

He exited through the side door, checking sightlines before disappearing into pedestrian traffic. The implications of his question lingered. Parks was investigating all angles, including her potential involvement in Hutchinson's death.

The television continued coverage of the "suicide," the official narrative solidifying with each carefully worded statement. The coffee shop filled with tourists oblivious to the corruption discussion that had just occurred at table seven.

Lawson walked to her car. Morning heat pressed against her skin. The clean officers list remained vivid in her memory. Names crossed out. Systematic removal of honest cops to protect corruption.

Monica had been right to trust no one. To create insurance policies hidden in multiple locations. To document the pattern while searching for its source.

"Our place." The phrase circled her thoughts. Not the fountain. Not the waterfront. Somewhere only Lawson would recognize. Somewhere connected to their relationship yet hidden from watchful eyes.

Five years searching for justice, and the answer remained locked in two words she couldn't decipher.

chapter
nineteen

LAWSON KNEW something was wrong before she inserted her key. The doorframe displayed a hairline fracture near the lock. Almost imperceptible unless you were looking for it. She'd been a detective long enough to recognize the subtle signs of forced entry later concealed with professional care.

She drew her weapon and pressed her back against the wall beside the door. Her neighbors wouldn't notice—Mrs. Abernathy across the hall was visiting her daughter in Florida, and the medical student next door worked hospital night shifts. Lawson took a steadying breath and turned the key with her left hand, weapon ready in her right.

The door swung open silently. She'd oiled the hinges last weekend, a habit from years of living alone. The apartment lay in perfect stillness. No movement disturbed the air. No sound beyond the refrigerator's electrical hum. She entered in a tactical crouch, sweeping her weapon across the entryway and living room.

Everything looked normal. Disturbingly normal. Her coffee mug remained on the side table where she'd left it that morning. Mail stacked neatly on the kitchen counter. Dishes drying in the rack. Nothing obviously disturbed or missing.

She cleared each room methodically. Bathroom empty. Guest bedroom undisturbed. Her bedroom appeared exactly as she'd left it—

bed hastily made, clothes draped over the chair, and backup weapon in the lockbox secured to her nightstand.

The apartment contained no intruders, yet someone had definitely entered. The subtle fracture in the doorframe proved it. Lawson holstered her weapon and began a more thorough examination. Professional instinct rather than random paranoia guided her search.

Her laptop sat on the coffee table, positioned at precisely the same angle she'd left it. She opened it and checked the browser history. Nothing unfamiliar appeared in the log, but someone with sufficient skill could cover their digital tracks.

The kitchen drawers revealed nothing missing. Silverware remained organized according to her particular system. Cabinets showed no signs of disturbance. The refrigerator contained the same half-empty containers and questionable leftovers from earlier in the week.

Lawson moved to her bedroom closet, where she kept a fireproof box containing important documents. Birth certificate. Property deed. Insurance policies. She entered the combination and checked the contents. Everything remained in place, including the envelope of cash she kept for emergencies.

"What were you looking for?" she murmured to the empty room.

Her gaze traveled upward, scanning the ceiling corners almost as an afterthought. The small black device blended with the smoke detector housing. Anyone else might have missed it. She retrieved a chair from the kitchen and stood on it to examine the object more closely.

A wireless camera. Professional grade. Battery powered with remote viewing capability. The kind used by security firms and surveillance professionals. She didn't touch it, recognizing the importance of preserving evidence.

She returned to the living room, examining ceiling corners with new attention. Another camera watched from above the bookshelf. A third monitored the front door. Her apartment had been transformed into a surveillance operation without her knowledge.

How long had the cameras been there? Days? Weeks? She tried to remember anything unusual upon returning home recently. Any sign she might have dismissed as paranoia. Nothing specific came to mind, which suggested the installation had happened recently.

Her phone chimed with a notification. Social media alert for Leah Blackwell's account. She opened it with growing unease.

The image showed a wooden keepsake box sitting on an unfamiliar countertop. The box lid was open, revealing intimate contents—letters, birthday cards, and photographs from her relationship with Monica. Weekend trips to Charleston. Private moments never meant for public view. The distinctive maple wood box with brass hinges was unmistakably hers—the one she kept hidden beneath her bed.

The caption read: "Where she hides her guilt. Detective Lawson's secret shrine to her partner. What else is she concealing? Episode 5: 'The Partner's Lies' drops tomorrow."

Lawson stared at the image, blood rushing in her ears. The invasion extended beyond physical space into her most private memories. Someone, or maybe even Blackwell herself, had entered her apartment, stolen her personal belongings, and provided the material to Blackwell. The wooden box contained items never entered into evidence. Never shared with anyone. The tangible remnants of a relationship she'd kept hidden even after Monica's death.

She rushed to her bedroom and dropped to her knees, lifting the dust ruffle. The empty space confirmed her fear. The box was gone. Someone had found and taken it.

She sat heavily on the bed, mind racing through implications. The intruder hadn't stolen valuables. Hadn't vandalized or destroyed. They'd come specifically for the wooden box. To gather intelligence. To provide Blackwell with ammunition for her podcast narrative.

Her security system included a basic camera monitoring the front door. She retrieved her phone and opened the app, scrolling back through recorded entries. Three visitors appeared during her absence today—the mail carrier at 10:17 AM, a package delivery at 11:45 AM, and at 1:32 PM, a figure she didn't recognize.

The timestamp placed the visitor during her coffee meeting with Parks. The figure wore a delivery uniform complete with cap pulled low. They approached her door carrying a small package. Instead of knocking, they examined the lock briefly before producing a small pry tool. With quick, practiced movements, they wedged it between the door and frame, forcing the lock mechanism to give way. They slipped inside, the entire process taking less than twenty seconds. Professional efficiency that left only the slightest damage to the doorframe—damage they attempted to conceal before leaving.

The exit footage showed the same figure leaving twenty-seven minutes later. A wooden box tucked under their arm where the package had been. Just smooth, purposeful movement suggesting a completed mission.

Lawson zoomed in on the grainy image. The delivery uniform offered perfect cover—neighbors accustomed to seeing various services throughout the day would notice nothing unusual. The cap and turned face prevented clear identification. Even height and build remained ambiguous beneath the loose-fitting uniform.

Lawson checked her phone again. Blackwell's post had already accumulated thousands of likes and comments.

She called Claire, who answered on the second ring.

"My apartment's been compromised." Lawson kept her voice steady despite the internal turmoil. "Someone installed surveillance cameras and stole my personal items. Blackwell just posted images of them online."

"Are you still there?" Claire's voice sharpened with concern.

"Yes. They're gone."

"Leave immediately." Papers rustled in the background. "Hotel tonight. Cash only. No credit cards."

"I need to document the cameras as evidence."

"Evidence for whom?" Claire's question carried pointed implications. "The department that's actively burying Hutchinson's murder? The Chief who ordered Parks to stand down?"

Lawson recognized the rational argument despite her investigative instincts. "I'll pack a bag."

"Use my beach house." Keys jingled through the phone. "Address is 1775 Tybee Island Drive. Security code 5241. No one knows I own it except my financial advisor."

"Rental under a corporate name?"

"LLC with privacy protections." Claire understood operational security. "Stock the kitchen from different stores. Alternate routes getting there. Basic protocols."

"Thank you."

"Don't thank me yet." Claire's voice lowered. "Blackwell's post shows your mementos from Monica. How personal were those items?"

The wooden box contained birthday cards with intimate messages. Weekend getaway photos showing a clear romantic connection. Notes they'd exchanged during workdays. Tangible evidence of everything she'd concealed for five years.

"Enough to construct a narrative." Lawson glanced at the camera in the corner. "Enough to paint me as someone with motive."

"Start packing. I'll meet you at the beach house after court." Claire ended the call without further discussion.

Lawson moved with deliberate efficiency. She grabbed the emergency go-bag from her closet—three days of clothes, basic toiletries, burner phone, and five hundred dollars cash. Standard preparation for any detective who'd worked enough cases involving witnesses who disappeared overnight.

She added her laptop and Monica's journal. The wooden box Blackwell had already exposed was gone, but she needed to maintain control of what evidence remained in her possession.

The surveillance cameras remained in place. She left them untouched, recognizing their value as evidence if a legitimate investigation ever became possible. Someone watching would see her packing overnight essentials—behavior that could be interpreted as routine rather than flight.

Her phone vibrated with another notification. Not social media but a text from an unknown number: *Running won't help. The truth follows wherever you go.*

The message contained no identifying information. No signature or context. Just the ominous warning from someone monitoring her movements in real time.

Lawson finished packing with heightened awareness of the cameras tracking her actions. She maintained casual movements while her mind categorized possibilities. The intruder had professional equipment, building access, and technological sophistication. Not a random criminal but a targeted operation.

The same organization that had systematically removed clean officers from the department. The same hidden power that had orchestrated Monica's death and Hutchinson's murder. Now their attention focused directly on her.

dead air episode 5:

"The Officer's Statement."

[Electronic theme music fades in, then quiets under narration]
 LEAH BLACKWELL: Welcome back to Dead Air. I'm Leah Blackwell.
 Throughout our investigation into Detective Monica Landry's murder, one document has remained central: the official statement given by her partner, Detective Erin Lawson. Today, we examine that statement against physical evidence from the scene and newly discovered witness accounts that contradict the official narrative.
 [Brief pause]
 LEAH: After multiple requests, we obtained a complete copy of Detective Lawson's statement through a Freedom of Information lawsuit. The document provides her account of what happened at the warehouse on August 17th, five years ago. Let me read the most pertinent sections:
 [Reading from document] "I arrived at the warehouse at approximately 11:00 p.m. after receiving a text from Detective Landry requesting the meeting. I parked my vehicle and approached the loading dock area where I observed my partner standing alone. Before we could speak, a bright light activated, temporarily blinding me. When my vision cleared, Detective Landry had been shot. I did not see the shooter or identify any suspects. I immediately called for assistance while attempting to provide emergency medical aid."

LEAH: This statement formed the foundation of the official investigation. It appears straightforward – a sudden ambush leaving no opportunity to identify the attacker. But multiple evidence points contradict this account.

[Sound of shuffling papers]

LEAH: First, surveillance footage from a business across the street shows Detective Lawson's vehicle arriving at 10:47 p.m. – thirteen minutes earlier than her statement claims. The same footage shows her remaining in her car for nearly five minutes before approaching the warehouse.

LEAH: When we presented this discrepancy to forensic investigator Dr. Eliza Mercer, her assessment was troubling:

DR. MERCER: Time discrepancies often indicate memory issues or intentional falsification. A thirteen-minute difference is significant. That's ample time for additional interactions or observations not included in the statement.

[Brief pause]

LEAH: Second, Detective Lawson's statement claims she "observed Detective Landry standing alone" before the floodlight activated. This contradicts the medical examiner's report, which determined Detective Landry was shot from an elevated position, likely the second-floor window of the warehouse.

LEAH: I asked retired homicide detective Oliver Williams to review both documents:

WILLIAMS: The angle of entry described in the autopsy report is inconsistent with a shooter at ground level. The trajectory indicates the shots came from approximately fifteen feet above the victim. If Detective Landry was standing when first observed, and the shooter was in that elevated position, they would have been visible to anyone approaching from the parking lot.

[Music intensifies]

LEAH: Third, and perhaps most troubling, is what Detective Lawson's statement omits entirely. Multiple witnesses at the Driftwood Tavern confirm she consumed several whiskeys in the hours before meeting her partner—a detail never mentioned to investigators.

LEAH: Tommy Reynolds, a regular at the Driftwood, provided this account:

TOMMY: She was at the bar from early evening. Had at least four whiskeys that I saw. Checking her phone a lot. Left suddenly after getting some kind of message. Seemed upset about something.

LEAH: The bartender, who requested anonymity, corroborated this account:

BARTENDER (voice disguised): Detective Lawson was a regular. That night she drank more than usual. Four, maybe five straight whiskeys. No food. Left around 10:30, maybe 11:00. Definitely shouldn't have been driving.

LEAH: When asked if Detective Lawson appeared intoxicated, the bartender was unequivocal:

BARTENDER: Absolutely. Slurring words by the end. Unsteady when she stood up. I considered saying something about driving, but ... you know ... she was a cop.

[Brief pause]

LEAH: These witnesses paint a very different picture than the official narrative. Detective Lawson, potentially impaired, arrived at a remote location to meet her partner after weeks of professional tension between them.

LEAH: I contacted the lead investigator who took Detective Lawson's statement, now-retired Detective James Morton:

MORTON: Standard procedure requires sobriety assessment for officers involved in shootings or traumatic incidents. I don't recall conducting one with Detective Lawson, but it was a chaotic scene. Captain Richardson took command early, might have made that determination.

LEAH: When asked if Captain Richardson directed any unusual procedures that night, Detective Morton became noticeably uncomfortable:

MORTON: I've been retired three years. My memory isn't what it used to be. What I can say is that Captain Richardson was particularly protective of Detective Lawson throughout the investigation. Professional courtesy for an officer who'd just lost her partner.

[Music shifts]

LEAH: Fourth, Detective Lawson's statement describes attempting "emergency medical aid" after the shooting. This contradicts first responder reports documenting that Detective Landry received one gunshot wound to the chest at close range—injuries that caused catastrophic damage to her heart and lungs, resulting in death within minutes.

LEAH: Paramedic Vincent Torres, first on scene that night:

TORRES: By the time we arrived, Detective Landry had no pulse, no respiration. Detective Lawson was kneeling beside her, covered in blood, but there was no actual medical intervention happening. Just holding her. Trauma response, probably. We see it often with partners.

LEAH: Torres noted that Detective Lawson appeared disoriented and unresponsive to basic questions—consistent with both traumatic shock and potential alcohol impairment.

[Brief pause]

LEAH: Perhaps most significant is what Detective Lawson's statement doesn't mention at all—her personal relationship with Monica Landry. Multiple sources within the department confirm the partners were more than colleagues.

SPD SOURCE (voice disguised): Everyone knew they were together. Not officially, of course. Department policy prohibits romantic relationships between partners. But they weren't exactly subtle. Arrived together, left together. Weekend trips. You do the math.

LEAH: This relationship adds critical context to the events leading up to that night. According to colleagues, the tension between Detectives Landry and Lawson in those final weeks wasn't just professional—it was personal.

FORMER COLLEAGUE (voice disguised): They had some kind of falling out. Monica started working odd hours, avoiding Lawson. Lawson started drinking more, staying late at the Driftwood. Whatever happened between them wasn't just about the Rafferty case.

[Music becomes more pointed]

LEAH: This brings us to the fundamental question: why did Detective Lawson omit these critical details from her official statement? Why exclude her relationship with Monica? Why not mention her activities before arriving at the warehouse?

LEAH: I put these questions directly to forensic psychologist Dr. Natalie Kim:

DR. KIM: Omissions in witness statements typically serve two purposes: self-protection or protection of others. When witnesses exclude potentially incriminating details, it's often to distance themselves from culpability or to shield someone else from scrutiny.

LEAH: When asked specifically about Detective Lawson's statement:

DR. KIM: Without speaking to her directly, I can only observe that the omissions create a specific narrative—one that minimizes her involvement and emotional connection to the victim while maximizing the randomness of the attack. Whether this was conscious deception or trauma-induced memory distortion would require direct assessment.

[Brief pause]

LEAH: Yet her actions in the five years since Monica's death tell quite a story. Detective Lawson received multiple disciplinary citations for unauthorized investigation into her partner's case. She was temporarily suspended for accessing sealed files related to the Rafferty investigation. Her personnel record shows increasing isolation, confrontational behavior with supervisors, and documented alcohol issues during work hours.

LEAH: These are not the actions of someone at peace with the official narrative. They suggest someone haunted by knowledge they can't reconcile with what they've told the world.

[Music softens]

LEAH: Tomorrow, I'm meeting with Rachel Banks, Monica Landry's sister, who has agreed to share previously undisclosed personal documents that may shed light on Monica's state of mind in those final weeks.

LEAH: In our next episode, we'll examine Ray Hutchinson's confession, recorded just days before his death in what police have ruled a suicide. His account contradicts everything we thought we knew about Monica Landry's murder and who orchestrated it.

[Music builds]

LEAH: This is Dead Air. The truth doesn't stay buried forever.

[Theme music plays out]

chapter
twenty

CLAIRE'S BEACH house stood three rows back from the shoreline on Tybee Island. Weathered cedar siding blended with neighboring vacation properties. Palm trees swayed along the gravel driveway where Lawson parked after a circuitous drive from Savannah.

The security keypad accepted the code without issue. Inside, the house smelled of disuse and air freshener. Hardwood floors gleamed beneath area rugs. Coastal-themed artwork decorated walls painted in neutral blues and tans. Generic enough to serve as a vacation rental but tasteful enough to reflect Claire's sensibilities.

Lawson dropped her bag beside the couch and conducted a thorough sweep. Bedrooms clear. Bathrooms empty. Kitchen untouched since the cleaning service last visited. No surveillance devices hiding in light fixtures or air vents. No signs of intrusion.

Windows offered views of neighboring houses but provided sufficient privacy with drawn blinds. The rear deck faced a small garden rather than the beach, offering concealed outdoor space.

She unpacked methodically. Clothes in the guest bedroom dresser. Laptop on the kitchen counter. Monica's journal secured in the nightstand drawer. In the quiet routine of unpacking, the reality of what had been stolen from her finally set in.

Blackwell possessed her most intimate memories now. By tomorrow morning, millions of podcast listeners would hear about her relationship with Monica. Evidence she'd denied for five years, now exposed for public consumption.

The kitchen cabinets revealed basic supplies—canned goods, pasta, coffee. The refrigerator stood empty except for condiments. She knew she should drive to town for groceries. Should establish security protocols. Should contact Parks about Hutchinson's murder investigation.

Instead, she found herself studying the drink cart in the living room. Crystal decanters containing amber liquid. Polished glasses arranged in neat rows. Five months sober suddenly felt like an arbitrary achievement compared to the immediate need for chemical oblivion.

She opened the nearest decanter and sniffed. Bourbon. Top shelf, from the smoothness wafting toward her. Her hand trembled slightly as she poured two fingers into a tumbler. The liquid caught the afternoon sunlight streaming through windows, transforming ordinary alcohol into liquid gold.

"Just one," she muttered to the empty house. The familiar justification that had preceded countless nights lost to memory.

The first sip burned like truth. The second spread warmth through her chest. By the third, the bourbon tasted like coming home to a place she'd never truly left.

She carried the glass to the deck, settling into an Adirondack chair overlooking the garden. Birds flitted between overgrown bushes. Wind rustled palm fronds against the evening sky. The tumbler emptied faster than intended.

One became two. Two became three. Three blurred into continuous refills as sunset painted the sky in watercolor streaks of orange and purple. Alcohol unlocked memories she'd carefully compartmentalized. Monica laughing during their Charleston weekend. Monica sleeping beside her, dark hair spread across white pillowcases. Monica arguing passionately about justice and corruption before everything fell apart.

The sliding glass door opened behind her. Claire's voice cut through bourbon-induced haze. "I see you found the bar cart."

Lawson didn't turn. "Quality selection."

"My father's collection." Claire's heels clicked across the deck boards. She placed a grocery bag on the side table and claimed the adjacent chair. "I brought food. Real food."

"Not hungry."

"Clearly." Claire eyed the tumbler in Lawson's hand. "How many is that?"

"Lost count."

"I can tell." Claire removed her blazer and draped it over the chair back. Court attire exchanged for evening casualness. "Want to talk about it?"

"About what?" Lawson gestured broadly with her glass. "My apartment being invaded? My private memories stolen? Hutchinson's murder? Monica's death? Pick a tragedy."

"Start with why today drove you back to drinking after five months sober."

The bourbon had dismantled too many internal barriers for effective deflection. "She's going to tell everyone about us. About Monica and me."

"Your relationship wasn't a crime."

"It was to the department." Lawson stared into her glass. "Partners aren't supposed to be involved. Professional boundaries and all that administrative bullshit."

"That doesn't explain your reaction." Claire's gaze remained steady. "There's something else."

The alcohol pushed words past filters that sobriety maintained. "I was drinking the night she died."

Claire sighed. "I know, Erin. I listened to the podcast."

Lawson shook her head. "No, I wasn't just drinking. I was *drinking*."

"What are you trying to tell me?" Claire asked slowly.

"Four whiskeys at the Driftwood before driving to the warehouse." The confession spilled out after five years of silence. "We'd been fighting. Hadn't spoken in two weeks. She texted about meeting, about having information on Rafferty. I went straight from the bar."

"You were impaired at the crime scene." Claire's voice remained neutral despite the bombshell revelation.

"Reaction time slowed. Observation skills compromised." Lawson's self-condemnation carried the weight of five years' guilt. "I saw things I couldn't process. Details lost to alcohol."

"What things?"

"Car parked behind the warehouse. Dark sedan. Thought it belonged to Monica's source." Lawson closed her eyes, forcing memories through alcohol's distortion. "Someone got out as I arrived. Familiar walk. I couldn't place it then. Still can't."

"Did you tell investigators?"

"Told them about the shooter. The floodlight. The gunshots." Lawson shook her head. "Not about the car. Not about seeing someone before the shooting started. Not about recognizing something in their movement."

"Why not?"

"Because admitting I saw someone meant admitting I could have identified them if I'd been sober." The tumbler trembled in her hand. "Because Richardson removed my intoxication from the official report. Protected me from suspension or worse."

Claire leaned forward. "This person you saw. Details? Anything?"

"Dark clothing. Baseball cap." Lawson strained against memory's limitations. "License plate visible in headlights. Partial view before the floodlight blinded me. G84 ... something. First three digits only."

"Male? Female?"

"Couldn't tell. Distance was too great. Light too poor." Lawson drained her glass. "Just the walk. Something distinctive about it."

"Like what?"

"Slight hesitation of the right foot. Almost imperceptible limp." She gestured vaguely. "Military bearing otherwise. Deliberate movement. Kind of like the person on the footage."

Claire absorbed this information with an attorney's calculation. "Footage? What footage?"

Bourbon blurred certainty into vague association. "Security footage from Hutchinson's building. Hooded figure had similar movement pattern."

"You never included this in your statement."

"How could I?" Lawson's laugh held no humor. "Detective arrives drunk to meeting where partner dies. Fails to identify potential suspect due to impairment. It makes a compelling headline."

"It's compelling evidence." Claire's expression hardened. "Evidence deliberately withheld from investigators."

"Evidence compromised by bourbon and guilt."

"Evidence Blackwell would use to destroy your credibility if she knew." Claire stood and took the empty glass from Lawson's hand. "You're done drinking for tonight."

Lawson didn't resist. The alcohol had already accomplished its purpose—dismantling the walls around memories she'd carefully contained for five years. "Monica deserved better than me as backup that night."

"Maybe." Claire's voice softened. "Or maybe it wouldn't have changed anything."

"We'll never know."

"No, but we can focus on what we do know." Claire disappeared inside, returning moments later with water and a sandwich. "Eat something. Sober up enough to think clearly."

Lawson accepted the offering without enthusiasm. Food would dull the alcohol's edge, returning her to a reality she'd tried to escape. The sandwich tasted like sawdust, but she forced herself to eat while Claire watched with unmasked concern.

"The partial plate." Claire pulled out her phone. "G84. Could be thousands of vehicles."

"Likely a government plate." Lawson's police instincts functioned despite intoxication. "Formatting matched state vehicle standard."

"Narrows it considerably." Claire made notes in her phone. "Especially if we cross-reference with department vehicles assigned five years ago."

"Records are restricted without warrant."

"There are alternative methods to access vehicle registration databases." Claire's vague reference suggested less-than-legal approaches. "Fiona has contacts in the transportation department."

"Fiona." Lawson closed her eyes as the deck tilted beneath her. The bourbon's full effect arriving. "Can she be trusted?"

"Her motivations align with ours for now." Claire helped Lawson to her feet. "You need to lie down before you fall down."

The journey from deck to bedroom passed in disjointed fragments.

Lawson's coordination deteriorated with each step. Claire's steady hand guided her through the house to the guest bedroom. The mattress received her collapsing form with silent judgment.

"Waste of five months of sobriety," Lawson muttered into the pillow.

"One setback doesn't erase progress." Claire placed water on the nightstand. "Sleep it off. We'll talk when you're coherent."

Darkness claimed portions of awareness as Lawson fought for consciousness. Time stretched and compressed. Claire's voice drifted from another room. Phone conversation with indistinct responses.

The front door opened. A new voice entered the house. Fiona's distinctive tone, carrying through walls.

"She's out cold?"

"Bourbon overload." Claire's response floated from the kitchen. "She provided some information, though. Partial plate from the night Landry died."

"Government vehicle?"

"Likely department issue."

Drawers opened and closed. Refrigerator door. Domestic sounds punctuated by professional discussion.

"Hutchinson agreed to meet tomorrow," Fiona said, her tone brisk but fluid. "We'll see him in the Savannah office."

"Really?" Claire sounded surprised.

"Strictly off the record."

The conversation continued, but Lawson's grasp on consciousness slipped further. Fragments reached her through her alcoholic fog.

"... brother's involvement ..."

" ... department corruption ..."

" ... meeting Hutchinson tomorrow morning ..."

Lawson struggled against the encroaching blackness. They were meeting Hutchinson tomorrow? The dead narcotics detective? The confusion swirled as darkness claimed her completely.

Her last coherent thought came from that part of her that wished the darkness might be permanent. Easier than facing tomorrow's revelations with newly exposed vulnerabilities and five months of sobriety abandoned in a single afternoon of weakness.

chapter twenty-one

MORNING ARRIVED WITH CRUEL INTENSITY. Sunlight streamed through blinds Lawson hadn't closed, stabbing directly into her bourbon-abused brain. She rolled away from the window, encountering a water glass and aspirin on the nightstand. Claire had anticipated her morning needs.

The bedside clock read 9:17 a.m. Nearly fourteen hours since her first drink. Her mouth tasted like something had died in it. Her head throbbed with each heartbeat. The price of abandoned sobriety, collected in full.

Bathroom rituals occurred on autopilot. Cold shower. Teeth brushed twice. Clean clothes from her go-bag. Each movement deliberate to minimize discomfort. The mirror reflected bloodshot eyes and skin that hadn't received adequate hydration. Punishment for weakness visible in every pore.

Voices drifted from the kitchen. Claire and Fiona engaged in a hushed but intense conversation. The scent of coffee permeated the house, drawing Lawson forward despite the desire to hide in hangover shame.

"She lives," Fiona announced as Lawson appeared in the doorway. No judgment colored her tone, just matter-of-fact observation.

Claire pushed a steaming mug across the counter. "Black. Strong enough to resurrect the dead."

"Feels appropriate." Lawson claimed the offering with unsteady hands. "Why are you both up so early?"

"Conference call with Thomas Hutchinson at ten." Claire checked her watch. "Twenty-eight minutes from now."

The swirling voices from last night finally began to make sense. "Thomas Hutchinson? Ray's brother?"

"The very same." Fiona leaned against the refrigerator, tablet propped against her chest. "Senior partner at Hutchinson & Associates. Arranged through his executive assistant after considerable negotiation."

"How did you manage that?"

"Mentioned potential story connections between his firm and Blackwell's podcast." Fiona's smile didn't reach her eyes. "Suggested press coverage might follow certain angles regardless of his participation."

"Polite professional blackmail." Claire prepared her own coffee. "Diplomatic pressure to address questions before they become public speculation."

Lawson's hungover brain struggled to process the implications. "He agreed to speak with journalists about his dead brother?"

"For fifteen minutes only." Fiona consulted her tablet. "Via conference call rather than an in-person meeting. No recording permitted."

"I want to be on the call."

Claire and Fiona exchanged glances.

"Bad idea." Claire shook her head. "If he knows you're listening, he'll say nothing substantive."

"He doesn't need to know." Lawson sipped her coffee, the caffeine activating dormant neurons. "Speaker phone. I'll stay silent."

"Risky." Fiona frowned. "Lawyers develop paranoia as a professional skill. He'll sense an audience."

"I need to hear his voice." Lawson set her mug down firmly. "Need to gauge his reactions directly."

Another silent exchange between the two women. Some unspoken communication passed between them before Claire nodded. "Okay. But absolute silence from you."

"Understood."

The minutes ticked by with agonizing slowness. Lawson consumed three glasses of water and another coffee while reviewing Fiona's notes on Thomas Hutchinson. Harvard Law. Clerked for a Supreme Court justice. Built Hutchinson & Associates from a regional practice to a national powerhouse specializing in corporate crisis management. Divorced twice. No children. Fifteen years older than his half-brother Ray.

At precisely 9:59 a.m., Fiona's laptop chimed with an incoming call notification. She connected and activated the speaker. "Fiona Stevens and Claire Stevens for Thomas Hutchinson."

"One moment while I connect you to Mr. Hutchinson's line." The woman's voice was crisp and professional but had an underlying weariness to it. "Mr. Hutchinson is finishing another call."

Soft classical music replaced the assistant's voice. Bach, Lawson thought, though her musical knowledge remained limited to what Monica had attempted teaching her years ago.

"Remember," Claire whispered to Lawson. "Complete silence."

The music ended abruptly. "The Stevens' sisters." Male voice. Deeper than expected. Smooth as aged whiskey, with none of the regional drawl his brother possessed. "Thank you for your patience. Thomas Hutchinson here."

"Appreciate you making time during difficult circumstances, Mr. Hutchinson." Fiona slipped into professional journalist mode. "Our condolences regarding your brother."

"Kind of you to say." A practiced pause. "Though I suspect condolences aren't your primary motivation for this conversation."

"We're investigating connections between your firm and Leah Blackwell's podcast." Fiona moved directly to substance. "Specifically, financial support channeled through Equinox Media Solutions."

A soft chuckle emerged from the speaker. "Direct approach. A refreshing change from legal equivocation."

"Do you deny the financial connection?" Claire asked.

"I categorically deny any direct funding from Hutchinson & Associates to Ms. Blackwell's podcast endeavors." His tone remained casual despite the formal language. "Though I can't speak to what individual partners might support through personal charitable foundations or media investments."

Lawson recognized the careful parsing. Denial of direct funding while acknowledging potential indirect support. Corporate lawyer precision in creating plausible deniability.

"Ms. Blackwell clerked at your firm." Fiona pressed forward. "Immediately after her judicial clerkship."

"Briefly, yes. One of dozens of promising young attorneys who pass through our associate program annually."

"Did you personally work with her?"

"Minimal interaction." Keyboard clicks sounded in the background. "Her performance reviews indicate solid research capabilities but limited client interaction skills. Hence her relatively short tenure with us."

"Yet her podcast specifically targets the case involving your brother." Claire interjected.

Silence stretched for several seconds. When Hutchinson spoke again, his tone had cooled noticeably. "My brother Raymond was troubled. Had been for years. His relationship with Detective Landry compounded existing personal issues."

"Troubled how?" Fiona asked.

"Obsessive tendencies. Difficulty maintaining professional boundaries." Hutchinson's voice lowered slightly. "The situation with Monica was becoming too much."

"Too much?" Claire echoed the phrase.

"I've said more than I intended already." The keyboard clicking stopped. "Family matters remain private despite public interest."

"Your brother confessed to murdering Detective Landry." Fiona's statement hung in the air between them. "Yet, evidence suggests his suicide was staged."

"Dangerous speculation, Ms. Stevens." Hutchinson's response came too quickly. "I'd caution against publishing unsubstantiated theories about an active investigation."

"The timing raises questions." Claire adopted her cross-examination tone. "Your brother dies hours after being identified as romantically involved with Monica Landry. Evidence suggesting murder disguised as suicide emerges. Meanwhile, a podcast with connections to your firm controls the public narrative."

"Coincidences appear significant until proven otherwise." Hutchinson's response sounded rehearsed. "Raymond's death represents tragedy, not conspiracy."

Lawson studied the laptop as if it might reveal Hutchinson's facial expressions. His voice carried a subtle tension beneath his practiced casualness. The lawyer answered questions while revealing nothing substantive—professional misdirection elevated to an art form.

A door opened on Hutchinson's end of the call. A muffled female voice spoke urgently in the background. "Sir, I apologize for the interruption. She found the second recording."

Papers shuffled. A chair creaked. When Hutchinson returned to the call, his voice carried tightly controlled alarm. "Ladies, I apologize for the abrupt conclusion, but an urgent client matter requires immediate attention."

"We have additional questions about your brother's connection to departmental corruption." Fiona attempted to extend the conversation.

"Perhaps another time." Professional politeness barely masked his desire to end the call. "I trust this conversation addressed your immediate concerns."

"Mr. Hutchinson—"

"Again, your condolences are appreciated during this difficult period of personal grief." The words were rushed together. "Good day."

The call disconnected as silence filled Claire's beach house kitchen.

"Well, that was abrupt." Fiona stared at her laptop screen. "Second recording?"

"Whatever it is sent him running." Claire tapped her fingers against the counter. "Something more important than controlling his brother's narrative."

Lawson processed the conversation while nursing her coffee. Hutchinson had revealed little beyond careful denials and vague references to his brother's "troubles." Professional crisis management applied to personal tragedy.

"He was nervous." Lawson broke her silence. "Controlled, but definitely nervous."

"Agreed." Fiona made notes on her tablet. "Especially when his assistant interrupted about finding a recording."

"What recording would warrant that reaction?" Claire frowned. "Something connected to Ray's death?"

"Or Monica's murder." Lawson set her empty mug in the sink. "Blackwell mentioned unnamed sources providing sealed evidence. What if Ray recorded something before he died?"

"Insurance policy." Fiona nodded slowly. "Protection against whoever was pulling his strings."

"Which his brother's firm is now desperately trying to contain." Claire completed the logical progression.

Lawson's phone vibrated with a notification. Dead Air Productions announcement: *Episode 6: "The Second Recording" broadcasting LIVE tonight at 6 p,m, Truth that someone killed to suppress.*

She showed the screen to Claire and Fiona. "Seems Blackwell found whatever Hutchinson's assistant was panicking about."

"Live broadcast." Fiona's eyebrows rose. "Breaking usual podcast release patterns. She's afraid someone might stop her."

"Or capitalizing on dramatic timing." Claire's skepticism remained intact. "Maximum audience engagement through artificial urgency."

"Either way, she has something Hutchinson wants contained." Lawson scrolled through additional notification details. "Something worth killing his brother to protect."

Fiona gathered her equipment with practiced efficiency. "I need to get back to the Tribune. Prepare coverage for whatever bombshell drops tonight."

"Stay here." Claire's suggestion carried undertones of command. "It's safer to work remotely until we know what that recording contains."

"I can't file stories from beach house isolation." Fiona shook her head. "Professional risk comes with the territory."

The women maintained eye contact for several heartbeats before Claire conceded with a nod. "Check in every hour. Any sign of surveillance or unusual attention, come straight back here."

"Yes, Mother." Fiona's sarcasm masked genuine appreciation for concern. "Lawson should stay put, though. Her connection to both murders makes her the most vulnerable target."

"Agreed." Claire turned to Lawson. "You're officially on beach house arrest until further notice."

Lawson didn't argue. Her hangover combined with revelation fatigue left little energy for resistance. "What about Parks? He should know about the recording." She hesitated, thinking about his last words to her. How long would their interests be aligned? Were they still?

"I'll contact him through secure channels." Claire moved toward her laptop. "An anonymous tip to his personal email rather than the department address."

Fiona departed with promises to return before the podcast aired. Claire retreated to the home office for client calls that couldn't wait despite murder investigations and corruption conspiracies. Normal professional obligations, continuing alongside extraordinary circumstances.

Lawson found herself alone on the deck, listening to the waves break against the distant shoreline. Six hours until Blackwell's live broadcast. Six hours to prepare for whatever revelation threatened Thomas Hutchinson enough to abruptly abandon careful damage control.

Her phone remained silent despite the notification settings. No messages from Parks. No further social media updates from Blackwell. Just the looming promise of "The Second Recording" and its unknown contents.

chapter
twenty-two

THE CLOCK on Claire's living room wall inched toward 6 p.m. with excruciating slowness. Lawson paced across hardwood floors while Fiona arranged recording equipment beside Claire's laptop. Outside, afternoon sunlight faded toward evening, painting Tybee Island in golden hues that belied the tension within the beach house.

"Stop wearing tracks in my floor." Claire emerged from the kitchen carrying a tray of sandwiches nobody would eat and coffee everyone would need. "Anxiety won't make time move faster."

"Professional habit." Lawson continued her circuit between windows. "Pre-raid ritual from tactical days."

Fiona checked the audio levels on her digital recorder. "Whatever Blackwell found, she's breaking standard podcast protocol to air it. No pre-production. No careful editing. Live broadcast risks technical failures, legal complications—"

"And prevents anyone from stopping the release." Lawson completed the thought. "Whatever this second recording contains, she's afraid of intervention."

Claire arranged food on the coffee table with precise movements. "Five minutes to air. Shall we place bets on what bombshell drops?"

"Not funny." Lawson claimed a chair facing the laptop. The Dead Air podcast webpage displayed a simple countdown timer against a black background. Professional design maintaining suspense until the broadcast began.

"Hutchinson abandoned careful damage control the moment his assistant mentioned the recording." Fiona positioned her secondary microphone. "Something beyond his brother's suicide note exists."

"Something worth killing for." Claire settled onto the couch, legal pad balanced on her knee. "Question becomes whose voice we'll hear."

The timer reached zero. The screen transitioned to simple audio visualization waves pulsing with ambient background noise. Blackwell's voice emerged after several seconds of silence.

"Good evening. I'm Leah Blackwell. This is Dead Air, broadcasting live for the first time in our program's history."

Her voice sounded different than previous episodes. Raw. Unpolished. The carefully constructed narrative persona replaced by genuine urgency.

"Tonight's episode deviates from our standard format. No scripted introduction. No carefully edited segments. Just truth that powerful people have killed to suppress."

Lawson exchanged glances with Claire. Blackwell's tone carried something beyond journalistic intensity. Genuine fear beneath that professional delivery.

"Five years ago, Detective Monica Landry was murdered at an abandoned warehouse in Savannah. Official investigation concluded with her partner, Detective Erin Lawson, as sole witness to an unidentified shooter who escaped into the night."

Fiona adjusted recording levels as background noise increased on the broadcast. Blackwell wasn't in her usual studio. The audio captured ambient sounds—distant traffic, air conditioning hum, occasional rustling papers.

"Two days ago, Detective Ray Hutchinson died in his apartment. Official ruling: suicide with a confession note claiming responsibility for Landry's murder. Case closed with a convenient narrative resolution."

Papers shuffled over the broadcast. Blackwell paused, seemingly organizing materials in real time rather than following a prepared script.

"Evidence suggests neither official narrative reflects truth. Detective Landry was investigating departmental corruption before her death.

Detective Hutchinson's suicide shows forensic inconsistencies suggesting a staged scene. Connections exist between both deaths, separated by five years but linked through institutional corruption."

Lawson leaned closer to the laptop. Blackwell's voice maintained professional control while incorporating an urgency previous episodes lacked.

"Yesterday, I received an encrypted file from an anonymous source within the Savannah Police Department. The file contained an audio recording never entered into evidence. A voicemail left on Detective Landry's phone the night before her murder."

Claire scribbled notes on her legal pad. Lawson remained motionless, every sense focused on Blackwell's words.

"I will play this recording unedited. The voice belongs to Detective Ray Hutchinson."

Static crackled through the laptop speakers. A male voice emerged through the electronic distortion. Ray Hutchinson's distinctive drawl, slightly slurred as if speaking through alcohol or extreme emotion.

"Monica, it's Ray. We need to talk. Things have gone too far. They know about us. Know what you've been investigating. I can't protect you anymore. Meet me tomorrow night. Usual place. Eight p.m. Come alone. No Lawson. Not if you want to survive this. I'm sorry about everything. So damn sorry."

The recording ended. Silence filled both the broadcast and Claire's living room. Lawson's hands gripped her knees with white-knuckle pressure. The voicemail confirmed what Blackwell had suggested in earlier episodes—Monica and Ray's relationship extending beyond professional boundaries.

"This voicemail never appeared in the official evidence." Blackwell's voice returned after the momentary silence. "Never mentioned in the investigation reports. Never presented during case reviews. Deliberately suppressed to maintain the official narrative."

"She's building toward something bigger." Fiona whispered. "Setting the foundation for the main revelation."

Blackwell continued. "The meeting referenced occurred twenty-four hours after this voicemail. Not at eight p.m. as suggested, but at eleven p.m. Not at their 'usual place' but at the abandoned warehouse where Detective Landry died."

"Why change the time and location?" Claire's question hung in the air.

"Detective Hutchinson's suicide note confessed to arranging Monica Landry's murder." Papers shuffled again. Blackwell cleared her throat before continuing.

"Yet, an examination of handwriting from the suicide note shows inconsistencies with Hutchinson's known writing samples. Evidence of forgery appears upon expert analysis. Someone wanted his confession to appear genuine while silencing him permanently."

"Shit." The word escaped Lawson involuntarily. "She's saying the confession was legitimate, but the suicide was murder."

"Which means—" Claire began.

"Which means Hutchinson killed Monica, then someone killed him to prevent further revelations." Fiona completed the thought. "Tying up loose ends."

Blackwell's voice grew more intense. "The second recording I received yesterday provides final confirmation. An audio file extracted from Detective Hutchinson's personal cloud storage. Created two days before his death. His actual confession, in his own words, unaltered and unabridged."

"She has Ray confessing on tape." Claire's expression showed rare surprise. "Recorded before his murder."

Lawson felt her pulse quickening. After five years pursuing shadows and suspicions, concrete evidence finally emerged. Ray Hutchinson's confession would close Monica's case with certainty rather than a convenient narrative.

"Before playing this recording, context remains essential." Blackwell's broadcast continued. "Detective Hutchinson worked in the Narcotics division during the period when Monica Landry investigated departmental corruption. Evidence suggests he participated in protecting certain drug operations while eliminating competition. Financial records show unexplained deposits to offshore accounts linked to his identity."

"The recording you're about to hear contains Detective Hutchinson's actual confession. His admission to participating in Monica Landry's murder under direction from someone within the department leadership. The identity of this individual—"

A loud crash interrupted Blackwell mid-sentence. Something heavy falling against a microphone or recording equipment. Muffled voices emerged through the broadcast—at least two people besides Blackwell herself.

"What the hell are you—" Blackwell's voice cut off abruptly.

Scuffling sounds filled the broadcast. Objects falling. A chair scraping across the floor. A door slamming with enough force to distort the audio levels.

"Get away from me!" Blackwell's voice returned, distant from the microphone. Fear replaced professional control. "Tom said—"

Another crash. Glass breaking. A scream, cut short. Heavy footsteps approached the microphone.

"You shouldn't have trusted him." A male voice. Too distorted to identify. "Some mentors betray their students."

The broadcast cut to silence. The audio visualization waves flatlined across the screen. Seconds later, an automated message appeared: "Technical difficulties. Broadcast temporarily suspended."

Lawson, Claire, and Fiona sat frozen in shock. The laptop speakers emitted soft static as the Dead Air website attempted to reestablish connection.

"Did we just—" Fiona broke the silence first.

"Witness Blackwell's abduction or possible murder?" Claire finished her question. "Appears so."

"Play it back." Lawson moved toward the laptop. "The last ten seconds before cutoff."

Fiona accessed her recording, rewinding to the final moments. They listened again to the crash, the scream, the approaching footsteps. The mysterious voice delivering a cryptic warning about mentors betraying students.

"'Tom said—'." Claire focused on Blackwell's interrupted question. "Thomas Hutchinson?"

"It doesn't make sense." Lawson shook her head. "We were on a call with him this morning. He called from his New York number. His assistant was there, too."

"Unless he hopped on a private flight. Big law money wouldn't be hard to do." Fiona suggested an alternative. "Realized he needed to be here in person to stop whatever happened next."

"Technical difficulties." Claire's voice dripped with skepticism. "Euphemism for an apparent violent abduction during a live broadcast."

Lawson stared at the message while processing the implications. "She was about to name Monica's killer. Someone who directed Ray Hutchinson's actions. Someone with enough authority to ensure evidence disappeared afterward."

"And enough power to orchestrate Ray's murder when he became a liability." Fiona added the logical extension. "The same person who just silenced Blackwell before she could play the second recording."

Claire retrieved her phone. "Who's your contact that can help? Did you say his name was Parks? This requires immediate police response regardless of departmental politics."

"No." Lawson's response came sharper than intended. "We don't know who to trust inside the department. The person who ordered Monica's death could be anyone with sufficient authority."

"Including Parks?" Fiona raised an eyebrow.

"I don't think so." Lawson considered the evidence Parks had shared. His questions about corruption. His careful documentation of evidence mishandling. "But certainty costs lives at this point."

Claire set her phone down without dialing. "What's our next move then?"

The Dead Air website remained unchanged. No further updates appeared despite five minutes passing since the broadcast interruption. Lawson stood and resumed pacing, her mind processing fragments from Blackwell's presentation.

"Blackwell said the second recording came from Ray's personal cloud storage." She thought aloud while moving. "A digital location accessible from anywhere."

"If we can identify his accounts." Fiona nodded slowly. "Digital forensics might—"

"His brother would have access." Claire interrupted. "A family member could claim inheritance rights to digital assets."

"Meaning Thomas Hutchinson likely has the recording Blackwell was about to play." Lawson completed the thought. "The same recording his assistant warned him about during our call."

Fiona gathered her equipment with sudden urgency. "I need to get to the Chronicle. Pull everything we have on Thomas Hutchinson's movements today. Cross-reference with potential broadcast locations Blackwell might use."

"Too dangerous alone." Claire objected. "Whoever took Blackwell won't hesitate—"

"A public newsroom offers safety in numbers." Fiona continued packing. "The Chronicle's security protocols exist for journalists' protection during sensitive investigations."

The argument continued while Lawson replayed the final moments of the broadcast in her mind. Something about the male voice triggered faint recognition. Not enough to identify with certainty, but a familiar cadence beneath the distortion.

"You shouldn't have trusted him. Some mentors betray their students."

The phrasing itself provided a potential clue. A mentor relationship. A betrayal dynamic. A connection to law enforcement or the legal profession where mentorship structures existed formally.

Her phone vibrated with an incoming message. Parks' number: *Blackwell's broadcast location identified. River Street Parking Garage. Level 4. Meet me there in one hour.*

"Parks just texted." Lawson interrupted Claire and Fiona's ongoing debate. "They've found where Blackwell was broadcasting from. He wants me to meet him at the River Street Parking Garage."

Claire's expression shifted to concern. "Could be a trap. We don't know who to trust right now."

"Maybe the real killer is trying to lure you out." Fiona moved to Lawson's side, reading the message over her shoulder. "After what we just heard happen to Blackwell—"

"If that's the case, it is what it is." Lawson pocketed her phone with resolute determination. "I want to know the truth. Five years is long enough."

"You can't seriously be considering meeting him alone." Claire stood, her voice sharpening with alarm. "Not after witnessing a live abduction."

"I need answers." Lawson moved toward her jacket draped over a nearby chair. "Parks has been straight with me so far. If they've found where Blackwell was taken—"

"And if they haven't?" Fiona challenged. "If someone has his phone? If he's been compromised?"

Lawson paused, considering the possibilities. Every investigative instinct acknowledged the danger. Yet the alternative—remaining in hiding while answers slipped further away—felt intolerable after five years of searching.

"I'm going." Her voice left no room for debate.

Claire and Fiona exchanged glances, more silent communication passing between them before Claire nodded firmly.

"Then we're coming with you." Claire reached for her own jacket.

Lawson recognized the determined set of both women's expressions. The same determination that had driven Claire to overturn wrongful convictions and Fiona to pursue stories others abandoned. Arguing would waste valuable preparation time.

"Fine," she conceded with reluctance that masked genuine relief. "But we do this professionally. Entry strategy. Communication protocol. Extraction plan if things go sideways."

"I have gear in my car." Fiona patted her equipment bag. "Including a portable scanner for police frequencies."

"I know the building layout." Claire grabbed her keys from the counter. "A colleague represented the property management company during a liability case three years ago."

Lawson felt a surge of unexpected gratitude as they moved with coordinated purpose toward the door. Whatever waited at the parking garage—trap or truth—she no longer faced it alone.

After five years of solitary pursuit, she had allies willing to risk their safety alongside her. The weight of Monica's death, carried alone for so long, now was distributed across willing shoulders.

Some burdens became lighter when shared with the right people.

chapter
twenty-three

THE RIVER STREET Parking Garage loomed over the cobblestone streets, a brutalist concrete structure at odds with Savannah's historic architecture. Yellow police tape stretched across the Level 4 entrance, fluttering in the evening breeze. Patrol cars with flashing lights crowded the ramp leading upward, their red and blue glow reflecting off surrounding buildings.

"So much for a trap," Claire remarked as they approached the scene. She gestured toward the dozen officers securing the perimeter and processing evidence.

Fiona scanned the assembly of official vehicles. "Half the department turned out for this. Something about a journalist's abduction attracts serious attention."

The public nature of the scene contradicted their earlier fears of ambush. Uniformed officers directed traffic. Bystanders gathered along the sidewalk, phones raised to capture whatever drama unfolded. A news van from the local television affiliate had already set up for a live broadcast at street level.

Lawson badged the officer controlling access, who checked her credentials against his clipboard before reluctantly lifting the tape. "Lieutenant Parks is expecting you, Detective. Fourth floor, north corner."

They rode the elevator in silence, each preparing for whatever awaited above. The doors opened onto organized chaos. Crime scene technicians photographed blood spatter across a concrete pillar. Evidence markers dotted the floor surrounding what appeared to be a makeshift broadcasting station—folding table, laptop, microphone setup, portable lighting equipment.

Parks stood at the center, directing the investigation with efficient authority. He spotted Lawson immediately, breaking away from a conversation with a forensics technician to intercept her group.

"You brought company." His gaze swept over Claire and Fiona with professional assessment.

"They insisted," Lawson replied. "What happened?"

"Still piecing it together." Parks guided them toward the makeshift broadcast area, careful to avoid contaminating evidence paths. "Security camera footage shows Blackwell and her assistant arriving approximately ninety minutes before broadcast."

"Professional planning." Lawson studied the blood pattern on the pillar. "Any sign of her?"

"Blood but no body." Parks lowered his voice. "Chief Wallace personally called this in as a high-priority investigation, but with specific instructions."

"Let me guess. I'm not welcome."

"You're technically a suspect." Parks handed her a preliminary report. "Wallace cited your connection to the Monica Landry case and potential motive to silence Blackwell before she revealed damaging information about you."

"That's absurd," Claire interjected. "Lawson's been with us since before the broadcast began."

"I'm not the one making these decisions." Parks kept his jaw tight, the disagreement flashing for a second before he smothered it. "Officially, you shouldn't be here at all, Detective."

"You're the one who called me here," Lawson shot back.

Across the crime scene, a young man sat on a concrete barrier, wrapped in a shock blanket despite the humid evening air. Mid-twenties, hipster beard, oversized glasses, his expression vacant while a uniformed officer attempted to take his statement. He clutched a laptop against his chest like a shield.

"Blackwell's assistant?" Lawson nodded toward the young man.

"Dylan Everett." Parks consulted his notes. "Audio engineer and production assistant for Dead Air. Found him knocked out cold."

Fiona studied the assistant with journalistic interest. "He's protecting that laptop like it contains gold."

"Evidence techs are waiting on a warrant before seizing it." Parks checked his watch. "Should come through any minute."

Claire straightened her blazer. "I'll handle this."

She approached the assistant with confident strides, lawyer mode fully engaged. Parks raised an eyebrow but didn't interfere as Claire introduced herself to both the assistant and the officer taking his statement.

"Is she going to—"

"Get information before the police confiscate everything?" Lawson finished Parks' question. "Almost certainly."

They watched as Claire spoke intently to Dylan, who nodded repeatedly before unlocking his laptop. The officer looked uncertain but stepped back as Claire sat beside the assistant, both now focused on the screen.

"Clever," Parks admitted. "The kid might talk to a friendly attorney before police pressure shuts him down."

Lawson turned her attention back to the crime scene. "Blood spatter analysis?"

"Consistent with blunt force trauma. Not immediately fatal based on volume and distribution." Parks pointed toward a knocked-over chair. "Attacker approached from behind. First blow stunned but didn't incapacitate. Trace evidence suggests a struggle and the vic's movement toward that pillar where the second impact occurred."

"Professional?"

"Very." Parks directed her attention to subtle scuff marks near the elevator. "Controlled extraction. No panicked movements or hesitation patterns. They knew exactly when and how to grab her."

Fiona joined them after photographing the scene with her professional camera. "Security in this building is a joke. Multiple blind spots in camera coverage. Stairwells without monitoring. Several potential extraction routes."

"Perfect location for a planned abduction." Parks nodded in agreement. "Question becomes, how did they know Blackwell would broadcast from here?"

"Inside information." Lawson studied the makeshift studio setup. "Someone knew her schedule."

Claire returned from her conversation with Dylan, expression tense with urgency. "We need to watch this now."

She led them to a quiet corner away from the main investigation activity. Dylan followed reluctantly, still clutching his laptop but now willing to share its contents. He opened a media player showing a document titled "Episode 7 Draft Script - The Cop Who Killed the Truth."

"Blackwell was working on the next episode even before broadcasting tonight's." Claire pointed to the timestamp. "Last edited three hours ago."

Dylan spoke for the first time, voice barely above a whisper. "She always prepared multiple episodes in advance. Said it was insurance in case something happened to her."

"Smart woman." Fiona positioned herself to record the screen with her phone.

Dylan scrolled through the document, revealing bullet-point notes rather than a polished script. Sections highlighted in yellow indicated incomplete research. Red text marked areas required additional source verification.

"There." Lawson pointed to a section labeled "Richardson Connection."

Dylan clicked on the subheading, expanding a section of detailed notes about former Captain Tom Richardson. Connections to the Rafferty investigation. Meeting schedules with Ray Hutchinson during periods when evidence disappeared from the case files. Financial transactions between offshore accounts linked to shell companies controlled by Thomas Hutchinson's law firm.

"Jesus," Fiona whispered. "She was building a case against Richardson."

"Not just him." Dylan continued scrolling to reveal additional sections. Notes about Chief Wallace's rapid promotion after Monica's case went cold. Questions about Judge Byrd's financial connections to businesses investigated during the Rafferty case."

"The corruption network Monica discovered. Blackwell found the same evidence and followed it to the top of the department." Lawson felt ice forming in her chest as pieces connected.

"Wait." Claire pointed to another section. "There's your name."

The section titled "Lawson's Omissions" contained a detailed analysis of discrepancies in Lawson's official statement after Monica's death. Notes about her relationship with Monica, the drinking before the warehouse meeting, suspicious behavior in the months following the murder.

Then, a highlighted section made Lawson's breath catch: "Second Recording confirms Richardson present at warehouse. Voice analysis matches warning to Lawson."

"She had proof Richardson was there that night. Audio confirmation he was present when Monica died."

Parks read over her shoulder, expression hardening with each revealed detail. "Richardson mentored both of you, didn't he? You and Landry?"

"First year on homicide." Lawson nodded slowly. "He specifically requested us for his division."

"You shouldn't have trusted him. Some mentors betray their students." Fiona quoted the words from the interrupted broadcast. "The voice on the podcast."

Dylan clicked to another section of the document. "She has the recording here."

He opened an audio file embedded in the document. The computer speakers emitted Richardson's distinctive voice, unmistakable.

"Ray, it's done. Clean up and get out. I'll handle Lawson when she arrives."

The short clip ended. Silence fell over their small group as the implications crystallized.

"Richardson set the whole thing up." Lawson struggled to process the betrayal. "Orchestrated Monica's murder. Used Ray as the triggerman. Planned to deal with me next."

"But something went wrong." Parks added the logical conclusion. "You arrived earlier than expected, or he lost his opportunity."

"Then spent five years burying evidence and blocking the investigation." Claire completed the picture. "Until Blackwell started digging it all up again."

A commotion at the elevator drew their attention. Chief Wallace emerged surrounded by administrative staff and senior officers. His gaze locked onto their small group immediately, expression darkening at the sight of Lawson.

"Lieutenant Parks." Wallace's voice carried across the crime scene, freezing activity throughout the floor. "Why is Detective Lawson contaminating my crime scene after explicit instructions to exclude her from this investigation?"

Parks straightened to his full height. "I take full responsibility, sir. Detective Lawson has provided valuable context regarding the victim's investigation."

"That context makes her a person of interest." Wallace approached with measured steps. His entourage followed like courtiers behind royalty. "Ms. Blackwell's podcast directly implicated Detective Lawson in misconduct related to the Landry murder."

Dylan quietly closed his laptop as the confrontation unfolded, protecting the evidence they'd just discovered.

"With respect, sir," Parks maintained a professional tone despite the public challenge to his authority, "Detective Lawson has an alibi for the time of Blackwell's abduction. I've verified her whereabouts personally."

Wallace's expression hardened. "Lieutenant, this is not an Internal Affairs matter. This is a criminal investigation that falls under my direct authority."

"With respect, sir," Parks stood his ground, "the potential involvement of department personnel makes this precisely an Internal Affairs matter. My division has jurisdiction whenever officers' conduct comes into question."

Wallace's voice lowered dangerously. "And I'm determining that Detective Lawson's presence compromises this investigation."

"Standard IA protocol allows me to interview all relevant personnel," Parks countered. "Detective Lawson's insights on the Blackwell investigation are critical, given her connection to the Landry case."

The power play unfolded with practiced efficiency.

Without the ability to force Parks to leave, Wallace turned to Lawson. "Detective," Wallace continued, "consider yourself on administrative leave pending internal review of your connection to this case. Surrender your badge and service weapon to Captain Reynolds before leaving the scene."

Claire stepped forward. "My client will comply under protest and with full reservation of rights. Any disciplinary action will be challenged through appropriate legal channels."

"Your client?" Wallace's eyebrow rose. "Is Detective Lawson in need of legal representation, Ms. Stevens?"

"Everyone deserves counsel when facing unfounded accusations." Claire's professional demeanor matched Wallace's bureaucratic armor. "Particularly when those accusations appear designed to obstruct justice rather than pursue it."

The chief's face flushed with barely contained anger. "Careful, Counselor. Interfering with a police investigation carries serious consequences."

"So does witness tampering and evidence suppression." Claire squared her shoulders. "Both of which I've documented extensively since arriving at this scene."

The standoff crackled with tension. Officers throughout the crime scene had abandoned any pretense of work, watching the confrontation unfold with professional interest.

Lawson unclipped her badge and removed her service weapon, presenting both to Captain Reynolds with precise movements that maintained her dignity despite the public humiliation.

"I expect a receipt for my property, Captain." Her voice remained steady through years of practice dealing with hostile situations.

Reynolds provided the required documentation without comment. His expression revealed nothing about his personal opinion regarding the chief's actions.

"Now, if there's nothing else," Claire gathered her belongings with deliberate movements, "my client will be leaving as instructed."

Wallace watched through narrowed eyes as they prepared to depart.

As they walked toward the elevator, Dylan fell into step beside them, laptop still clutched against his chest. The young man had recognized the sudden shift in the political winds and made his choice about which side offered better protection.

Parks hung back slightly, appearing to maintain a professional distance while actually creating an opportunity to speak privately. "I'll keep you informed despite Wallace's games. We both know what this is about now."

"Richardson." Lawson kept her voice barely above a whisper. "He's still controlling things from retirement."

"Through Wallace and others." Parks nodded subtly. "The corruption network your partner discovered five years ago remains active."

"We need that recording." Lawson glanced toward Dylan and his protected laptop. "It's concrete evidence linking Richardson to Monica's murder."

"Get somewhere safe first. Wallace will have you followed." Parks maintained his escort posture as they reached the elevator. "I'll contact you through secure channels when I can."

The elevator doors opened. Lawson, Claire, Fiona, and Dylan stepped inside, leaving Parks behind. As the doors closed, Lawson caught his final whispered advice.

"Trust no one in uniform. Not anymore."

The elevator descended toward the street level, where curious onlookers and the media waited. Lawson felt the weight of her missing badge and service weapon like phantom limbs. Administrative leave. Public removal from the case. Wallace's heavy-handed tactics, designed to isolate and neutralize her.

Yet something unexpected had happened in the process. Their group had expanded to include Dylan and his protected evidence. Parks had subtly declared his allegiance to the truth rather than the chain of command.

Most importantly, they now had names. Richardson. Wallace. Byrd. The architecture of corruption Monica had died exposing. The powerful figures who had orchestrated her murder and continued protecting their interests five years later.

The elevator reached the ground level. Doors opened to camera flashes and shouted questions from reporters who had somehow learned of Lawson's suspension already.

Claire took the lead, professional shield deploying automatically. "No comments at this time. My client maintains her innocence of any wrongdoing and expects full reinstatement following proper review procedures."

They pushed through the media gauntlet toward Claire's car parked at the curb. Fiona kept Dylan close, protecting both him and his crucial laptop from the cameras and questions.

Lawson moved through the chaos with mechanical precision, mind already processing next steps rather than dwelling on present humiliation. Richardson had orchestrated Monica's death. Had likely ordered Blackwell's abduction. Would come for Lawson next once he realized she had discovered the truth.

The game had changed completely. No longer a quest for justice through official channels but a fight for survival against the very institution she had served for over a decade.

Some battles couldn't be won within the system.

Sometimes you had to burn everything down to expose the truth.

chapter
twenty-four

MORNING NEWS BROADCASTS blared from the television in Claire's beach house living room. Each channel displayed the same footage: Lawson exiting the parking garage, surrounded by cameras and shouted questions. The ticker at the bottom of the screen spelled out her new status with brutal simplicity: "Detective Erin Lawson Named Person of Interest in Leah Blackwell Disappearance."

"Turn it off." Lawson stood in the kitchen doorway, coffee mug gripped tightly in her hand. Three hours of restless sleep had done nothing to diminish yesterday's exhaustion.

Fiona ignored the request, increasing the volume instead. "We need to know what they're saying."

The anchor's professionally concerned voice filled the room. "The Savannah Police Department has confirmed that Detective Erin Lawson has been suspended pending investigation into her possible connection to podcast host Leah Blackwell's disappearance. Sources within the department suggest Detective Lawson had motive to silence Blackwell before damaging revelations about her partner's death could be made public."

"Sources within the department." Claire emerged from the guest bedroom, already dressed for court despite the early hour. "Wallace is controlling the narrative."

Social media updates scrolled across the bottom of the screen.

#FindLeah had been trending nationwide since last night's interrupted broadcast. Celebrity tweets demanding justice. Podcast fans organizing virtual vigils. Armchair detectives, dissecting every frame of the abduction audio.

"They're painting me as the villain." Lawson watched her own image flash across the screen—her official department photo juxtaposed with security footage of her entering the parking garage. The visual framing suggested guilt before any evidence had been presented.

"Public opinion trial before actual investigation." Fiona typed furiously on her laptop. "Classic misdirection tactic."

The television switched to a press conference outside police headquarters. Chief Wallace stood at a podium surrounded by uniformed officers, his expression grave with manufactured concern.

"We are pursuing all leads in Ms. Blackwell's disappearance. Detective Lawson's suspension is standard procedure when an officer becomes central to an ongoing investigation. I want to assure the public that this department is committed to finding Ms. Blackwell and bringing those responsible to justice, regardless of who they may be."

Carefully crafted statements. Plausible deniability wrapped in procedural justification. Wallace's performance hit every necessary note to appear thorough while actually obstructing real investigation.

"He's good." Claire's grudging professional assessment cut through the tension. "Building reasonable doubt about department motives while simultaneously directing attention toward you."

Lawson set her coffee down before she could throw it at the screen. "Where's Dylan? He has the evidence that could counter this narrative."

"Not answering calls since last night." Fiona closed her laptop with a decisive snap. "Texts go unread. Voicemail full."

"Could he have been taken too?" The possibility sent a chill through the room.

"Or spooked into hiding." Claire retrieved her briefcase from beside the couch. "Young man suddenly holding evidence in a high-profile abduction with police corruption overtones. Fight or flight would naturally trigger."

Fiona's phone pinged with an incoming message. She checked it, expression shifting from concern to satisfaction. "The Chronicle's editor just approved my article. Publishing in fifteen minutes online, tomorrow's front page print edition."

"What article?"

"The one detailing your alibi during Blackwell's abduction, the Chief's suspicious rush to name you a person of interest, and serious questions about the department's handling of both Blackwell and Landry investigations." Fiona displayed her phone screen showing the headline: "Detective Scapegoated in Podcast Host Disappearance: Corruption Questions Mount."

"They approved that?" Claire appeared genuinely surprised.

"I have documentation." Fiona's smile carried professional pride. "Witness statements confirming your whereabouts. Parks' preliminary assessment contradicting the Chief's public statements. Records of Wallace's questionable promotions after the Landry case went cold."

"You're putting yourself at risk." Lawson understood the professional consequences Fiona faced by challenging powerful institutions. "Wallace will retaliate."

"Let him try." Fiona returned to her laptop. "Tribune's legal department welcomes the opportunity. First Amendment battles make careers in journalism."

Claire checked her watch. "I need to file motions challenging your suspension before the courthouse closes. The administrative hearing is scheduled for tomorrow morning."

"I need to see Richardson first." The decision had formed during the sleepless hours before dawn. "He's at the center of this somehow."

"Absolutely not." Claire's lawyer voice emerged, the tone she likely used with difficult clients. "Approaching a potential suspect compromises your position and risks additional administrative charges."

"He knows what happened to Monica." Lawson moved toward the door. "Maybe what happened to Blackwell too."

"You have no badge, no authority, and a target on your back." Fiona joined Claire's opposition. "Wallace would love nothing more than to charge you with harassment or interference."

"I'll be careful." Lawson grabbed her jacket from the hook beside the door. "Just a conversation."

"At least wait until my article publishes." Fiona gestured toward her laptop screen. "Give the department something else to worry about before you make yourself more visible."

The logic made sense, but patience had never been Lawson's strength. Five years waiting for justice had depleted her capacity for further delay. "Richardson needs to know we're onto him."

"And if he's involved in Blackwell's disappearance?" Claire blocked the doorway. "You'd be walking into the lion's den alone."

"Then I'll bring a chair and whip." Lawson gently moved past her. "I've faced worse."

Further arguments followed her to the door. Professional concerns from Claire. Practical cautions from Fiona. Lawson absorbed their warnings without altering her course. Some confrontations couldn't be delegated or delayed.

The drive to Richardson's house consumed forty minutes. Magnolia Way looked different in daylight—manicured lawns and carefully pruned trees creating a façade of ordered tranquility. Richardson's colonial revival still projected authority with its imposing columns and symmetrical windows.

Lawson parked across the street, studying the property for signs of activity. Richardson's car was missing from the driveway. Newspapers collected on the porch. Window blinds partially closed against morning sunlight.

She approached cautiously, professional instincts cataloging potential threats despite her suspended status. The doorbell chimed inside the house, its sound muffled through thick wooden doors. Footsteps approached from within.

Amy Richardson opened the door halfway, security chain still in place. The former captain's wife looked older than Lawson remembered—new lines etched around eyes that remained sharp with intelligence.

"Detective Lawson." No surprise colored her voice. "I wondered when you might appear."

"Mrs. Richardson. Is your husband home?"

"Tom's on his annual fishing trip." Amy's expression revealed nothing. "Chattooga River. Same week every year."

"Convenient timing."

"Scheduled months in advance." Amy's gaze remained steady. "Is there something I can help you with?"

"When did he leave?"

"Three days ago. Returns Friday." Amy's hand rested on the door edge, ready to close it if necessary. "I can give you the name of the lodge if it's important."

"It's important." Lawson studied the woman's face for signs of deception. "A podcast host investigating your husband's connection to Monica Landry's murder has disappeared."

Not even a flicker of reaction crossed Amy's features. Either she knew nothing or possessed remarkable control. "That sounds like a matter for the police."

"I am the police."

"Not according to this morning's news." Amy's matter-of-fact delivery carried no malice, just acknowledgment of widely broadcast information. "Your suspension was mentioned specifically."

"Administrative leave pending investigation." The correction sounded hollow even to Lawson's ears.

"Then I suggest you allow active officers to handle their duties." Amy began closing the door. "I'll tell Tom you stopped by."

"Did he ever mention Monica?" Lawson asked quickly, before the door could close completely. "Or Ray Hutchinson?"

Amy paused, door half-closed between them. "My husband mentored dozens of officers during his career, Detective. He rarely discussed individual cases or personnel matters at home."

"Even after Hutchinson's suicide?"

"Especially then." Amy's expression softened slightly. "Tom believed in maintaining professional boundaries. Something you might consider during your administrative leave."

The door closed with quiet finality. Lawson stood on the porch, frustrated by the encounter's lack of productive information. Amy Richardson either genuinely knew nothing or had mastered the art of polite stonewalling through decades of marriage to a police captain.

Three days ago. Before Blackwell's abduction. Before Hutchinson's murder, staged as suicide. The timeline potentially provided Richardson with an alibi.

Unless the fishing trip was a fabrication. A cover story maintained by a loyal wife while Richardson operated from the shadows.

Lawson returned to her car, mulling possibilities. Richardson could have orchestrated everything from a distance. Digital communications. Trusted subordinates carrying out orders. Physical absence providing plausible deniability while events unfolded according to plan.

Her phone vibrated with an incoming call. Fiona's number.

"The article just published." Fiona's voice carried the excited tension of a journalist who had just fired a significant shot across powerful bows. "Chronicle's server traffic quadrupled in five minutes."

"Any official response?"

"Department spokesperson says they 'don't comment on speculative reporting' but 'stand by their investigation procedures.'" Fiona's satisfaction came through. "Social media's exploding. #CorruptSavannahPD trending alongside #FindLeah."

"Any sign of Dylan?"

"Still nothing." Fiona's tone shifted to concern. "Claire's filing a missing person report, but without evidence of foul play, it won't get priority."

"Evidence keeps disappearing." Lawson started her car, watching Richardson's house in the rearview mirror. "First Blackwell, now potentially her assistant."

"What about Richardson?"

"Allegedly fishing. Chattooga River. Left three days ago according to his wife."

"Convenient." Fiona's skepticism matched Lawson's own. "I'll have a contact check lodges in that area, confirm the reservation."

"Good. I'm heading back now."

"Be careful. Wallace called a press conference for noon. Likely responding to my article."

"Looking forward to his creative interpretation of facts." Lawson pulled away from the curb, keeping Richardson's house in view until distance obscured it. "See you soon."

chapter
twenty-five

EVENING SHADOWS LENGTHENED across the beach house living room. Fiona's laptop displayed multiple news sites simultaneously, each featuring variations of the same headline: "Missing Podcast Host Investigation Intensifies." Takeout containers littered the coffee table, evidence of meals hastily consumed between strategy sessions and evidence reviews.

Lawson paced the perimeter of the room, unable to maintain stillness despite physical exhaustion. Thirty-six hours without proper sleep had transformed nervous energy into a persistent background hum.

"Amy Richardson claims he's been fishing for three days." She recounted the morning's confrontation for the third time, details unchanged despite Claire's careful questioning. "Chattooga River. Annual trip, according to her."

"And you believe this?" Claire looked up from piles of documents spread across the dining table.

"I believe she believes it." Lawson stopped at the window, scanning the street for unfamiliar vehicles or surveillance positions. Paranoia had become operational procedure since the parking garage confrontation. "Whether it's true is another question entirely."

Claire rubbed her eyes, their slightly bloodshot appearance a result of hours of focused reading. "I might have something that helps contextualize Richardson's potential involvement."

"Might have?" Fiona looked up from her laptop. "You've been buried in those papers for three hours."

"Because what I have shouldn't be in my possession." Claire's expression suggested professional lines crossed for exceptional circumstances. "My judicial contacts provided access to Richardson's complete personnel file. Including sections redacted from public records requests."

Lawson stopped pacing. "That's confidential department information."

"Hence my careful handling and review before sharing." Claire gestured toward the chair opposite her. "You'll want to sit for this."

The dining table held neat stacks of documents, each bearing official department letterhead. Performance reviews. Transfer orders. Commendations. Disciplinary actions. The administrative architecture of a thirty-year police career laid bare for examination.

"I analyzed for patterns rather than isolated incidents." Claire's lawyer preciseness emerged in her systematic presentation. "Richardson's career shows repetition of events that raises significant questions."

She pushed forward the first document set. "Seven transfers to different precincts over thirty years. Each followed incidents where officers under his command died or disappeared under questionable circumstances."

Lawson examined the transfer orders. Dates matched critical periods in departmental history. Officer-involved shootings with conflicting witness statements. Internal investigations that ended inconclusively. Cases that faded from public attention without resolution.

"Each transfer came with a promotion or increased responsibility." Claire indicated relevant sections, highlighted in yellow. "Rising through the ranks with remarkable speed compared to peers with similar experience and qualifications."

"Career advancement built on convenient tragedies." Fiona moved to the table, professional interest engaged. "Classic pattern for someone systematically eliminating obstacles."

"That's one interpretation." Claire pushed forward another document stack. "But these suggest alternative possibilities."

Commendation letters filled these pages. Citations for exposing corrupt officers. Recognition for maintaining departmental integrity during difficult periods. Awards for ethical leadership presented by community oversight committees.

"He exposed corruption?" Lawson struggled to reconcile these documents with her understanding of Richardson's character.

"Selectively." Claire tapped a specific commendation. "Always officers outside his direct command. Always with substantial evidence provided anonymously to internal affairs. Never cases connected to his previous assignments."

"Playing both sides." Fiona's journalist mind connected patterns quickly. "Building a reputation as corruption fighter while protecting his own operations."

"Or deeper game." Claire arranged the documents in chronological order. "Creating controlled exposure of minor corruption to deflect attention from larger systemic issues."

Lawson studied the timeline Claire had constructed. Richardson's career mapped against department scandals and reforms. Each exposure he orchestrated coincided precisely to times when public scrutiny threatened to expand beyond his control.

"Sacrificing pawns to protect more valuable pieces." The chess metaphor emerged naturally from the strategic pattern. "Making himself appear heroic while actually consolidating power."

"Exactly." Claire extracted a folder from her briefcase, placing it carefully at the center of the table. "This is the most concerning element. Psychiatric evaluation conducted ten years ago following an officer-involved shooting under his command."

"Department-mandated assessment?"

"Required after his officer killed a suspect under questionable circumstances." Claire opened the folder with evident reluctance. "The evaluation notes are ... troubling."

The psychological assessment spanned multiple pages. Clinical language describing personality traits and behavioral tendencies. Standardized test results presented in graphs and percentiles. Then, the psychiatrist's narrative assessment, highlighted sections standing out against the clinical jargon.

"Subject displays characteristics consistent with survivor's guilt stemming from early career trauma." Lawson read aloud. "Compounded by messiah complex regarding departmental integrity and personal responsibility for justice outcomes."

Fiona leaned closer to read another section. "Demonstrates rigid moral framework with self as ultimate arbiter of ethical boundaries. Rejects institutional limitations when they conflict with personal justice model."

The final highlighted section chilled the room despite the warm evening. Claire pointed to the psychiatrist's concluding observation: "Subject capable of extreme actions if believes justified by greater good. Recommending ongoing therapeutic intervention and leadership role review."

"He rejected the recommended therapy." Claire flipped to the final page. "Signature here refusing further sessions, citing departmental priorities requiring his full attention."

"And continued rising through the ranks despite this assessment." Lawson felt pieces clicking into place within her understanding of Richardson. "Because he was effective at maintaining appearance of departmental integrity while actually controlling which corruption was exposed."

"The perfect shield." Fiona's voice carried reluctant admiration for the strategic brilliance. "Reputation as corruption fighter protecting his own operations."

Claire closed the file with a decisive movement. "There's one more thing. The address listed for emergency contact differs from his Magnolia Way residence."

She slid a photocopy across the table. Property deed for a cabin twenty miles outside Savannah city limits. Remote location accessible by a single private road. Purchased fifteen years ago through a family trust rather than under Richardson's personal name.

"Officially a weekend retreat." Claire tapped the document. "But utility records show consistent electrical usage patterns regardless of season or occupancy claims."

"A secondary operations base." Lawson studied the location coordinates. "Private. Isolated. Perfect for activities that can't happen at his primary residence."

"Or perfect fishing alibi location with no witnesses to confirm or deny his presence." Fiona added the logical alternative.

The television volume suddenly increased as breaking news graphics flashed across the screen. Fiona grabbed the remote, raising the sound further as the anchor's grave expression filled the frame.

"Breaking news in the Leah Blackwell disappearance investigation. The Savannah Police Department has issued an arrest warrant for suspended Detective Erin Lawson, officially naming her as primary suspect in the podcast host's abduction. Chief Wallace released the following statement just moments ago."

The screen switched to Wallace at department headquarters, standing before assembled press with practiced solemnity.

"Evidence recovered from the crime scene has established Detective Lawson's direct involvement in Ms. Blackwell's disappearance. We are currently executing search warrants at multiple locations. I urge Detective Lawson to surrender peacefully to avoid further complications in what has become a disturbing case of police misconduct."

The anchor returned, reading from a teleprompter with professional concern. "Sources within the department indicate digital evidence links Detective Lawson directly to the crime scene hours before the abduction. Authorities ask anyone with information regarding her whereabouts to contact the special task force established for this investigation."

Lawson's phone rang, Parks' number appearing on the screen. She answered immediately, putting it on speaker.

"They're fabricating evidence." Parks' voice carried urgency without panic. "Wallace ordered digital forensics to create timestamp modifications showing you at the scene earlier yesterday. They're executing a warrant at your apartment right now."

"What evidence are they planting?" Claire's question cut straight to the critical concern.

"Don't know specifics. I'm locked out of the investigation completely." Background noise suggested Parks was moving while speaking. "But they'll find whatever they need to make the charges stick."

"I need to turn myself in." Lawson spoke the words without fully believing them. "Fight this through proper channels."

"Absolutely not." Parks' response came sharp and immediate. "Wallace has compromised the entire chain of evidence. You'll be in custody before your attorney can file the first motion."

Claire nodded agreement. "He's right. They're moving too quickly, too publicly. This isn't about proper investigation."

"It's about controlling the narrative." Fiona's journalist assessment aligned with their concerns. "Making you the scapegoat before Blackwell's actual abductors can be identified."

"Go somewhere they won't look." Parks' voice lowered further. "I'll work from inside as long as I can. Find out what really happened to Blackwell."

The call ended abruptly. The three women stared at each other across the suddenly silent living room. The television continued displaying Lawson's department photograph beside footage of the parking garage crime scene, visual storytelling designed to establish guilt in public perception.

"They'll check here first." Claire moved toward her laptop with decisive purpose. "My ownership of this property isn't difficult to trace given our professional connection."

"We need somewhere they won't immediately search." Fiona began gathering their research materials, efficiently organizing papers into manageable stacks.

Lawson looked down at the property deed still resting on the table. Richardson's cabin address stared back at her, an option both dangerous and logical.

"I'm going to this cabin." She tapped the document decisively. "Amy said he'd be there fishing. I need to confront him directly."

"With an arrest warrant out for you?" Claire's expression reflected immediate concern. "That's either incredibly brave or completely reckless."

"Maybe both." Lawson gathered the personnel file into its folder. "But I'm done playing this game through intermediaries and evidence trails. Richardson has answers about Monica's death, and I'm going to get them face to face."

"You realize you'll likely be arrested in the process," Fiona said, journalist's analytical detachment giving way to genuine concern.

"If that happens, it happens." Lawson's decision had formed with crystalline clarity. "Five years is long enough. I need to look Richardson in the eyes and hear the truth from him directly."

"At least let us come with you." Claire's objection came automatically. "Legally and strategically, you shouldn't go alone."

"I need you working official channels." Lawson countered with equal conviction. "Filing motions challenging the warrant. Questioning evidence handling procedures. Maintaining legal pressure on Wallace's operation."

"And I need to keep publishing." Fiona added her strategic assessment. "Each article forces them to respond publicly, potentially creating contradictions we can exploit."

The television switched to helicopter footage of police vehicles surrounding Lawson's apartment building and SWAT team members positioned at entrances.

"They're creating a spectacle to reinforce guilt narrative." Fiona's media literacy provided immediate context. "Knowing you're not there but generating footage that suggests imminent capture."

"Which means you have limited time before they expand the search perimeter." Claire moved toward her bedroom. "I'll prepare some supplies while you map the route to Richardson's cabin."

Lawson studied the property maps showing Richardson's cabin location. Remote enough for privacy. Accessible enough for practical occupation. Perfect balance for someone maintaining a separate operational base away from his primary residence.

Her official law enforcement career might be over with Wallace's public statement. No administrative hearing would easily reverse a warrant issued with such public certainty. But that didn't change her fundamental purpose—finding the truth about Monica's death, regardless of personal consequences.

"If I get arrested trying to confront Richardson, so be it." Lawson folded the map decisively. "But I'm done chasing shadows and evidence fragments. It's time for direct confrontation."

Claire returned with a small bag. "At least take these essentials. And promise you'll call before doing anything rash."

"Define rash." A hint of Lawson's dry humor surfaced despite the circumstances.

"Charging into a potentially dangerous situation without backup or legal protection." Claire's concern was palpable. "Richardson's psychological profile suggests someone capable of extreme actions when cornered."

"I've spent my career handling dangerous suspects." Lawson accepted the bag with genuine appreciation for Claire's concern. "One retired police captain doesn't scare me."

"It should." Claire tapped the psychiatric evaluation. "Especially one with a messiah complex and the connections to act on it."

The television continued displaying Lawson's department photograph beside footage of the parking garage crime scene, visual storytelling designed to establish guilt in public perception.

Lawson gathered the most critical evidence documents, focusing on Richardson's psychiatric evaluation and property records. Five years pursuing justice through proper channels had led to this moment—a direct confrontation with the man potentially responsible for Monica's death, while herself facing arrest for a crime she didn't commit.

The irony wasn't lost on her. But some truths required looking their keepers in the eye, regardless of personal risk.

Some investigations could only be completed by stepping outside the system that contained them.

chapter
twenty-six

PINE TREES CROWDED the narrow dirt road leading to Richardson's cabin. Lawson navigated the final mile with headlights off, moonlight providing just enough visibility to avoid the deeper ruts and potholes. The borrowed car—Claire's second vehicle, kept for emergencies—handled the rough terrain better than expected.

The cabin appeared through a break in the trees. Simple construction. Two stories with a wraparound porch. Cedar siding weathered to silver-gray. A single light glowed through the front window. Richardson's SUV sat in the gravel driveway, confirming Amy's fishing trip story contained at least partial truth.

Lawson parked behind a stand of trees fifty yards from the structure. Standard approach protocol ingrained through years of tactical training. She surveyed the property through binoculars, noting multiple sight lines and potential cover positions. No other vehicles visible. No movement outside the building.

The woods surrounding her felt alive with night sounds. Crickets. A distant owl. Wind rustling through pine needles. The perfect backdrop to mask her footsteps as she approached the cabin with practiced caution. The weight of her backup weapon—the one Wallace hadn't confiscated—pressed reassuringly against her ankle.

Wooden steps creaked despite her careful ascent to the porch. The cabin door stood partially open, warm light spilling across weathered boards. An invitation. Or a trap.

"Come in, Lawson." Richardson's voice carried from inside. "You've come this far. Might as well finish it."

She pushed the door open with her fingertips, maintaining position outside the threshold. Richardson sat at a wooden table centered in the main room. A service weapon rested on the surface before him, pointed toward the empty chair opposite. His appearance startled her—three days of stubble shadowed his jaw. Dark circles underlined bloodshot eyes. The pressed shirts and perfect posture replaced by rumpled flannel and slouched shoulders.

"I'm not armed." He gestured toward the empty chair. "Well, not in hand anyway. Figured we might need protection before this conversation ends."

"Protection from what?" Lawson remained in the doorway, assessing angles and distances.

"Depends on who finds us first." Richardson nodded toward the chair again. "Sit down. You didn't drive all this way to stand in the doorway."

Lawson entered but remained standing, maintaining the tactical advantage of mobility. The cabin interior reflected its owner—organized, utilitarian, devoid of unnecessary decoration. A fishing rod leaned in one corner. Maps covered one wall, red pins marking locations across Savannah and surrounding counties.

"I knew you'd come." Richardson studied her with weary resignation. "You always were smart. Too smart to believe the official narrative."

"Which official narrative?" Lawson maintained distance between them. "Monica's murder? Hutchinson's suicide? Blackwell's abduction? My arrest warrant?"

"All manufactured from the same template." Richardson's hand rested inches from his weapon. "Control the story. Eliminate loose ends. Maintain the operation."

"The operation you helped run." The accusation emerged sharper than intended.

"The operation I infiltrated." Richardson corrected with unexpected calmness. "There's a distinction worth understanding before you judge too quickly."

"Convince me."

Richardson reached slowly toward a folder beside his weapon. Lawson tensed, hand moving instinctively toward her ankle holster. He froze, then continued with deliberate transparency, opening the folder to reveal photographs and documents.

"Monica discovered something bigger than either of us anticipated." He pushed the folder toward her. "Not just corrupt cops taking bribes. A structured criminal network with protection from both investigation and prosecution."

Lawson approached cautiously, glancing at the contents while maintaining awareness of Richardson's position. Surveillance photos. Financial records. Organizational charts with names connected by relationship lines. Monica's handwriting filled the margins with questions and observations.

"The Rafferty case opened the door," Richardson continued while she examined the materials. "Monica followed money trails beyond street-level dealers to offshore accounts and shell companies. Found the same corporate entities protecting different criminal operations across jurisdictions."

"You knew about this." Lawson looked up from the documents.

"Not initially." Richardson shook his head. "I discovered fragments after her death. Pieces she'd hidden in case something happened to her. Took years to assemble the complete picture."

"And you did nothing." The accusation carried five years of accumulated anger.

"I did everything possible without getting killed in the process." Richardson's voice hardened. "Gathered evidence. Identified network members. Worked to understand who controlled the operation."

"While officers died. While evidence disappeared. While cases went cold."

"While I played the long game." Richardson tapped a photograph showing Thomas Hutchinson emerging from the courthouse. "The leader wasn't a cop. It was someone who could control both investigations and prosecutions. Someone above departmental politics."

"Thomas Hutchinson." The name emerged as a statement rather than a question.

"Senior partner at Hutchinson & Associates." Richardson confirmed with a tight nod. "Corporate attorney with connections throughout the judicial system. Campaign contributor to judges and district attorneys. Legal counsel to businesses used for laundering operations proceeds."

Lawson studied the organizational chart Monica had created. Names connected through financial transactions and case interactions. Thomas Hutchinson was positioned at the top, with tendrils extending down through the police department, the district attorney's office, and local government.

"Monica discovered who was leading it." Richardson's voice softened with something resembling respect. "She traced the connections all the way to the top. But I never knew until after her death. I just received orders through the chain, never understanding how high it reached."

"Why should I believe you weren't part of it?" Lawson finally claimed the chair opposite Richardson, proximity to the evidence outweighing tactical considerations.

Richardson extracted a small recorder from his pocket. "Because I've been gathering evidence against them for five years."

He pressed play. A conversation between Thomas Hutchinson and Chief Wallace emerged from the tiny speaker. Discussion of evidence suppression in a recent narcotics case. Careful language about "procedural complications" and "witness reliability issues." Professional code for systematic obstruction.

"I've recorded dozens of conversations." Richardson stopped the playback. "Built case files on fifteen officers still active in the department. Documented judicial interference in twenty-eight criminal prosecutions. Assembled everything needed to dismantle the entire operation."

"Yet you never brought it forward." Lawson couldn't keep accusation from her tone.

"Bringing it forward meant exposing Monica's murder." Richardson met her gaze directly. "Which meant exposing your relationship with her. Your drinking the night she died. Everything I had protected you from."

Lawson leaned back, processing implications of Richardson's knowledge. "You told me you didn't know about us."

"I lied. Of course I knew." A hint of paternal disappointment colored his response. "I requested you both for my division. Monitored your development as partners. Noticed when professional boundaries shifted to personal involvement."

"And said nothing."

"Department policy on partner relationships didn't interest me." Richardson shrugged. "Your effectiveness as investigators mattered more than administrative regulations."

Lawson processed this revelation while examining more of Monica's documents. The evidence before her represented years of careful investigation. Monica's initial discoveries. Richardson's subsequent expansion. A comprehensive map of corruption extending from street-level enforcement through the highest levels of the local judicial system.

"Ray Hutchinson killed Monica." Richardson's statement drew her attention back to him. "On his brother's orders. After she discovered their connection and threatened exposure."

"And you let him get away with it." The accusation carried five years of bottled rage.

"I protected you." Richardson's response came with unexpected intensity. "You loved her. They would have killed you too if they believed you shared her knowledge."

"So you buried evidence. Redirected the investigation. Ensured her case went cold."

"I kept you alive while building a case that could actually succeed." Richardson leaned forward. "Monica died because she moved too quickly with insufficient protection. I wasn't going to let you make the same mistake."

Lawson struggled to reconcile this version of Richardson with the calculating manipulator her investigation had suggested. The evidence before her supported his claims of working against the corruption network. Yet his methods had effectively obstructed justice for Monica's murderer. And Claire's discovery still loomed: a career marked by seven transfers, each shadowed by suspicious deaths or disappearances. Was that a trail of coincidence—or a pattern deliberately planted to conceal his real work? "What about Blackwell?" She redirected to current events. "Ray Hutchinson's supposed suicide? My arrest warrant?"

"Thomas Hutchinson protecting his operation." Richardson's expression darkened. "Blackwell discovered too much. Found connections Monica had documented. Started asking questions that threatened the entire network."

"Including Ray's confession recording."

"Which Thomas couldn't allow to become public." Richardson nodded. "Ray had become a liability after Monica's murder. Guilt made him unpredictable. When Blackwell found him, Thomas decided both problems needed permanent resolution."

"He had his own brother killed." The calculated ruthlessness chilled Lawson despite her anger.

"Business decision." Richardson's clinical assessment reflected years observing the organization's operation. "Thomas values the network above all else. Family connections became irrelevant once Ray threatened operational security."

"And Blackwell?"

"Likely dead." Richardson's blunt assessment carried no emotional inflection. "Thomas doesn't leave loose ends when eliminating threats."

"You sound certain for someone claiming to work against them."

"Five years studying their methods provides clarity about operational patterns." Richardson tapped another folder on the table. "My testimony against Thomas. Complete confession of my knowledge about the organization. Insurance policy in case something happens to me."

"Why tell me this now?" Lawson struggled to process everything Richardson had revealed. "Why not bring this evidence forward through proper channels?"

"Because there are no proper channels anymore." Richardson gestured toward the window. "Wallace controls the department. Thomas influences the district attorney."

"So you've been playing double agent." The realization crystallized as she examined more evidence. "Appearing to work within the system while actually gathering evidence against it."

"The only approach with potential for success." Richardson

nodded. "Direct confrontation gets you killed. Ask Monica. Ask Blackwell."

"Yet here you sit, telling me everything." Lawson noted the contradiction. "Revealing your undercover operation to a detective with an active arrest warrant."

"Because we've run out of time." Richardson's expression hardened. "Thomas knows I've been investigating him. Ray likely revealed my questions before his death. They'll come for me next. Probably you as well."

"Then why not run? Disappear with your evidence?"

"Because running means they win." Something of the commanding officer Lawson had once respected emerged in Richardson's posture. "I've spent thirty years upholding the law. I won't abandon that commitment now when it matters most."

The cabin fell silent except for the ticking of a wall clock. Lawson studied Richardson across the table, searching for deception in his expression.

"I was protecting you." Richardson repeated, softer this time. "You loved her. They'd have killed you too."

"If you're telling the truth—" Lawson began.

"I am." Richardson interrupted with quiet certainty.

"Then we need to move this evidence somewhere secure. Before Thomas realizes you've shared it with me."

Richardson's expression relaxed slightly at her implied acceptance of his explanation. "I have copies secured with my attorney. Instructions to release everything if I don't check in daily."

"Not enough." Lawson gestured toward the folders. "Thomas has resources to intercept attorney communications. We need multiple distribution channels beyond his influence."

"We?" Richardson raised an eyebrow.

"Five years ago, Monica died investigating this network." Lawson met his gaze directly. "I'm finishing what she started, with or without your help."

For the first time since her arrival, Richardson smiled. Not his professional expression used for departmental functions, but something genuine carrying unexpected warmth.

"She would have appreciated your persistence." He gathered the folders into a larger evidence container. "Even when it bordered on recklessness."

"She would have expected nothing less." Lawson reached for the container, decades of anger toward Richardson not entirely displaced but temporarily suspended by shared purpose.

Outside, a twig snapped in the darkness. Both froze, professional instincts instantly alert. Richardson moved to the window, careful to remain outside direct sight lines.

"Vehicle approaching." His whisper carried urgent warning. "Lights off. Professional driving pattern."

Lawson joined him at the window, maintaining a similar tactical position. Moonlight revealed a dark SUV navigating the dirt road. No headlights. No identifying markings visible at this distance.

"Thomas sending a cleanup crew?" She kept her voice equally low.

"Or Wallace's team tracking your location." Richardson moved toward his weapon. "Either way, this conversation just got more complicated."

They watched in tense silence as the vehicle slowed near the final bend in the road. Its headlights suddenly activated, illuminating a reflective sign Lawson hadn't noticed during her approach. The SUV paused for several seconds, then executed a three-point turn.

"They're leaving." Richardson's confusion matched her own.

The vehicle retreated back up the dirt road, red taillights diminishing until they disappeared around a distant curve.

"Wrong address?" Lawson ventured, the tension in her shoulders easing slightly.

"Or locals who realized they'd taken the wrong turn." Richardson returned his weapon to the table. "These backroads all look the same at night if you don't know them well."

"We should still move this evidence somewhere secure." Lawson gestured toward the folders. "Even if that wasn't Thomas's team or Wallace's officers, they'll be looking for both of us soon enough."

Richardson nodded, gathering the files back into their container. "Five years of investigation. Everything needed to bring down Thomas Hutchinson's entire operation."

chapter
twenty-seven

RAIN PATTERED against the beach house windows. Claire paced between kitchen and living room, phone clutched in her hand. Twenty-seven hours since Lawson had left for Richardson's cabin. Twenty-six hours since her last text: *Arrived. Will update when possible.*

Fiona sat cross-legged on the couch, laptop balanced precariously as she worked through multiple browser tabs. Dark circles shadowed her eyes. Neither woman had slept properly since Lawson's departure.

"She should have called by now." Claire checked her phone again, confirming what she already knew. No missed calls. No new messages.

"Phone signal can be spotty in those backwoods." Fiona didn't look up from her screen. "Or she turned it off to avoid location tracking."

"Or she's been arrested. Or worse."

"Not arrested." Fiona finally glanced up. "That would make headlines. Wallace would parade her in front of cameras immediately."

The possibility neither woman voiced hung between them. If Lawson had confronted Richardson and things had gone badly, they might never know what happened.

Claire's phone vibrated. She answered before the first ring completed.

"Lawson?"

"It's me." Lawson's voice came through distorted by a poor connection. "Limited signal. Can't talk long."

"Are you safe? Did you find Richardson?"

"Yes, to both. Richardson has evidence about Thomas Hutchinson's operation. Monica uncovered it before she died." Static interrupted the connection momentarily. "Need you to check something. Criminal cases dismissed during Hutchinson's tenure as a defense attorney."

"Already working that angle." Claire put the call on speaker. "What about Richardson?"

"He's been playing double agent. Building a case against Hutchinson for years." More static crackled through the connection. "Will explain everything when I get back. Signal failing. Don't try to call —I'll contact you."

The line went dead. Claire stared at the phone, relief battling with fresh concern. Lawson, alive and apparently working with Richardson rather than against him. New information that changed their understanding of the former captain's role in events.

"She didn't sound like a hostage." Fiona returned to her laptop. "And that bit about Thomas Hutchinson confirms what I've been finding."

"Which is?"

Fiona turned her screen toward Claire. "Flight records from Savannah private airport. Thomas Hutchinson's personal jet departed yesterday afternoon. Destination Belize."

"Non-extradition country." Claire scanned the flight manifest Fiona had somehow obtained. "Convenient timing given Blackwell's abduction and the subsequent media attention."

"Very." Fiona clicked to another screen. "Airport security footage makes it more interesting."

The video showed Thomas Hutchinson approaching his jet on the tarmac. Tall, distinguished, wearing an expensive suit despite traveling. Executive confidence in every movement. Behind him walked a second figure—hooded, stumbling slightly. A security officer gripped this person's arm, guiding them toward the aircraft steps.

"That build matches Leah Blackwell." Claire leaned closer to the screen. "The height. The slight frame."

"Exactly." Fiona froze the frame, zooming in on the hooded figure.

"Note the resistance in her posture. The security guard's grip forcing compliance."

"Not a willing passenger."

"Not even slightly." Fiona forwarded through additional footage showing both figures boarding. "Thomas Hutchinson leaving the country with what appears to be a kidnapped journalist the day after she threatened to expose his operation."

Claire grabbed her phone again. "I need to contact my federal connections. This requires Interpol involvement."

"Already sent the footage to FBI contacts at the Chronicle." Fiona continued working through her remaining tabs. "But the trail went cold after landing in Belize. A private car met the plane. No airport cameras captured where they went afterward."

Claire made calls while Fiona continued her digital investigation. Legal authorities. Law enforcement contacts. Judicial colleagues who might expedite international cooperation. Each conversation added layers of bureaucratic complexity without actionable progress.

"Getting proper channels to acknowledge this will take days." Claire set her phone down after the sixth call. "By then, Hutchinson could be anywhere."

"Which is precisely the point." Fiona closed one laptop and opened another. "He's using time and jurisdictional barriers to his advantage."

Rain intensified outside, drumming against the roof with increasing urgency. The weather matched their mood—dark, turbulent, promising worse to come.

Claire moved to her briefcase, extracting files she'd gathered before Lawson's departure. Legal documents spread across the dining table in methodical arrangement. Case numbers. Court dates. Judicial rulings. The administrative architecture of justice system manipulation.

"I pulled sealed records from court." Claire arranged documents chronologically. "Cases where Thomas Hutchinson represented defendants with charges mysteriously dropped."

"Sealed records? How'd you get your hands on those?" Fiona joined her at the table.

"Let's call it professional courtesy from clerks who owe me favors." Claire pointed to the pattern emerging from the documents. "Twenty-seven cases over fifteen years. Charges ranging from money laundering to drug trafficking. All dismissed due to 'evidentiary issues' or 'procedural violations.'"

Fiona examined the documents. "Same defendants appearing under different corporate entities. Shell companies dissolving and reforming with similar ownership structures."

"All benefiting the Vartanian family." Claire tapped a name appearing throughout the documents. "Old-world crime organization with modern business methods. Using legal channels to protect illegal operations."

"Monica connected these dots?" Fiona asked.

"According to what Lawson just said about Richardson's evidence." Claire arranged another document set. "Monica discovered the pattern during the Rafferty investigation. Thomas Hutchinson provided legal protection while his brother Ray facilitated operations within the police department."

"Perfect system." Fiona's tone carried reluctant admiration for the criminal efficiency. "Legal counsel controlling which cases proceed to trial. Departmental influence determining which evidence gets collected or lost."

"Monica threatened the entire structure by documenting connections between supposedly separate entities."

Fiona's phone buzzed with an incoming message. "My editor needs a statement about Wallace's press conference."

"What press conference?"

"Apparently happening now." Fiona grabbed the remote, turning on the television.

Chief Wallace stood before the assembled media, his expression professionally grave. Behind him stood Captain Reynolds and several uniformed officers, forming a visual backdrop of departmental authority.

"The investigation into Leah Blackwell's disappearance continues with all available resources. We are pursuing several promising leads regarding Detective Lawson's involvement. Additionally, we have issued a material witness warrant for former Captain Thomas Richardson, who may possess relevant information."

"They're expanding the net." Claire recognized the tactical approach from previous high-profile cases. "Creating the appearance of a comprehensive investigation while actually controlling the narrative."

"Standard deflection strategy." Fiona typed notes while watching. "Focus public attention on Lawson and Richardson to distract from Thomas Hutchinson's disappearance."

Wallace continued addressing the assembled reporters. "We ask the public to remain vigilant. Both Detective Lawson and Captain Richardson should be considered persons of interest in an ongoing kidnapping investigation. Anyone with information regarding their whereabouts should contact the dedicated task force immediately."

A reporter raised her hand. "Chief Wallace, sources indicate Thomas Hutchinson left the country yesterday on his private jet. Is there any connection between his departure and Ms. Blackwell's disappearance?"

Wallace's expression revealed momentary surprise before professional control reasserted itself. "We have no information suggesting Mr. Hutchinson's travel plans relate to this investigation. As a prominent attorney with international clients, his movements abroad are routine and documented."

"Documented like taking a kidnapped podcast host with him?" Fiona muttered toward the screen.

"Do you plan to question Mr. Hutchinson regarding his brother's suicide?" Another reporter pressed the issue.

"The department extends appropriate professional courtesy to a grieving family member." Wallace's deflection came smoothly. "Mr. Hutchinson has cooperated fully with investigators regarding his brother's death, which has been conclusively ruled suicide."

Claire muted the television as Wallace began repeating talking points about ongoing investigation priorities. "He's lying about Hutchinson's cooperation."

"Of course he is." Fiona returned to her laptop. "The question becomes how deeply Wallace is involved in Hutchinson's operation."

Claire considered this question while organizing the legal documents. "Financial records might show a connection. Judges received payments through consulting contracts with Hutchinson-affiliated firms. Wallace could have similar arrangements."

"Worth investigating." Fiona noted the approach for future research. "Though direct financial links might be better concealed for someone with departmental authority."

The beach house phone rang—landline rather than either woman's cell. They exchanged glances. Few people knew this number. Fewer still would use it rather than their personal contacts.

Claire answered cautiously. "Hello?"

"Ms. Morgan." Male voice, professional tone. "This is Agent Komarov, FBI Organized Crime Task Force. We received information regarding Thomas Hutchinson's departure from your colleague at the Chronicle."

"Yes." Claire kept her response neutral while signaling Fiona to trace the call.

"We've confirmed the footage shows a potential kidnapping situation. Interpol has been notified." Komarov continued without awaiting a response. "We need to speak with Detective Lawson regarding her knowledge of Hutchinson's operation."

"Detective Lawson isn't available." Claire chose her words carefully. "She's pursuing leads related to the Blackwell abduction."

"Is she with former Captain Richardson?" Komarov's directness suggested significant background knowledge.

"I can't confirm her current location." Claire maintained professional distance. "But I can facilitate contact when she's available."

"Ms. Morgan." Komarov's tone shifted slightly. "We're not coordinating with local authorities given the potential for compromise. Detective Lawson isn't our target—Hutchinson is. Any information she has could help locate Ms. Blackwell before the situation deteriorates further."

Fiona nodded across the room, confirming the call originated from legitimate FBI numbers. Claire made a rapid decision.

"I'll pass along your contact information. That's all I can promise."

"Understood." Komarov provided a direct line and secure email. "Please emphasize time sensitivity. Hutchinson has extensive resources abroad. Each hour reduces our chances of successful recovery."

The call ended. Claire relayed the conversation to Fiona, who added the information to their expanding investigation board. Photographs.

Documents. Timeline elements. The visual organization of complex case connections spread across the living room wall.

"Federal involvement changes the equation." Fiona taped another document into place. "Local corruption can't easily obstruct an FBI organized crime investigation."

"Unless they've been compromised too." Claire's experience with high-level cases had eliminated naïve trust in institutional integrity. "We need independent verification before risking Lawson's position."

Rain continued battering the beach house windows. Darkness arrived earlier than usual under heavy cloud cover. Claire turned on additional lights while Fiona prepared coffee. Neither woman suggested sleep despite clear exhaustion.

"Richardson claimed to be building a case against Hutchinson for years." Claire processed this information aloud while reviewing documents. "If legitimate, his evidence combined with Lawson's knowledge could provide a foundation for federal prosecution."

"Big if." Fiona remained skeptical. "Richardson concealed evidence after Monica's murder. Redirected investigation away from the Hutchinson connection. Actions that directly obstructed justice."

"Claiming undercover operation now." Claire considered tactical implications. "Double agent narrative provides retroactive justification for questionable actions."

"A convenient explanation." Fiona's journalistic skepticism emerged fully. "Or a legitimate long-game approach to bringing down a sophisticated criminal enterprise."

Richardson's true motivations remained uncertain despite Lawson's brief update. The former captain had manipulated investigations and concealed evidence for years. Whether those actions served justice or obstructed it remained to be determined by evidence not yet fully examined.

Fiona's laptop emitted a distinctive chime—the alert tone she'd set specifically for the Dead Air podcast updates. Her head snapped up, fingers immediately navigating to the notification.

"Claire. Dead Air is going live again. Five minutes from now."

"What?" Claire abandoned the documents, moving quickly to

Fiona's side. "How is that possible if Blackwell's with Hutchinson in Belize?"

"It could be automated content." Fiona refreshed the page, confirming the alert. "Or someone else broadcasting under the podcast brand."

"Or Blackwell found a way to transmit." Claire grabbed her phone, typing rapidly. "I'm alerting Komarov. This could provide location data if they can trace the broadcast origin."

The Dead Air website displayed a simple countdown timer against a black background. Three minutes and forty-seven seconds remaining until broadcast. No additional information provided context for the unexpected resurrection.

"Should we call Lawson?" Fiona asked, already preparing recording equipment to capture whatever might emerge.

"No time." Claire gestured toward the timer. "And we don't know if her position is secure. Better to record everything and analyze it before potentially compromising her location."

Both women fell silent as the countdown approached zero.

chapter
twenty-eight

RAIN HAMMERED AGAINST THE WINDSHIELD. Lawson navigated the back roads toward Savannah, Richardson's evidence secured in a waterproof case beside her. Their parting had been oddly formal—professional respect not fully extinguished by years of suspicion. He'd remained at the cabin to organize additional materials while she transported the most critical evidence to Claire for safekeeping.

Her phone chimed with an unfamiliar notification tone. The sound cut through the steady drum of rain, drawing her attention to the passenger seat where the device rested. The Dead Air podcast icon flashed on the screen. Live broadcast notification.

Lawson pulled onto the shoulder, positioning the car beneath a highway overpass for better protection from the downpour. Engine idling, she grabbed the phone with sudden urgency. How could the podcast be broadcasting again? Blackwell remained missing, presumably in Thomas Hutchinson's custody across international borders.

She tapped the notification. The Dead Air website loaded, audio visualization waves pulsing with an active broadcast already in progress. Not Blackwell's voice but a familiar male tone emerged from the tiny speaker.

"—repeat, this is Dylan Everett, audio engineer and producer for Dead Air podcast." The young man's voice carried none of the shock-numbed quality from the parking garage crime scene. Instead, he spoke with determined clarity. "Leah Blackwell suspected she was being watched for weeks before her abduction. She created contingency protocols in case something happened to her."

Lawson increased the volume, leaning closer to capture every word through the competing sounds of rain and distant traffic.

"This automated system begins releasing files twenty-four hours after Leah fails to enter her security code." Dylan continued explaining. "I've verified the content authenticity through digital signatures embedded in the files. What you're about to hear comes directly from Leah's secured cloud storage, untouched since her disappearance."

A brief silence, followed by an electronic tone. Dylan's voice returned with procedural instructions.

"New files will publish hourly on this server. Each contains evidence Leah compiled during her investigation into Monica Landry's murder. Rather than broadcasting these files sequentially, we're making them available for immediate download to prevent potential interference with the distribution system."

Lawson opened the podcast's website on her phone browser. A file repository appeared beneath the live broadcast window, with the first file already available for download. It bore a simple label: Hutchinson_-Judge_Recording.mp3.

She downloaded it while Dylan continued his introduction.

"Leah created this dead man's switch because she understood the risks of her investigation. The evidence she uncovered revealed corruption extending through Savannah's entire justice system. If you're listening to this, it means those corrupted elements have taken action against her."

The first downloaded file completed. Lawson opened it while keeping the live broadcast running in the background. Thomas Hutchinson's distinctive voice emerged through her phone speaker.

"Judge, I appreciate your careful consideration of our motion to suppress." His professional tone carried the subtle undercurrent of a familiar relationship. "The evidence chain procedural issues you identified saved considerable trial preparation resources."

A female voice responded with equal professional polish. "The court simply applies appropriate procedural standards, Mr. Hutchinson.

When evidence collection fails to meet those standards, the law requires appropriate remedy."

"Your judicial wisdom serves justice admirably." Hutchinson's voice carried knowing weight. "The foundation's annual contribution will reflect our continued appreciation for the court's attention to procedural details."

The recording ended. Clear evidence of inappropriate relationship between defense attorney and judge. Subtle corruption cloaked in professional courtesy language. Exactly the sort of exchange that appeared innocent in isolation but damning within a larger pattern.

Dylan's voice returned on the live broadcast. "Leah documented dozens of similar conversations. Evidence of systematic case manipulation through judicial influence. Each hourly file release will provide additional documentation of the corruption network Monica Landry discovered before her murder."

The broadcast continued with technical details about file authentication methods. Lawson returned to the repository page, discovering a second file already available: Hutchinson_Meeting_Photos.zip.

She downloaded and opened it. The compressed folder contained high-resolution surveillance photographs. Thomas Hutchinson meeting various Savannah officials in locations distant from public view. Parking garages. Private dining rooms. Boat docks. Each image time-stamped and geotagged with precise location data.

The most recent photos showed Thomas Hutchinson with Chief Wallace three days before Blackwell's abduction. Both men examined documents in Wallace's personal vehicle parked behind a restaurant closed for renovation, a meeting location selected for privacy rather than convenience.

Dylan's voice continued providing context for the releases. "Leah catalogued these connections for months. Built evidence chains documenting how Thomas Hutchinson's influence network operated across departments. The hourly releases will continue until all files have been distributed."

Lawson scrolled through additional photographs. Hutchinson with a district attorney at a hunting cabin registered to neither man.

Hutchinson with banking executives whose institutions appeared in Monica's financial investigation notes.

The corruption network visualized through methodical surveillance documentation. Exactly the evidence Monica had begun assembling before her murder. Connections that had threatened Thomas Hutchinson's entire operation.

Dylan's broadcast continued with increased urgency. "The final file contains Leah's direct message. Recorded the day before her abduction. Unfortunately, the file shows signs of corruption—only fragments remain accessible. Our technical team continues working to recover the complete content."

The repository updated again. A new file appeared: Blackwell_Final_Message.mp3.

Lawson downloaded it immediately, anticipation building as the progress bar filled. The file opened automatically.

Static filled her car's interior before resolving into Blackwell's voice—fragmented, cutting in and out between bursts of electronic distortion.

"—discovered the connection—" Static interrupted. "—Thomas Hutchinson orchestrating—" More disruption. "—killed Monica when she—" The voice strengthened momentarily. "If you're hearing this, trust Lawson. She wasn't involved—" Final fragment emerged with surprising clarity. "The real evidence is where it all began."

The recording ended. Lawson replayed it immediately, straining to capture additional words between static bursts. The message remained frustratingly incomplete.

Trust Lawson. The direct endorsement carried significant implication. Blackwell had concluded Lawson wasn't involved in Monica's death or subsequent cover-up, despite earlier podcast episodes questioning her potential culpability.

The real evidence is where it all began. The cryptic final statement suggested a location containing additional proof beyond what the hourly files would reveal. But where had it all begun? The warehouse where Monica died? The Rafferty case that initiated her investigation? Some other starting point Blackwell had discovered?

Dylan's voice returned to the live broadcast. "These releases will continue hourly until all secured files have been distributed. Leah created multiple distribution channels to ensure the evidence reaches proper authorities regardless of local interference. The complete archive has been transmitted to federal agencies and international journalists through scheduled delivery systems."

Smart precaution. Thomas Hutchinson might control local law enforcement and the judiciary, but his influence had limits against federal investigation and international media scrutiny. The distributed evidence created overlapping protection layers that would survive even if individual recipients were compromised.

Dylan continued, his voice gaining confidence through technical explanation. "Technical analysis of the corrupted final file continues. Updates will be provided through this channel as recovery efforts progress. For security reasons, this live broadcast will now conclude. Further communications will occur through automated file releases."

The broadcast ended. Audio visualization waves flattened into a static line across the phone screen. Lawson sat in silence broken only by rain and occasional vehicles passing on the highway above.

Blackwell's dead man's switch had activated, releasing evidence accumulated over months. Each hourly file would further damage Thomas Hutchinson's operation and the corruption network protecting it. The automated system would continue functioning regardless of what happened to Blackwell herself.

Lawson started the engine again, pulling back onto the rain-slick road toward Savannah. The evidence from Richardson combined with Blackwell's automated releases created comprehensive documentation of the corruption Monica had died investigating. The truth would emerge through channels Thomas Hutchinson couldn't control.

But Blackwell's final message suggested something more remained hidden. Critical evidence at the place "where it all began."

chapter
twenty-nine

THE ABANDONED PAPER mill warehouse squatted against the night sky like a decaying monument to industrial obsolescence. Its jagged silhouette cut a menacing shape against the cloud-scattered stars, broken windows reflecting moonlight in sharp, dangerous glints. Lawson parked beside the loading dock where Monica had bled out five years ago; the concrete still stained despite countless rainstorms. The rain had stopped an hour earlier, leaving the air thick with humidity, and the metallic scent of wet asphalt mingled with rusting metal.

She killed the engine and sat for a moment, listening to the tick of cooling metal and the distant sound of highway traffic. This place held ghosts—Monica's most prominently, but also the ghost of who Lawson herself had been before that night. The officer who believed in the system. The woman who thought love could be compartmentalized away from duty.

With deliberate movements, she retrieved her phone and typed a message to Parks: *At the warehouse. Found something in Blackwell's files. Meet me here.*

The screen illuminated her face in the darkness as she waited. His response came within minutes: *On my way. Don't go in alone. 15 minutes out.*

Fifteen minutes. Lawson debated waiting in the car, then decided against it. Time remained their scarcest resource. She stepped out into humid air that clung to her skin like a damp shroud. Her flashlight beam cut through the darkness as she began circling the building's perimeter, searching for signs of recent activity while mentally mapping possible approaches.

Weeds choked the loading bay where the ambulance had parked that night, pushing through cracked concrete with nature's inexorable patience. Yellow police tape fragments still clung to rusted metal poles, faded to almost white after years of sun exposure. Graffiti covered most accessible wall surfaces, vivid blues and reds forming territorial markers for local gangs claiming this abandoned territory.

Windows on the upper floors gaped like dead eyes, glass long since shattered by vandals or weather. Wind whispered through empty frames, creating eerie whistles that raised the hair on Lawson's neck despite her professional detachment.

The real evidence is where it all began.

Blackwell's final message echoed through her mind as she examined the structure's decaying exterior. This warehouse represented more than abandoned industrial space. It marked the spot where Monica had died investigating corruption that reached the highest levels of Savannah's justice system. Ground zero—the place where truth collided with power and lost.

Lawson completed her circuit of the building's exterior, noting three viable entry points beyond the main doors. Old security habits die hard. Always know your exits. Always map your approaches. Assume hostility until proven otherwise. The tactical training Monica had teased her about still guided her movements after all these years.

Headlights swept across the lot, illuminating decades of industrial debris scattered across cracked asphalt. Parks emerged from his department vehicle, flashlight in hand and service weapon visible on his hip. He approached with the measured, cautious movements of someone who'd learned not to trust abandoned buildings or the shadows they contained.

"Been here long?" he asked, voice low despite the isolation.

"Ten minutes. Just scanning the perimeter." She gestured toward the building's weather-beaten facade. "No signs of recent activity. Place looks exactly as it should after five years." Parks swept his beam across broken windows and shadowed doorways, professional assessment in his narrowed gaze. "Any activity while you waited?"

"Dead." Lawson gestured toward the main entrance where metal doors hung partially open, hinges long since rusted into permanent positions. "But Blackwell's message suggested something here connects to Monica's investigation. Something that began here and continued elsewhere."

"What exactly are we looking for?" Parks turned his attention to the building's interior, visible in fragments through broken windows.

"Evidence someone hid after Monica died. Something that proves the connection to Thomas Hutchinson." Lawson moved toward the entrance, gun remaining holstered but hand resting near it from professional habit. "Something worth killing for five years ago and still worth killing for today."

They entered through the main doors, metal groaning in protest as Lawson pushed them wider to allow passage. Parks' flashlight carved paths through darkness filled with debris and decay, illuminating fallen ceiling tiles and pigeon droppings that crunched beneath their careful steps. Industrial equipment sat in forgotten clusters, covered in rust and bird waste. Metal stairs led to catwalks overlooking the main floor where shadows pooled like black water.

The smell hit immediately—mildew and rodent droppings mixed with the distinctive chemical tang of long-abandoned industrial processes. Lawson breathed shallowly, memories flooding back of that night five years ago when this same smell had filled her nostrils as she knelt beside Monica's bleeding body.

"Monica kept a journal." Lawson's voice echoed in the cavernous space, bouncing back altered by the building's hollow interior. "Final entry mentioned meeting Ray Hutchinson here. But she also wrote about proof being in 'our place.' I've been trying to figure out what that meant."

Parks stepped carefully around a fallen beam. "Your place meaning what exactly?"

"Private location. Somewhere meaningful to our relationship." Lawson swept her own flashlight across the concrete floor, searching for anything that might qualify as a hiding spot. Water pooled in uneven depressions, reflecting their lights in distorted patterns. "Could be here in some hidden corner. Could be somewhere else entirely. The clue is frustratingly vague."

"If Blackwell found something connecting this place to evidence, it has to be significant." Parks' voice carried the measured tone of someone working through a puzzle methodically. "Something not obvious in the original investigation."

They moved deeper into the building, stepping carefully around broken machinery and scattered debris. The warehouse floor stretched for nearly an acre, shadows concealing distant corners despite their powerful flashlights. Parks examined structural elements while Lawson focused on areas that might conceal evidence. Wall panels. Maintenance access points. Any place where something could be hidden away from casual discovery.

"Monica was methodical." Lawson checked behind a rusted control panel, finding nothing but mouse droppings and dust. "If she hid something here, she would have ensured it remained secure regardless of who might search later."

"Including those who killed her?" Parks asked the obvious question.

"Especially them." Lawson moved to another section, checking electrical panels and ventilation ducts. "The question is whether she hid it on a previous visit here."

They continued their search in widening circles, documenting possible hiding spots while finding nothing of obvious evidentiary value. The warehouse held decades of industrial history layered beneath recent abandonment—broken tools, scattered paperwork, occasional signs of transient occupation. Nothing connecting directly to Monica or Ray Hutchinson.

"Here." Parks' voice carried from the building's far corner, excitement breaking through his professional reserve. "Fresh crime scene tape on a door. That seems odd. The crime happened five years ago, but this looks almost brand new."

Lawson crossed the uneven floor quickly, joining him beside a steel door marked BASEMENT ACCESS. Yellow tape sealed the frame with official departmental markings, but the adhesive showed recent application. Bright plastic contrasted sharply with the warehouse's general decay, edges still crisp rather than frayed by time and elements.

"Someone secured this recently." She examined the tape more closely, running her fingers along the adhesive edge. "Within the last few weeks. The factory closed fifteen years ago. The murder happened five years ago. There's no legitimate reason for fresh crime scene tape."

"Could be department evidence preservation." Parks tested the door handle beneath the tape, finding it secured but not locked. "Or someone protecting what's down there."

Lawson studied the tape placement—professional application following department protocols. "Whoever placed this had training. Knew proper procedures." She produced a folding knife from her pocket, blade glinting in the flashlight beam. "Only one way to find out what they're protecting."

Parks hesitated, professional ethics visibly battling investigative curiosity. "Breaking crime scene tape violates multiple regulations. If this is legitimate department security..."

"Then I'll add it to my growing list of procedural violations." Lawson sliced through the tape with quick, decisive strokes. "So does murder. So does evidence tampering. So does kidnapping a journalist." She met his gaze directly. "I'm already facing an arrest warrant. What's one more violation if it gets us closer to the truth?"

The steel door opened with metallic protest, hinges grinding after years of disuse. Beyond lay concrete steps descending into absolute darkness deeper than their flashlight beams could penetrate. Stale air drifted upward from the opening, carrying scents of mold and something chemical that made her nose burn slightly.

"Careful." Parks tested the first step with his weight. "Structure could be compromised after all these years."

Lawson began the descent, concrete solid beneath her boots despite superficial crumbling at the edges. "This building was constructed in the 1940s. They built foundations to last back then."

Parks followed her down the narrow staircase, both flashlights creating overlapping pools of illumination that revealed the surprisingly well-preserved space below. The basement stretched farther than expected, concrete walls lined with metal shelving units that held plastic containers and cardboard boxes. The organization suggested purpose rather than abandonment—systematic storage rather than forgotten materials.

"This isn't abandoned storage." Parks read labels attached to the nearest containers, surprise evident in his voice. "These are evidence boxes. Case numbers. Property descriptions. All organized like department archives."

Lawson examined box after box, confirming his assessment. Each contained evidence from cases supposedly closed or destroyed according to official records. Drug seizures that should have been incinerated. Weapons that should have been melted down. Cash and valuables that should have been returned to owners or processed through department procedures. Documents that should have been shredded after retention periods expired.

"Someone's been stockpiling evidence instead of destroying it." She opened a container labeled with Ray Hutchinson's badge number, contents neatly arranged inside with professional organization. "Look at this."

Inside lay packets of cocaine marked with DEA seizure tags. Accompanying paperwork showed the drugs should have been destroyed eighteen months ago following case closure. Instead, they sat preserved in climate-controlled storage beneath an abandoned warehouse, inventory sheets updated with recent dates.

"This is extensive." Parks moved to another shelving unit, opening containers with increasing urgency. "Financial records here. Bank statements. Wire transfer documentation. All from cases Thomas Hutchinson defended successfully through evidence suppression motions."

"He was selling evidence back to his clients." The scheme crystallized in Lawson's mind as she examined more containers. "Using his brother's departmental access to recover seized assets after cases closed. Returning them for additional payment beyond legal fees."

"Perfect system." Parks photographed evidence labels with his phone, documenting the discovery methodically despite the overwhelming volume. "Legal fees plus recovery fees. Double profit from the same criminal enterprise. The department thinks the evidence has been destroyed, clients recover valuable assets, and Hutchinson profits twice from the same case."

They worked through the storage area systematically, documenting contents that represented years of methodical evidence theft and resale. Each container held proof of corruption extending beyond individual cases into wholesale manipulation of the justice system. The basement had been converted into unofficial evidence storage—a shadow archive where seized materials disappeared before official destruction.

"Over here." Parks called from the basement's far corner, voice echoing against concrete walls. "Something embedded in the wall. Different from the shelving system."

Lawson joined him beside a section where concrete showed fresh repair work. A square foot of wall displayed newer material than surrounding areas, slightly different color indicating recent application. Parks worked his fingertips around the edges until mortar crumbled away, revealing a small cavity containing a plastic bag.

"Deliberate hiding spot." He extracted the bag carefully, preserving potential fingerprint evidence.

Inside the protective plastic, a micro SD card lay wrapped in additional protective material.

"Hidden recently." Parks examined the hiding spot more carefully, professional assessment evident in his methodical approach. "Concrete work maybe two weeks old. Someone knew something worth preserving was here."

Lawson pocketed the memory card, mind already processing possibilities. "Blackwell must have found this place. Hidden the card during her investigation."

"Or someone else entirely." Parks sealed the cavity with an evidence marker. "Someone who knew what was down here and wanted the record preserved."

They climbed back to the main floor, both processing the implications of the basement discovery. Evidence theft on a massive scale. Systematic corruption involving multiple department members. The complete subversion of the justice system procedures for profit.

"We need to secure this location." Parks sealed the basement door with tape from his equipment kit. "Document everything properly before someone realizes we've been here. This represents years of criminal activity."

"The memory card first." Lawson gestured toward the exit, suddenly eager to examine its contents. "Let's see what someone wanted us to find."

They returned to the parking lot, where Lawson retrieved her laptop from the car. The computer booted quickly as she connected the SD card. A single video file appeared on the screen, dated three days before Monica's death. She clicked play, and Monica's voice filled the car's interior through tinny speakers.

"I know what you've been doing." Monica stood in what appeared to be the same basement they'd just explored, facing someone outside the camera's frame. She looked determined but cautious, posture suggesting she conversed with a potential threat. "Selling evidence back to criminals. Using department resources to protect Thomas Hutchinson's clients."

The camera remained focused on Monica, but a male voice responded from off-screen. Lawson found the cadence familiar, but the speaker's identity remained elusive.

"You don't understand the bigger picture, Monica. This system protects more than it harms."

"Protects criminals. Harms victims. That's not justice." Monica's expression hardened, the determination Lawson remembered so well evident in her stance.

"Justice is complicated. Sometimes wrong methods serve right purposes."

Monica shook her head, rejection clear in her body language. "I have documentation. Financial records. Communications between you and Thomas Hutchinson. Everything needed to expose the entire operation."

The off-screen voice hardened, professional polish giving way to underlying threat. "Where's this documentation?"

"Secure location. Multiple copies. Insurance against exactly this situation." Monica's confidence suggested preparation against potential consequences.

"You're making a mistake, Monica. This can't continue."

"It won't. I'm taking everything to federal authorities. The corruption ends now."

The video cut to black. Lawson stared at the empty screen, Monica's final declaration hanging in the sudden silence. But Monica never got her chance to deliver the evidence to federal authorities. And the corruption continued for five more years.

Her phone chimed with another Dead Air podcast notification. A live broadcast, starting immediately.

"That's Blackwell." Parks leaned closer to read the alert, professional interest overcoming his earlier procedural concerns. "Thought she was in Belize with Thomas Hutchinson."

Lawson tapped the notification, opening the podcast website. But instead of Blackwell's voice, Leah Blackwell's face appeared on screen—bruised, exhausted, but undeniably alive. She sat in what appeared to be an empty room, speaking directly into a camera with desperate urgency.

"If you're watching this, I'm still alive. For now."

chapter
thirty

LAWSON'S FINGERS moved across her phone screen, attaching the video file to a message for Claire and Fiona. The recording of Monica's confrontation in that basement storage facility represented the breakthrough they'd been seeking for five years. Not just evidence of corruption, but a direct connection to whoever had orchestrated Monica's death.

"Sending this to Claire now." She typed a brief message that accompanied the video: *Found Monica's insurance policy. Voice on recording sounds familiar but can't place it. Need your legal expertise to identify and analyze implications.*

Parks leaned against the car's hood, his posture casual but his eyes constantly scanning the warehouse perimeter for any signs they'd been followed; professional vigilance never entirely abandoned despite the isolated location. The abandoned building loomed behind them like a weathered sentinel, its broken windows reflecting fragments of streetlight from the distant road.

"Whoever killed Monica knew about the evidence storage," he said, voice low despite the emptiness surrounding them. "Had to protect the basement operation. Too much incriminating material to leave exposed."

Lawson nodded, the same conclusion having formed in her mind minutes earlier. "Millions in drugs, weapons, financial records. The perfect blackmail material against half of Savannah's criminal organizations."

Her phone buzzed with an incoming call. Claire's number appeared on the screen, the attorney having obviously viewed the video immediately upon receiving it.

"Claire." Lawson answered, putting the call on speaker so Parks could participate.

Claire's voice carried sharp urgency without her usual measured legal cadence. "I'm watching the video now. The audio quality isn't perfect, but I recognize that voice."

"You can identify it?" Lawson straightened, adrenaline spiking through her system.

"Judge Elizabeth Byrd." No hesitation colored Claire's response. "I've argued cases before her for years. That cadence, that particular way she emphasizes certain words—that's definitely her voice."

Judge Byrd—the respected jurist who'd attempted to shut down Blackwell's podcast from the beginning. Who'd positioned herself as protecting ongoing investigations while actually protecting herself. The pieces clicked into place with sickening clarity.

"That makes sense." Lawson processed the implications rapidly. "She pushed for the injunction against Blackwell's podcast. Claimed it would interfere with active investigations."

"Because she knew exactly where the investigation was heading." Claire's typing clicked through the phone connection, her multitasking evident even remotely. "I'm pulling her case assignments now. Cross-referencing with Thomas Hutchinson's client list from the Bar Association database."

Parks moved closer, listening to the conversation while maintaining watch on their surroundings. His tactical awareness never wavered despite his evident interest in the developing theory. The warehouse district remained empty except for occasional traffic on the distant highway, headlights cutting brief paths before disappearing around distant corners.

"How many of Hutchinson's cases appeared before Byrd?" Lawson asked, already suspecting the answer.

"Still calculating the final numbers." More typing sounds echoed through the connection. "But preliminary count shows significant statistical anomaly. Far beyond probability for random assignment within the district."

"She was directing cases to herself." Lawson's voice hardened with certainty.

"Or manipulating the assignment system to ensure Hutchinson's clients received favorable treatment. As chief judge, she controls docket assignments for the entire district." Claire's legal experience provided immediate understanding of the procedural mechanisms involved. "She could ensure particular cases landed on her calendar without obvious interference."

Lawson climbed into her car, starting the engine while keeping Claire on speaker. Parks remained outside for another minute, completing his security check before joining her in the passenger seat. His presence provided tactical reassurance as she processed this new information.

"Judge Byrd killed Monica to protect her arrangement with Thomas Hutchinson." The pieces assembled themselves with crystalline clarity in Lawson's mind. "Monica discovered the judicial corruption. Threatened to expose everything. Byrd couldn't allow that to happen."

"Which explains why key evidence went missing after Monica's death." Claire's voice carried grim satisfaction at solving the puzzle. "Byrd had judicial authority to access anything related to ongoing investigations."

"Including the basement storage facility." Lawson connected the final dot.

"Exactly." Papers rustled as Claire organized her findings. "She could authorize evidence transfers, approve destruction orders, manipulate any aspect of case processing. Perfect position to control every element of the justice system."

Lawson's phone chimed with another notification. Dead Air podcast update. The live broadcast that had appeared earlier was continuing, apparently broadcasting from some unknown location.

"Claire, I need to check something. Blackwell's broadcasting again."

"How is that possible if she's with Thomas Hutchinson in Belize?"

"Not sure. I'll call you back."

Lawson ended the call and tapped the podcast notification. The video stream loaded after brief buffering, showing Blackwell seated in what appeared to be an empty room with white walls. No windows visible in the frame. No identifying features to indicate location. Her face showed distinct bruising around both eyes, discoloration suggesting injuries at least twenty-four hours old. Her movements seemed sluggish, hands occasionally wandering before being corrected, suggesting chemical sedation or exhaustion.

"My name is Leah Blackwell." Her voice carried none of its usual professional authority. Words slurred slightly, confirming drug influence. "I want to retract statements made during my previous podcast episodes regarding the Savannah Police Department and Detective Erin Lawson."

The camera remained fixed on Blackwell's face in an uncomfortable close-up. Someone off-screen was clearly directing her words, forcing this public recantation under duress. The static framing suggested a camera fixed on a tripod rather than a professional production setup.

"My allegations were based on incomplete information and flawed analysis." Blackwell paused between sentences, struggling to maintain focus. Eyes occasionally drifting before snapping back to the camera. "The Savannah Police Department conducted thorough investigations into both Detective Landry's murder and Detective Hutchinson's suicide."

Parks leaned closer to the screen, professional assessment evident in his expression. "Forced statement. Classic hostage protocol. Reading prepared text under duress."

"But why broadcast it?" Lawson kept her eyes focused on Blackwell's face, looking for any signs of coded communication or hidden messaging. "They already have her in custody. Why risk exposure through public broadcast?"

"Public damage control. Discredit her previous reporting before anyone can act on the evidence she revealed through the automated releases." Parks' understanding of tactical motivation provided immediate insight. "Classic counterintelligence approach. Undermine the messenger after the message has spread."

Blackwell continued reading from what was obviously a prepared script, voice flattened of natural intonation. "I apologize for any harm caused by my irresponsible journalism. The podcast will cease production immediately."

Then, something changed in her expression. Her eyelids began moving in a rapid pattern. Not random blinking from exhaustion but systematic sequences with deliberate timing.

"She's signaling." Lawson grabbed a pen from the console, transcribing the blink patterns onto a napkin. "Morse code. She's using her eyelids to communicate."

F-I-N-D T-H-E J-U-D-G-E.

"Find the judge." Parks read over her shoulder as she decoded the message. "Does she know about Byrd? How would she have that information if she's being held by Hutchinson?"

The video stream ended abruptly mid-sentence. The Dead Air website returned to its standard homepage without additional content or announcements. No explanation for the broadcast or its sudden termination.

Lawson immediately called Claire back. "Did you see it? The broadcast?"

"I did. Recording it for evidence preservation."

"The blinking. It was Morse code. She signaled 'find the judge.'"

"Well, that aligns perfectly with what I just discovered." Claire's voice carried controlled excitement. "I just finished a quick analysis of Byrd's case history. Thirty-seven cases involving Thomas Hutchinson as defense counsel over the past eight years. All resulted in dismissals, reduced charges, or unusually advantageous plea agreements."

"Statistical impossibility."

"Beyond impossibility. Criminal conspiracy with documented pattern." Claire's typing resumed in the background. "I'm organizing everything into evidence packages for federal prosecutors. The pattern is so clear even a first-year law student could see it."

"How long will that take to process through official channels?"

"Hours for preliminary filing. Days for comprehensive presentation and formal action." Claire paused briefly. "But we have enough now to request immediate federal intervention based on corruption of judicial office."

Lawson considered their options while Parks conducted another security sweep of the area through the car windows. The evidence against Judge Byrd remained technically circumstantial but compelling in its consistency. Monica's video provided direct proof of corruption. Blackwell's coded message confirmed Byrd's central role in whatever was happening now.

"There's more." Claire's voice carried fresh urgency. "I found something else in Byrd's judicial record while searching case histories. She personally authorized the evidence transfer that moved Monica's case files to storage."

"Personally authorized?" Lawson straightened, the significance immediately apparent.

"Signed order dated three days after Monica's murder. Transferred all physical evidence to 'secure archive facility pending case resolution.'" Claire's disgust colored every word. "She was cleaning up her own crime scene using judicial authority."

"Using her position to obstruct investigation into her own criminal actions." Lawson completed the thought. "Perfect cover. No one questions a judge's evidence handling orders."

Parks gestured toward the road. "We should move. I'll ride with you."

"What about your car?" Lawson asked, glancing toward where Parks had parked on the other side of the lot.

"It's secure here. Too isolated for random theft, and I'd rather maintain our conversation than split up. I can grab it later after we decide our next move."

Lawson nodded in agreement as she started her engine while continuing the conversation with Claire. "What about federal contacts? Any response to the evidence packages you sent earlier about Hutchinson?"

"Agent Komarov confirmed receipt and indicated high-priority classification. FBI organized crime task force is reviewing everything." Claire's tone carried cautious optimism. "Federal wheels turn slowly, but they're turning."

"Not slowly enough for Thomas Hutchinson. He's had time to relocate Blackwell multiple times since reaching Belize."

"Which is why we need to move quickly on the Byrd angle." Claire's strategic thinking was fully engaged. "She's still in Savannah. Still operating under the assumption that her involvement remains hidden."

"What do you suggest?" Lawson navigated through empty streets, heading toward downtown without a conscious destination.

"Direct confrontation. Present the evidence. Force her to choose between cooperation and federal prosecution."

Parks shook his head, security training asserting itself. "Dangerous approach. Byrd has resources and connections we can't fully predict."

"Less dangerous than allowing her to continue operating." Claire's conviction strengthened. "Every day we delay gives her more opportunities to destroy evidence or eliminate witnesses."

Lawson weighed the options while driving toward the city center. Direct confrontation carried significant risks but offered the potential for immediate resolution. A federal investigation provided procedural safety but required time they might not have with Blackwell in immediate danger.

"Where would we find Byrd at this hour?" she asked.

"Home address is public record. But approaching her residence puts us in violation of numerous regulations." Claire's lawyer instincts warred with her desire for justice.

"We're already beyond regulations." Lawson reminded her. "I'm on the lam. You're harboring a fugitive. Parks is risking his career. At this point, direct action might be our only viable option."

"Valid point." Claire paused briefly. "I'm sending Byrd's address now. You can decide how to proceed."

The text arrived within seconds. Residential address in Savannah's historic district. Expensive neighborhood where judges and successful attorneys maintained their public images alongside old-money families.

"Claire, document everything we've discovered. Create multiple backup copies. If this confrontation goes wrong, make sure the evidence reaches federal authorities."

"Already handled." Claire's efficiency provided reassurance. "Every document, every recording, every connection has been transmitted to multiple secure locations. Nothing disappears even if we do."

"Good." Lawson ended the call and turned to Parks. "Ready to interview a judge?"

chapter
thirty-one

JUDGE BYRD'S estate sprawled across two acres in Savannah's most exclusive historic district. Wrought-iron gates guarded the entrance to grounds that belonged in architectural magazines. Manicured lawns stretched between century-old live oaks draped with Spanish moss. The main house rose three stories, its Federal-style columns and wraparound porches speaking of old money and established power.

Lawson parked two blocks away, positioning the car where they could observe the property through binoculars without attracting attention. The neighborhood slept peacefully around them—expensive homes occupied by people who trusted their security systems and assumed their wealth protected them from the violence that plagued less fortunate areas.

"Motion sensors on the gate posts." Parks studied the entrance through his field glasses. "Cameras covering the driveway approach. Professional security installation."

"Expected for a federal judge." Lawson scanned the grounds systematically. "Pool house behind the main residence. Guest cottage near the back fence. Multiple outbuildings."

"Any activity?"

"Lights on in the main house. Second floor, what looks like a home office." She adjusted focus, examining windows for movement. "Pool house is dark."

They settled into surveillance routine, taking turns monitoring the property while the other documented observations or contacted backup resources. The digital clock on the dashboard showed 11:47 p.m., late enough that most legitimate activity should have concluded.

"There." Parks pointed toward the estate's eastern boundary. "Movement near the fence line."

Lawson swung her binoculars toward the indicated area. A figure moved through shadows cast by oak trees, staying clear of the main driveway's lighting. Athletic build. Deliberate movements suggesting familiarity with the property layout.

"Professional approach pattern." She tracked the figure's progress toward the pool house. "Knows where the cameras are positioned."

The intruder reached the pool house without triggering any visible security responses. Instead of forcing entry, they produced what appeared to be a key.

"Authorized access." Parks lowered his binoculars. "Either Byrd's expecting someone or this person has legitimate access to the property."

"Or they've been here before. Either way, we need to get closer."

They approached on foot, leaving the car parked. The estate's perimeter fence stood eight feet tall, wrought iron with decorative spear points that would discourage casual intruders. Parks located a section where landscaping provided cover from the main house's sight lines.

"Boost me up." Lawson positioned herself against the fence base.

Parks interlaced his fingers, creating a step that allowed her to reach the top rail. She pulled herself over carefully, avoiding the sharp points, then dropped to the manicured grass on the other side. Parks followed with athletic efficiency.

They moved across the grounds using trees and landscaping for concealment. The pool house sat fifty yards from the main residence, connected by a flagstone path that wound between flower beds and ornamental shrubs.

Soft light emanated from the windows, but curtains prevented direct observation of the interior. Lawson approached from the side, finding a gap in the window covering that allowed limited viewing.

The interior had been converted from recreational space into something resembling a command center. Multiple computer monitors displayed surveillance feeds from various locations around Savannah. Recording equipment occupied a professional-grade rack system. Maps covered one wall with colored pins marking locations throughout the city.

"Surveillance hub." She whispered to Parks, who had positioned himself near the main entrance. "Someone's been watching multiple locations simultaneously."

A figure moved into view inside the pool house. Richardson, still wearing the casual clothes from their cabin meeting. He studied something on one of the monitors, adjusting controls.

But movement in the room's far corner drew Lawson's attention to another presence. A woman sat in a chair positioned against the back wall. Even from this angle, Lawson recognized the distinctive profile.

Leah Blackwell. Alive.

Lawson blinked hard, certain exhaustion was creating hallucinations. Blackwell was supposed to be in Belize with Thomas Hutchinson. They'd seen airport security footage of her boarding his private jet. Yet here she sat, twenty feet away in a judge's pool house.

"Parks." She grabbed his sleeve, pointing through the window. "Blackwell's inside."

His expression mirrored her confusion. "That's impossible. She left the country with Hutchinson."

"Unless someone else got on that plane." Lawson studied Blackwell's appearance through the glass. "Or this is someone else entirely."

But the more she observed, the more certain she became. Blackwell appeared alive but sedated. Her head lolled slightly to one side. Restraints secured her arms to the chair. An IV line connected to her left arm, suggesting ongoing chemical sedation to maintain compliance.

"She's been here the entire time." The implications crashed through Lawson's mind. "The airport footage was staged. Someone else wearing a hood to create a false trail."

Richardson moved to a cabinet, retrieving medical supplies. He checked the IV connection, adjusted flow rates, then returned to the monitoring station.

Parks positioned himself beside the window, confirming Lawson's observations. "He's been holding her here since the abduction."

"But why keep her alive?" Lawson studied the setup more carefully. "If this entire operation runs from the judge's property, why not eliminate the threat permanently?"

Richardson's attention shifted to one of the monitors displaying what appeared to be the main house's interior. He reached for a radio, speaking into it too quietly for them to overhear. After receiving a response, he moved toward the pool house entrance.

Lawson and Parks retreated to concealment behind a storage shed as Richardson emerged. He walked toward the main house, leaving Blackwell unguarded in the converted command center.

"Now." Lawson approached the pool house door.

Parks tested the handle. "Unlocked."

They entered with weapons drawn, conducting a rapid tactical sweep of the single-room space. Blackwell stirred as they approached her chair. Her eyes opened partially, pupils dilated from chemical sedation. She attempted to speak but only managed slurred syllables.

"Leah." Lawson knelt beside the chair, checking restraints and the IV connection. "We're here to help. Can you understand me?"

Blackwell nodded weakly, managing to form words with obvious effort. "You're ... Detective Lawson."

"How are you here? We saw footage of you leaving the country with Thomas Hutchinson."

"Decoy." Blackwell's speech improved slightly as consciousness returned. "Someone else ... wearing my clothes. I've been here ... since the parking garage."

"Richardson's been holding you prisoner?"

"Protecting me." Blackwell struggled to focus. "Byrd wanted me dead immediately. Richardson convinced her ... sedation provided better control."

The pool house door opened. Richardson entered alone, hands visible and empty. His expression carried exhaustion mixed with something resembling relief.

"I couldn't let her kill another one." He moved slowly, maintaining distance from their weapons. "Judge Byrd ordered Blackwell's execution after the podcast exposed too much."

Parks maintained a tactical position near the door while Lawson continued assisting Blackwell. "You had her this whole time. At the cabin, you never said a word."

"Because I wasn't certain you could be trusted yet." Richardson's voice carried a defensive edge. "Five years of watching corrupt officers betray investigations. I needed proof of your commitment before revealing Blackwell's location."

"Proof of my commitment?" Lawson's anger flared. "I've been hunting Monica's killer for five years."

"While drinking yourself into blackouts. While making tactical errors that compromised evidence." Richardson gestured toward the IV equipment. "I couldn't risk Blackwell's life on your emotional stability. When Amy told me you came looking for me, I drove out to the cabin to meet you there."

Blackwell stirred between them.

"By pretending to follow her orders while actually protecting you."

"The same approach I used after Monica's death." Richardson moved to the monitoring station, indicating screens that showed various Savannah locations. "Appear to cooperate while actually gathering evidence."

"You tested me at the cabin." Lawson processed the manipulation. "Gave me partial truth to see how I'd react."

"I gave you everything except Blackwell's location." Richardson met her gaze directly. "Your response confirmed what I'd hoped. You wanted justice more than revenge."

"You could have contacted federal authorities." Parks challenged Richardson's methods. "Proper channels exist for witness protection."

"Proper channels include compromised personnel." Richardson indicated specific monitors showing federal building entrances. "Byrd has connections throughout multiple agencies. Direct contact risked exposing Blackwell's location."

The surveillance screens suddenly shifted, showing new activity around the main house. Judge Byrd emerged from a side entrance, accompanied by two men in dark clothing. All three moved toward the pool house with weapons visible.

"She knows we're here." Richardson reached for a pistol secured beneath the monitoring console. "The motion sensors detected your approach."

Blackwell attempted to stand but collapsed back into the chair. "Can't ... legs won't work."

Lawson cut the restraints while Parks moved to the window. "Three subjects approaching. Thirty seconds out."

"We need to move." Lawson helped Blackwell to her feet, supporting her weight as circulation returned to sedated limbs.

"No." Blackwell gripped Lawson's arm with surprising strength. "I need to face her. End this."

"You can barely stand." Parks maintained watch through the window. "Twenty seconds."

"I have everything recorded." Blackwell pulled herself upright against the chair. "Her confession. The orders. All of it."

Richardson positioned himself beside the main entrance, weapon drawn. "Five years of playing her game. Time for truth."

Footsteps circled the building. Multiple positions.

"Detective Lawson." Byrd's voice carried through the walls, commanding and cold. "I know you're inside."

Parks moved away from the window, taking cover behind the equipment racks. "They've surrounded the building."

Lawson helped Blackwell toward the monitoring station, both women moving awkwardly as the journalist's sedated muscles struggled to respond. The screens displayed armed figures at each exit.

"Judge Byrd." Lawson called toward the door. "We have evidence of your involvement in Monica Landry's murder. Federal agents are already reviewing the documentation."

"Evidence obtained through illegal breaking and entering. Inadmissible in any court proceeding." Byrd's legal training showed in her immediate response. "Release Ms. Blackwell and surrender peacefully. This can still end without additional bloodshed."

Richardson checked his weapon's magazine. "She's not walking away from this. Not after Monica. Not after five years of cover-ups."

The door handle turned slowly. Locked, but not for long against determined intrusion. Metal scraped against metal as someone worked the mechanism from outside.

"Tom." Byrd's voice grew closer. "Bring her out. We're done with this charade."

"No more games, Elizabeth." Richardson called back through the door. "The federal agents have everything. Your operation ends tonight."

A sharp crack split the air as the lock mechanism gave way. The door swung open, revealing Judge Elizabeth Byrd flanked by two men in tactical gear.

"Detective Lawson. Mr. Richardson. Ms. Blackwell." Her gaze swept the room, cataloging positions and tactical advantages. "This ends now."

chapter
thirty-two

JUDGE ELIZABETH BYRD stepped into the pool house with measured confidence. Her tailored suit remained immaculate despite the late hour. Gray hair pulled into a perfect chignon. The same commanding presence she projected from the bench now filled the converted surveillance center.

The two men flanking her moved with military bearing. Tactical gear. Professional weapons handling. Eyes that swept the room, cataloging threats and escape routes before settling into overwatch positions. Their faces carried the blank expressions of soldiers who followed orders without question.

"Detective Lawson." Byrd's gaze found each person in turn. "Lieutenant Parks. Ms. Blackwell." Her attention lingered on Richardson. "Tom."

Richardson kept his weapon lowered but ready. "Elizabeth."

"Thirty years we've worked together. Through three police chiefs. Five district attorneys. Countless reforms and reorganizations." Byrd moved deeper into the room, apparently unconcerned by the firearms trained in her direction. "I'd hoped our partnership could continue."

"Partnership." Lawson shifted position, maintaining cover behind the equipment rack while supporting Blackwell's unsteady frame. The journalist's weight pressed against her shoulder, muscles still fighting sedative aftereffects. "You mean your criminal empire."

"I mean efficient administration of justice. This city's crime rate dropped forty percent during my tenure as chief judge. Drug trafficking decreased. Gang violence diminished. Public safety improved."

The surveillance monitors continued their silent vigil, displaying empty streets and vacant buildings across Savannah. Digital proof of the order Byrd claimed to maintain through corruption.

Parks stepped forward, weapon trained on the nearest tactical officer. His voice carried cold recognition. "You killed Bram Kowalski."

Byrd's expression flickered—the first crack in her judicial composure. "Detective Kowalski exceeded his operational parameters. Much like Detective Landry."

"He was investigating evidence tampering. Found your network's fingerprints all over major drug cases. You had him murdered to protect your operation." Parks' grip tightened on his weapon, three years of suppressed rage threatening to surface. "Made it look like a drunk driving accident."

"Detective Kowalski was troubled. Personal problems led to self-destructive behavior. Tragic but hardly uncommon among law enforcement personnel." Byrd's legal training provided smooth deflection despite the accusation's accuracy.

"Bram didn't drink. You know that. I know that. Everyone who worked with him knew that." Parks took another step forward, professional control warring with personal fury. "But alcohol appeared in his blood anyway. Convenient how evidence works when you control the system."

Lawson watched Parks process the confirmation of his partner's murder. The same cold rage she'd carried for five years now reflected in his expression. Two cops united by the systematic elimination of their partners.

"You've been cleaning house for years," Parks continued, voice gaining strength. "Any cop who got too close to your protection racket ended up dead or transferred. Bram documented the pattern before you killed him."

"Detective Parks, your emotional investment in this matter compromises your judgment. Professional detachment serves justice better than personal vendetta." Byrd's judicial tone remained steady despite the mounting accusations.

"Justice?" Parks laughed without humor. "You perverted everything law enforcement represents. Turned the courts into a protection service for criminals who could afford your fees."

"By managing chaos." Byrd gestured toward the screens with judicial precision. "Random enforcement creates random results. Systematic oversight produces systematic improvement. Thomas Hutchinson's clients operated within defined parameters. Limited territorial boundaries. Restricted product distribution. Controlled violence levels. Their cooperation ensured predictable criminal activity that law enforcement could manage effectively."

Richardson moved closer to the monitoring station, his weapon tracking Byrd's movements. "Tell them about Monica."

Byrd's composure cracked slightly. Professional mask slipping to reveal something colder beneath. "Detective Landry exceeded her operational boundaries."

"She was federal." Richardson's statement cut through the tension. "FBI informant. Recruited three years before her death."

Lawson's grip on Blackwell tightened involuntarily as pieces reshuffled in her mind. Monica's meticulous documentation. Her systematic evidence gathering. The careful investigation techniques that had impressed veteran detectives.

"You knew?" Parks directed the question toward Richardson, his voice carrying disbelief and growing understanding.

"I recruited her." Richardson's weapon remained trained on Byrd while he spoke. "The Bureau needed inside access to investigate judicial corruption. Monica volunteered."

"Jesus." Lawson's voice emerged as barely a whisper. "Monica was working undercover the entire time."

"The Rafferty case was bait." Understanding crystallized as she processed the implications. "Designed to expose the corruption network."

"Monica was supposed to gather evidence slowly. Build comprehensive documentation over years." Richardson's voice carried old pain and fresh regret. "Long-term penetration of the judicial protection system.

But she discovered Thomas Hutchinson's connection to you, Elizabeth. She couldn't resist moving quickly once she understood the scope."

A muscle twitched along Byrd's jawline, the only visible crack in her judicial veneer. "She threatened twenty years of careful work. Systematic improvement of public safety through managed criminal cooperation. The greater good required protective measures."

"So you ordered her death." Lawson's words hung in the air like smoke.

"I authorized necessary intervention." Byrd's legal precision maintained even here, every word chosen for maximum deniability. "The operation served community interests. Individual sacrifice preserved collective benefit. Standard cost-benefit analysis applied to administrative decision-making."

The clinical description of Monica's murder chilled the room. Byrd discussing federal agent assassination with the same detachment she applied to sentencing guidelines.

Blackwell struggled against the lingering sedation, fighting to contribute. "You killed a federal agent investigating your corruption."

"I eliminated a threat to public order." Byrd's voice hardened further. "Monica Landry's idealistic pursuit of abstract justice would have destroyed effective crime management. Returned chaos to streets we'd pacified through intelligent cooperation with manageable criminal elements."

Parks absorbed this casual admission of multiple murders. Bram's death wasn't an isolated incident but part of systematic elimination spanning years. The scope of Byrd's criminal enterprise exceeded even his most pessimistic estimates.

"Bram was twenty-eight years old," Parks said quietly. "Had a fiancée. Planned to propose the weekend after he died. She still visits his grave twice a week, wondering what she did wrong to make him start drinking."

"Tragic consequences of necessary administrative decisions." Byrd's clinical response revealed a complete absence of remorse.

The standoff crystallized around competing philosophies of justice —Byrd's utilitarian corruption against the fundamental principles that had already driven good cops to their deaths. Parks's shoulders squared, his gaze locked on Byrd with a steadiness that made Lawson understand why Bram had once trusted him. Some truths demanded exposure regardless of personal cost. Richardson adjusted his grip on his weapon, professional training warring with personal emotion. "The Bureau knows everything now. Your operation ends tonight regardless of what happens in this room."

"Does it?" Byrd smiled without warmth, the expression transforming her distinguished features into something predatory. "Agent Komarov receives his intelligence through carefully managed channels. Federal task force operations require judicial oversight for warrant approval. My cooperation enables their investigative success."

The implication was staggering. Any federal investigation would be compromised from its inception. Byrd controlled both criminal prosecution and federal oversight through her judicial authority and institutional connections.

"You've been feeding them selected information." Parks grasped the scope of her influence. "Managing what they discover."

"Directing their attention toward appropriate targets while protecting valuable community assets." Byrd's confirmation carried professional pride in bureaucratic manipulation. "Thomas Hutchinson's network provides social stability. Federal agents eliminate disruptive criminal elements. Everyone benefits from coordinated enforcement strategies."

"Except the victims of the crimes you've protected." Lawson's anger built with each revelation. Five years of pursuing justice while the system itself worked against resolution.

"Except cops like Bram who believed in actual justice," Parks added, his voice hardening with each word. "Who thought evidence should convict the guilty instead of protecting them."

"Acceptable casualties in service of greater community safety." Byrd's judicial demeanor remained intact despite the moral bankruptcy of her position. "Individual justice balanced against collective security. Your partners simply lacked appropriate scope of vision."

The casual dismissal of Bram's life as "acceptable casualty" snapped something fundamental in Parks' psychological restraint. Three years of methodical investigation. Three years of patient evidence gathering.

Three years of professional conduct while his partner's killer walked free.

His weapon swung toward Byrd. "You're going to pay for what you did to him."

"Lieutenant Parks." Richardson's sharp command cut through the rising tension. "Don't let her make you into what she is."

Parks froze, finger on the trigger, professional training warring with personal vendetta. Killing Byrd would provide emotional satisfaction but betray everything Bram had died fighting for. Justice through law, not vigilante execution.

"Bram would want you to do this right," Lawson said quietly. "Official channels. Legal process. The justice system working the way it's supposed to."

Parks held his position for several heartbeats, weapon trained on the woman who'd ordered his partner's death. Then, professional discipline reasserted itself. He lowered the gun slightly, though it remained ready.

The low hum of electronic equipment filled the momentary silence. The tactical officers shifted their weight but maintained unwavering focus.

Byrd clasped her hands in front of her, gold rings catching the harsh fluorescent light. "You should understand, Detective Lawson. Your career in law enforcement taught you the necessity of compromise. The real world operates through negotiation between idealism and reality."

"I never negotiated away justice," Lawson spat back.

"You merely defined it narrowly enough to preserve your conscience." Byrd's rebuke carried decades of judicial authority. "Your definition simply lacks appropriate scope."

Richardson moved another step closer, his weapon never wavering. "Monica recorded everything. Your orders. Your meetings with Thomas. Financial arrangements. The federal agents have complete documentation of your criminal conspiracy."

"They have carefully curated evidence supporting necessary prosecutions." Byrd's confidence suggested deeper corruption than any of them had imagined. "Agent Komarov will arrest appropriate suspects while protecting essential community operations. Federal bureaucracy responds to proper judicial guidance."

"Including you?"

"Judicial immunity protects legitimate exercise of administrative authority." Byrd's legal training provided multiple escape routes through institutional protection. "My cooperation with federal investigations demonstrates a commitment to justice rather than obstruction. Constitutional separation of powers prevents inappropriate interference with judicial independence."

Lawson absorbed the trap closing around them. Byrd had anticipated federal involvement. Prepared legal defenses. Compromised the investigation from within through her judicial connections. Monica's death served only to protect an operation that would continue functioning under federal protection.

A chill spread through the room despite the humid Savannah night. The stakes extended beyond individual survival into systemic corruption that might prove impossible to dismantle.

"There is another option." Byrd's voice softened marginally, judicial sternness giving way to pragmatic negotiation. "Recognition that current arrangements serve community interests better than chaotic alternatives."

"You're offering a deal." Lawson's disgust sharpened each word.

"I'm suggesting a realistic assessment of available choices." Byrd indicated the tactical officers positioned throughout the room with subtle hand gestures. "Ms. Blackwell's podcast created public attention that requires careful management. Detective Lawson's investigation threatens operational security through emotional rather than rational decision-making. Lieutenant Parks' internal affairs review compromises necessary departmental cooperation."

The silence stretched taut as piano wire. One of the tactical officers shifted position, the metal fixtures on his vest catching the overhead light. Outside, cicadas buzzed in relentless rhythm against the humid night.

Richardson kept his weapon trained on her center mass while processing the offer. "What kind of deal?"

"Complete silence regarding tonight's discoveries. Ms. Blackwell retracts her allegations through carefully crafted public statements emphasizing journalistic error and inadequate fact-checking. Detective

Lawson accepts transfer to a federal task force with appropriate compensation and career advancement. Lieutenant Parks receives promotion to captain with expanded authority over internal investigations."

"In exchange for covering up Monica's murder."

"In exchange for preserving systematic improvements to public safety that benefit thousands of law-abiding citizens." Byrd's justification carried absolute conviction. "Individual justice balanced against collective security. Philosophical principles applied to practical governance."

Blackwell struggled to speak through the lingering sedation, her voice gaining strength with each word. "And if we refuse?"

Byrd's expression returned to judicial coldness, the negotiating mask dropping to reveal bureaucratic ruthlessness. "Then this room becomes the site of a tragic confrontation. Detective Lawson, already facing arrest warrants for kidnapping, attacked federal personnel during a legitimate rescue operation. Lieutenant Parks and Mr. Richardson died attempting to protect a kidnapped journalist from an unstable colleague. Ms. Blackwell succumbed to injuries sustained during her extended captivity."

Byrd held the tactical advantage through her armed security. Controlled the narrative through her judicial authority. Possessed institutional power to justify whatever outcome served her purposes.

"The beauty of judicial authority," she continued, "lies in its official presumption of legitimacy. My word carries constitutional weight. Your accusations represent desperate attempts to avoid accountability for criminal behavior."

Richardson's weapon remained steady despite the impossible odds. Byrd checked an expensive watch, the diamond bezel glinting under the harsh lights. "Thirty seconds to decide. Cooperation ensures everyone leaves alive with enhanced career prospects. Continued resistance guarantees alternative resolutions with appropriate documentation."

chapter
thirty-three

THE THIRTY SECONDS stretched into infinity. Lawson's finger found her weapon's grip. Parks adjusted his stance. Richardson's breathing steadied into tactical rhythm. The tactical officers remained motionless, awaiting orders.

Blackwell pushed herself upright against the monitoring station. Her legs trembled from the sedatives, but her voice cut through the tension with surprising clarity.

"No."

Byrd's eyebrows rose. "Ms. Blackwell?"

"The truth matters." Blackwell gripped the edge of the equipment rack, knuckles white with effort. "Monica died for it. I won't dishonor that by accepting your deal."

"You're barely conscious. Hardly in a position to make rational decisions."

"Rational enough to know murder when I see it." Blackwell's strength grew with each word. "Your operation ends tonight. No deals. No cover-ups. No more victims."

Byrd's expression hardened into judicial finality. "Very well." She raised her hand toward the tactical officers. "Execute—"

Floodlights blazed outside the pool house. White-hot illumination transformed night into day through every window. Amplified voices boomed across the estate grounds.

"FBI! FEDERAL AGENTS! EVERYONE ON THE GROUND NOW!"

The tactical officers spun toward the windows, weapons rising. Byrd's hand froze mid-gesture as the situation collapsed around her carefully maintained control.

"Ma'am, we need to move." The nearest officer stepped toward Byrd.

"Stand down." Byrd's command carried absolute judicial authority. "I'll handle federal coordination."

"This is Special Agent Komarov. The property is surrounded. Exit with hands visible. No weapons. Comply immediately or face federal prosecution for obstruction."

Richardson kept his weapon trained on Byrd despite the chaos erupting around them. "Sounds like your federal connections aren't as solid as you claimed."

"Komarov follows proper channels." Byrd's confidence wavered for the first time. "Judicial oversight guides his investigation parameters."

The pool house door exploded inward. Federal agents in tactical gear flooded through the entrance, weapons trained on everyone inside. Red laser dots danced across walls and equipment. Professional voices barked commands, overlapping into controlled chaos.

"WEAPONS DOWN! HANDS VISIBLE! EVERYONE ON THE GROUND!"

Parks immediately dropped his pistol, hands rising above his head. "Lieutenant Parks, Internal Affairs. We're cooperating fully."

Lawson released her grip on her weapon but didn't drop it. "Detective Lawson. We have a federal informant and evidence of judicial corruption."

The lead agent swept his rifle across the room's occupants. Body armor marked with FBI identifiers. Face shield reflecting the harsh lighting. "Judge Byrd, you're under federal arrest for conspiracy, racketeering, and murder of a federal agent."

Byrd's gaze darted between the federal agents and the glass door leading to the rear garden. Her hand slipped inside her blazer, emerging with a small pistol. Before anyone could react, she fired once at the nearest light fixture. Glass shattered, plunging half the room into darkness.

"Shots fired! Everyone down!" The lead agent dropped to a crouch as his team scattered for cover.

In the momentary chaos, Byrd bolted toward the rear door, moving with surprising speed for her age. She crashed through the glass, disappearing into the darkness beyond.

"She's running!" Richardson shouted, already moving after her. "East side of the property!"

Lawson didn't hesitate. She vaulted over an overturned chair, following Richardson through the shattered doorway. Glass crunched under her boots as she sprinted into the night. Ahead, Byrd's pale suit caught moonlight as she raced toward a wooded area at the property's edge.

"Federal agents! This is Morrison. Suspect fleeing east toward the tree line. All units converge!" The radio call crackled behind them as the FBI team reorganized.

Richardson kept pace beside Lawson, weapon drawn. "She's heading for her escape route. Underground tunnel system. Connects to the river. Boat waiting."

"How do you know this?"

"Been watching her for years." Richardson's breathing remained controlled despite their sprint. "Documented every contingency plan. Every escape route."

Byrd reached the trees, disappearing into the shadows. Lawson and Richardson plunged after her, branches slapping against their faces. Somewhere behind them, federal agents shouted commands, flashlight beams cutting through the darkness as they organized pursuit.

"Left her tactical team behind," Richardson said. "They're just hired muscle. No loyalty once things go south."

Ahead, moonlight revealed a small stone outbuilding half-hidden by overgrown vegetation. Byrd yanked open its wooden door and disappeared inside.

"There!" Lawson increased her pace, Richardson matching her stride for stride.

They reached the outbuilding seconds later. Ancient gardening equipment hung from rusty hooks. A wheelbarrow lay overturned in one corner. The dirt floor showed clear footprints leading to what appeared to be a root cellar door.

Richardson pulled it open, revealing stone steps descending into darkness. "Stay with Parks and Blackwell," he told Lawson. "I'll track her through the tunnel."

"Not a chance." Lawson checked her weapon. "She killed my partner. I'm seeing this through."

"Then we go together." Richardson started down the steps. "Watch your footing. These tunnels were built during Prohibition. Not maintained in decades."

Lawson took one last look behind her. Federal agents were spreading through the garden, flashlights sweeping across the manicured lawn. Parks stood in the shattered doorway of the pool house, watching her disappear into the outbuilding. Then Lawson descended into darkness after Richardson, following the woman who had ordered Monica's death, the judge who had corrupted an entire justice system, the killer who had finally run out of legal protections to hide behind.

chapter
thirty-four

DARKNESS SWALLOWED them as they descended the stone steps. Damp air chilled Lawson's skin, carrying the earthy scent of decades-old brickwork and stagnant water. Richardson switched on a small tactical flashlight. The narrow beam revealed brick walls slick with moisture and a tunnel barely wide enough for two people to walk side by side.

"Watch your step," Richardson warned. "Floor's uneven."

Their footsteps echoed in the confined space. Water dripped somewhere ahead, a steady metronome counting seconds as they moved deeper beneath the estate. Lawson kept her weapon ready, eyes straining to detect movement beyond Richardson's light.

"These tunnels connect to the river?" she asked, voice hushed.

"Built during Prohibition for rum-running. The original owner smuggled liquor from ships to distribution points throughout Savannah." Richardson swept his light across moisture-stained walls. "Byrd discovered them when renovating the pool house. Maintained them as an emergency exit."

Ahead, footprints marked the muddy floor. Small, precise indentations from expensive heels. Byrd moving at speed despite the darkness and uneven terrain.

"She's familiar with this route," Lawson observed.

"Practiced it monthly, according to my surveillance." Richardson's breathing remained controlled despite their pace. "Thirty-minute direct path to a boathouse on the river."

The tunnel forked unexpectedly. Both paths disappeared into identical darkness. The footprints stopped at the junction, revealing where Byrd had paused to consider her options.

Richardson knelt, examining the ground. "Left tunnel's her usual route. Right leads to a maintenance shaft that emerges near the gatehouse."

"So which did she take?"

He pointed his light at barely perceptible marks in the mud. "Right tunnel. She's improvising."

They followed the narrower passage. The ceiling lowered, forcing them to hunch as they moved forward. Richardson's light revealed ancient support beams sagging beneath the weight of earth above. Decades of moisture had rotted the wood, leaving structural integrity questionable at best.

"This section wasn't properly maintained," Richardson said. "Byrd avoided it during practice runs."

A gunshot cracked through the tunnel. The bullet struck brick inches from Lawson's head, sending fragments stinging against her cheek. She dropped instinctively, pulling Richardson down with her.

"Kill the light!" she hissed.

Darkness enveloped them. Lawson blinked, waiting for her eyes to adjust. Twenty yards ahead, a faint glow revealed Byrd's position. The judge had found emergency lighting in this section, giving herself an advantage over her pursuers.

"Give up, Elizabeth," Richardson called. "Federal agents are stationed at both exits by now. Nowhere to go."

"Always an exit strategy, Tom." Byrd's voice echoed from ahead. "You taught me that during our first corruption investigation."

"That was different. We were pursuing justice then."

"We're still pursuing justice. My definition simply evolved beyond your limited perspective."

Richardson motioned to the right. A small alcove offered minimal cover. They shuffled sideways, pressing against damp brick.

"She has eight rounds in that pistol," Richardson whispered. "Beretta 21A Bobcat."

"How can you be so sure?" Lawson asked. "They come with seven-round magazines too."

"I gave her that gun as a gift when she made chief judge," Richardson said grimly. "Custom eight-round magazine. She's fired three so far."

Lawson calculated angles and distances. "We can't advance without light. She has position advantage."

"Not for long. That emergency lighting runs on battery backup. Twenty minutes maximum."

A fourth shot echoed through the tunnel. More warning than targeting.

"Lawson!" Byrd called. "Tell me something. Did you ever suspect Monica was working for the FBI?"

The question echoed against stone walls. Lawson remained silent.

"Your partner was a federal agent." Byrd's voice carried smug satisfaction. "Recruited by Richardson. She died working for the Bureau, not Savannah PD. They discarded her when operations became complicated."

"Shut up," Lawson muttered.

"You loved her, didn't you?" Byrd's words slithered through darkness. "Office romance against department policy. Kept it hidden while she investigated you and your colleagues."

"She wasn't investigating me."

"She investigated everyone, Detective. Her own partner included. Her lover. All potential suspects in the corruption network she mapped for her federal handlers."

Richardson placed a restraining hand on Lawson's arm. "She's baiting you. Trying to force movement she can target."

Another shot cracked through the tunnel. Five down. Three remaining.

"Richardson knows the truth," Byrd continued. "He recruited Monica. Managed her informant activities. Directed her investigation toward specific targets."

"Including you," Richardson called back.

"Including everyone expendable to your operation." Byrd's laugh echoed against stone. "I discovered her identity three weeks before she died. Confronted her with evidence of her betrayal."

"You ordered her execution," Lawson said, unable to stay silent.

"I authorized appropriate response to an operational threat." The distinction carried Byrd's judicial precision even now. "Her investigation jeopardized controlled criminal management systems that maintained public safety."

The emergency lights flickered briefly. Battery power diminishing.

"We need to move," Richardson whispered. "The lights will fail soon."

"Giving up position advantage," Lawson countered.

"She's stalling for time. Her boat's waiting. If she reaches the river, federal coverage becomes complicated by jurisdiction and water routes."

Lawson weighed options. Advancing meant exposure. Waiting meant Byrd's potential escape.

"I'll draw fire," Richardson said. "You advance under cover."

Before she could object, he darted across the tunnel. A sixth shot rang out. Richardson grunted, staggering against the opposite wall. Blood darkened his sleeve where the bullet had struck.

Lawson surged forward, using Richardson's distraction to close half the distance to Byrd. The emergency lights illuminated the judge's silhouette thirty feet ahead, weapon raised for her final shots.

"Drop the gun!" Lawson shouted. "Last chance, Byrd."

The judge fired her seventh shot. The bullet grazed Lawson's thigh, tearing fabric and skin in a burning line. She returned fire immediately. Two shots in rapid succession. The first missed. The second struck Byrd's shoulder, spinning her backward.

The emergency lights flickered again, then died completely. Darkness consumed the tunnel. Lawson activated her phone's flashlight, sweeping the beam ahead. Blood droplets marked Byrd's retreat, disappearing around a corner.

"Richardson?" Lawson called.

"Still breathing." His voice sounded strained. "Arm wound. Through and through. Keep moving. Don't lose her."

Lawson advanced carefully, following the blood trail. The tunnel opened into a larger chamber with brick arches supporting the ceiling. Ancient wooden crates lined the walls, remnants from Prohibition storage. A metal ladder rose through a shaft in the ceiling at the chamber's center.

Byrd stood beside the ladder, one hand pressed against her wounded shoulder. Blood soaked her expensive suit jacket, dripping onto the stone floor. Her weapon dangled uselessly in her other hand.

"End of the line," Lawson said, training her weapon on the judge's chest.

Byrd smiled without warmth. "The beginning of your education, Detective."

"Drop the gun."

The chamber's shadows shifted as flashlight beams probed from the tunnel entrance. Federal agents approaching, voices echoing through stone passages. Seconds remaining before the confrontation expanded beyond their control.

Byrd raised her weapon suddenly, aiming not at Lawson but at Richardson who had just appeared at the chamber entrance. With her eighth and final shot, she fired.

Two gunshots thundered through the chamber. Lawson discharged her weapon from training rather than will. Byrd's final bullet found its mark as Lawson's shot struck the judge center mass. The judge collapsed against the ladder, weapon clattering onto stone.

Richardson staggered backward, fresh blood spreading across his chest. The bullet had struck him over the heart, a mortal wound without immediate medical attention.

"Tom!" Lawson caught him as he fell. His weight dragged them both to the ground. Blood soaked through his shirt, hot against her supporting arm.

Federal agents swarmed into the chamber, weapons sweeping for threats. Agent Morrison led the team, assessing the scene with tactical efficiency.

"Two down! Need medical immediately!" he shouted into his radio.

Richardson gripped Lawson's arm with fading strength.

Medics rushed into the chamber, equipment bags in hand. They moved directly to Richardson, whose vital signs deteriorated visibly. Byrd lay motionless against the ladder, beyond saving.

Medics pushed Lawson aside, beginning emergency procedures. Blood soaked the stone beneath Richardson's body. His eyes remained fixed on hers as life ebbed from them.

"Case closes tonight," he managed before consciousness left him.

Agent Morrison led Lawson away as medical teams fought to stabilize Richardson for transport, the outcome already clear in the medics' expressions and frantic movements.

"Complete statement required," Morrison said. "Once you're medically cleared."

Lawson nodded mechanically, watching over her shoulder as Richardson's life drained onto centuries-old stone beneath a judge's estate.

Five years of investigation ended in underground darkness. Justice delivered through bullets and personal vengeance rather than judicial process.

chapter
thirty-five

WHITE HOSPITAL CORRIDORS stretched in sterile uniformity. Lawson navigated through them, guided by the nurse's directions. Critical Care Unit, third floor, Room 307. Richardson had survived surgery but remained in critical condition. The bullet had punctured his right lung and nicked an artery. Three hours of emergency procedures had stabilized him enough to transfer from operating room to recovery.

She paused outside his door. Through the narrow window, monitors blinked and recorded vital statistics in green. Richardson looked diminished against white sheets, tubes and wires connecting him to machines that sustained what his body could no longer manage alone.

The guard stationed outside nodded at her approach. Federal, not local police. The distinction mattered now that department corruption stood exposed. No one knew how deep Byrd's influence reached, how many officers still carried loyalty to the dead judge. Federal protection ensured Richardson lived long enough to testify.

"Agent Morrison cleared you for ten minutes." The guard checked his watch. "Doctor says he's conscious but heavily medicated. Don't expect much clarity."

Lawson pushed through the door. The antiseptic smell hit her first, then the rhythmic beeping of cardiac monitors. Richardson's eyes opened at her approach, recognition flickering across features gray with pain and medication.

"Erin." Her first name, not her rank. The formality that had defined their relationship for years stripped away by circumstance.

She pulled a chair to his bedside. "Doctor says the surgery went well."

"Doctors lie to comfort the dying." Richardson's voice emerged as a dry rasp, a shadow of his commanding tone. "I've got maybe hours. Internal bleeding they can't completely stop."

"You should rest. Save your strength."

Richardson's hand moved toward the morphine pump controlling his pain medication. He pressed the button to decrease the flow rather than increase it. "Need clarity. Need you to know everything before I'm gone."

The movement took visible effort. Sweat beaded across his forehead despite the room's chill. The decision to reduce pain medication for lucidity spoke to whatever urgency drove him.

"Listen carefully." He shifted, wincing as tubes pulled against his movement. "There's a safety deposit box at Savannah Trust Bank. Key taped under my desk drawer at home. Box contains everything about Monica's case. Everything I didn't tell you before."

"The FBI investigation records?"

"More than that." His breathing became shallow, each word measured against available oxygen. "My personal records. Things that never entered official files."

Lawson leaned closer. The cardiac monitor showed increased heart rate. "Richardson, whatever confession you're planning can wait until you recover."

"No recovery coming." His certainty carried absolute conviction. "I need you to understand what happened. Why it happened. The truth Monica died for."

She recognized the determination in his expression. The same stubbornness that had driven his career now focused on unburdening his conscience before death claimed him. Fighting him would waste precious energy he clearly intended to spend regardless of her protests.

"I'm listening."

"I recruited Monica for the FBI operation. Spotted her potential during her first year in Homicide. Smart. Detailed. Incorruptible." Pride colored his words despite his weakened state. "The Bureau needed someone inside who could document judicial corruption without raising suspicion. She volunteered immediately."

"That part I understand," Lawson said. "What I don't understand is why you concealed her status after her death. Why you redirected the investigation away from Byrd."

Richardson's fingers tightened on the sheet. "Because I killed her."

Lawson almost stood up, the shock hit her so hard. Three syllables that rewrote five years of history. The cardiac monitor registered Richardson's distress in accelerated beeping.

"Explain." The word emerged through clenched teeth.

"Monica discovered Byrd's connection to Thomas Hutchinson faster than anticipated. Started gathering evidence independently, outside approved channels." Richardson's voice strengthened with his confession's momentum. "She told me she'd uncovered direct financial links. Planned to take everything to the federal prosecutor immediately."

"Why was that a problem? Wasn't that the objective?"

"The operation timeline required six more months of surveillance. Building comprehensive network mapping before arrests. Taking down not just Byrd and Hutchinson but the entire organization." His eyes locked onto hers with surprising intensity. "Monica's accelerated timeline threatened the larger operation. My FBI handler ordered containment."

"Containment," Lawson repeated, the euphemism's meaning clear.

"Special Agent Charles Drummond. Twenty-two years with Bureau organized crime division. Specialized in long-term infiltration operations. He authorized extreme measures to protect the investigation. Ordered me to neutralize the threat Monica posed through premature exposure."

"You're saying the FBI ordered her murder."

"Not in those exact words." Richardson closed his eyes briefly, gathering strength. "Drummond said 'contain the situation by any means necessary' during our secure call that night. Bureau terminology with understood implications. Plausible deniability built into the language."

Lawson's fingers dug into her palms. "So you met her at the warehouse."

"So I let Byrd think the undercover agent was Monica. She ordered the hit, and I carried it out."

Richardson's breathing grew more labored. "I arrived before you. Set up the floodlight to create momentary blindness. Positioned myself behind the equipment shed."

The scene reconstructed itself in Lawson's mind. Monica arriving, uncertain, looking for her informant. Richardson waiting in darkness. The trap already set.

"She never saw me." His voice dropped lower, forcing Lawson to lean closer. "When she stepped into the light, I took the shot. Clean trajectory through vital organs. No possibility of survival.

"You were the perfect witness. Drunk. Distracted. Grieving your fight with her." Richardson nodded slightly. "I knew you wouldn't be able to get a clear visual that night. Your statement about an unidentified shooter aligned with operational needs."

The betrayal cascaded through Lawson's body. Five years investigating her partner's murder, never suspecting the killer sat across from her at department meetings. Guided her career. Protected her from consequences while concealing his own guilt.

"Why tell me this now?"

"Because Drummond authorized Monica's death, then abandoned the operation once she died." Anger brought color to Richardson's pale cheeks. "Bureau politics. Asset loss requiring explanation. Easier to terminate the investigation than acknowledge a federal agent died under their orders."

"In that lockbox, you'll find a digital recorder. Password is Monica's badge number. I recorded every conversation with Drummond. Insurance against Bureau abandonment." Richardson's eyes darted to the door, checking for potential interruption. "Last recording proves he authorized lethal action against a federal agent, then orchestrated the cover-up to protect his career."

"Why protect me all these years? Why not let me take the fall for her death?"

"Guilt." The word emerged as barely a whisper. "I killed your partner. Watched you destroy yourself seeking justice I prevented."

"Was it you, then? That broke into my apartment and stole the only reminders I had of Monica?"

"Set up on Byrd's orders. I imagine when they do a sweep of her house, they'll be entered into evidence and you can request to have it returned to you."

The heart monitor's rhythm accelerated again. A nurse appeared in the doorway, checking readings with professional concern.

"His heart rate's elevating. He needs rest." Her tone allowed no argument.

"Two more minutes," Richardson rasped. "Critical case information."

The nurse frowned but retreated to the hallway, leaving the door partially open.

Richardson turned back to Lawson, voice dropping to ensure privacy. "The safety deposit box should have what you need to see this through. Monica's original evidence that started everything."

"Everything I needed to solve her murder five years ago." Bitterness edged her words.

"Yes." No excuse offered. No justification attempted. Just acknowledgment of the damage done.

"Did Byrd know you were a double agent?"

Richardson looked pensive. "Maybe she had her suspicions, but even if she did, neither of us could expose the other without self-destruction." Richardson's mouth twisted into a pained grimace.

The monitoring equipment registered deteriorating vital signs. Richardson's breathing grew more labored with each exchange. The confession extracted a physical cost that accumulated with each revelation.

"Drummond still works for the Bureau. Washington field office. Decorated career built on operations I helped execute." Richardson grabbed her wrist with surprising strength. "He sacrificed Monica for career preservation. Then built promotions on her grave."

"I'll find him."

"Careful. He has resources. Protection from senior Bureau leadership." Richardson released her arm, strength fading visibly. "The recording provides leverage. Use it carefully."

Footsteps approached from the hallway. Richardson's wife entered, face drawn with exhaustion and fear. Her eyes registered Lawson's presence with momentary confusion before focusing on her husband's deteriorating condition.

"Tom." Amy moved to his bedside, taking his hand.

"I was just leaving," Lawson said, standing up.

Richardson's gaze held Lawson's for a final moment. "Remember what I said about the deposit box."

She nodded and turned to walk out. She paused at the doorway, turning back toward the man who had killed her partner and then spent years protecting her from the consequences of that action.

"Do you regret it?" she asked. "Any of it?"

"All of it," Richardson choked out.

Amy stroked his forehead. "You should go now, Detective."

Lawson stepped into the hallway, mind reeling with revelations that transformed everything she thought she understood about Monica's death. The mentor who recruited her for an FBI operation. The killer who executed her when she threatened operational timelines. The true betrayal ran deeper than anything she'd imagined during five years of investigation.

Richardson's monitors keened in alarm as she walked away. Medical personnel rushed toward his room with emergency equipment. The confession had cost him whatever strength remained.

chapter
thirty-six

LAWSON GRIPPED the steering wheel a little tighter as the bank's marble facade loomed ahead, morning sunlight glinting off its glass doors like a promise of cold finality. She'd barely slept after last night's hospital vigil, the echo of Richardson's rasping confession still clawing at the edges of her mind. Claire sat in the passenger seat, scrolling through her phone with that lawyer's focus, but her silence felt heavier than usual.

"You gonna tell me what's eating at you, or do I have to guess?" Lawson asked, pulling into the visitor lot and killing the engine.

Claire set her phone down, exhaling slowly. "Hospital called while you were in the shower this morning. Richardson passed at 4:17 a.m. Internal bleeding—they couldn't stabilize him."

Claire didn't need to tell Lawson the news. She knew it was inevitable, after seeing the tubes and the gray pallor last night. The man who'd pulled the trigger on Monica was gone, his secrets now just metal and paper waiting in a vault. Lawson nodded once, swallowing the churn in her gut. "One less ghost. Let's get what he left behind."

"What about the FBI handler he mentioned?" she asked as they stepped out, keeping her voice low even in the empty lot.

"Charles Drummond exists," Claire confirmed, falling into step beside her as they crossed toward the entrance, briefcase swinging at her side. "Twenty-six years with the Bureau. Currently Assistant Director of Organized Crime Division in Washington. Decorated career. Multiple commendations for successful operations against criminal enterprises."

"Built on Monica's grave, just like he said."

"Potentially." Claire's tone stayed neutral, lawyer's caution intact. "Without evidence, it's just Richardson's deathbed accusation."

The Savannah Trust Bank lobby gleamed with marble floors and mahogany counters. Morning light streamed through tall windows, reflecting off brass fixtures and illuminating the bank's logo etched into the wall behind the teller stations. Lawson approached the service desk, badge held discreetly at her side. Claire walked beside her, the click of her heels echoing in the high-ceilinged space.

"I need access to a safety deposit box," Lawson told the clerk, a young woman with her hair pulled into a tight bun. "Thomas Richardson is the account holder."

The clerk's expression shifted to professional sympathy. "I'm sorry, ma'am, but account holders must be present for access."

Claire stepped forward, placing a document on the counter. "Federal court order authorizing access. Detective Lawson is acting as an officer of the court in an ongoing federal investigation."

The clerk examined the paperwork, eyes widening slightly as she read through the legal language. "I'll need to verify this with the manager."

"Of course," Claire said.

They waited in silence while the clerk disappeared into a glass-walled office at the back of the lobby. Through the transparent walls, they watched the manager review the documents, make a phone call, then nod.

The manager emerged, a tall man with silver-streaked hair and a tailored suit. "Detective Lawson, Ms. Stevens. I understand you have a court order for Mr. Richardson's safety deposit box."

"That's correct," Lawson said.

Walsh nodded. "We'll need to document this access thoroughly. Please follow me to the vault area."

They followed him through a doorway that required both keycard and biometric access. The temperature dropped several degrees as they entered the vault corridor, the air conditioning maintaining the climate-controlled environment necessary for document preservation.

They reached the vault entrance where another employee waited with a signature log. Lawson signed the registry, documenting time and date of access. The bank employee used his key to open the outer vault door, revealing walls lined with numbered metal boxes of various sizes.

"Box 413," Walsh said, consulting the paperwork. "You'll need the customer key."

Lawson produced the key she'd retrieved from Richardson's home earlier that morning. Amy had been surprisingly cooperative, guiding her directly to the desk where Richardson had hidden it. Whether from grief or guilt, she'd asked no questions about its purpose.

The employee inserted his key into one lock while Lawson used Richardson's key in the other. Both turned simultaneously, and the drawer slid open with a metallic groan. Inside rested a rectangular steel container, approximately eighteen inches long and twelve inches wide.

"You can use Room 3," Walsh said, indicating a private viewing room off the main vault. "I'll be stationed outside should you need anything."

The viewing room contained a simple table and four chairs. No windows, no cameras. Complete privacy for customers examining their valuables. Lawson placed the container on the table as Claire closed the door behind them.

Lawson lifted the lid of the box, revealing meticulously organized contents. Multiple USB drives labeled by date. Manila folders with color-coded tabs. A portable hard drive secured in padded casing. Several small digital voice recorders.

"He prepared this thoroughly," Claire observed. "Everything cataloged and dated."

Lawson removed the first folder, labeled "FBI OPERATION: INITIAL DOCUMENTS." Inside she found official Bureau paperwork establishing Operation Harbor Justice, an undercover investigation into judicial corruption in the Southern District of Georgia. Monica's name appeared on the third page, listed as a recruited asset with Richardson as her handler. Both signatures at the bottom, dated five years and seven months ago.

"This confirms the operation existed," Claire said, examining the documents. "And that Monica worked for them."

"And that Richardson lied to me for years about knowing her involvement." Lawson set the folder aside and lifted the next one.

This folder contained surveillance photographs. Monica meeting with Richardson at locations away from the department. Monica photographing evidence in the warehouse basement. Monica sitting in her car outside Judge Byrd's residence, documenting visitors who arrived after midnight.

The third folder held financial records. Bank statements showing transfers between accounts controlled by Thomas Hutchinson and Judge Byrd. Offshore holdings under shell company names. Property purchases made through intermediaries that connected back to both Byrd and various criminal defendants whose cases she had dismissed.

Lawson moved methodically through the physical evidence, absorbing information that validated everything Richardson had confessed. The operation existed. Monica worked for the FBI. Byrd's corruption extended exactly as Richardson had described.

Claire inserted one of the USB drives into her laptop. "This appears to be Monica's personal case file. Notes on her investigation. Observations about department personnel she suspected were involved."

Lawson leaned over to view the screen. Monica's meticulous documentation methodology appeared in detailed spreadsheets and carefully structured reports. The organizational style Lawson had admired during their partnership now revealed as Bureau-trained investigative technique rather than personal habit.

"She documented Richardson's unusual behavior in the weeks before her death," Claire said, scrolling through a text document. "Noted that he seemed increasingly concerned about her timeline. Questioned whether he might be compromised."

"She suspected him?"

"Not of working against the operation. She worried he might be under pressure from someone in the Bureau to slow the investigation." Claire continued reading. "She references 'D' several times. Must be Drummond."

Lawson opened another folder, this one labeled "DEPARTMENT

CORRUPTION - ACTIVE." Inside were detailed files on individual officers, including financial records and surveillance photos. She flipped through several before stopping at a thick subfolder labeled "HUTCHINSON, RAY - NARCOTICS."

"Claire, look at this." She spread the contents across the table.

The file contained Ray Hutchinson's legitimate investigation into evidence tampering. Meticulous documentation of drugs that disappeared from evidence lockup. Financial records showing mysterious cash deposits into officers' accounts. Witness statements about pressure to alter testimony. Everything organized with the same methodical approach Monica had used.

"Ray was investigating the same corruption network," Claire said, scanning the documents. "Not participating in it."

"He was building a case against evidence tampering in Narcotics. Had been for months." Lawson found a handwritten note in Monica's writing: *Ray discovered the warehouse storage operation. Plans to go to Internal Affairs next week. Needs protection.*

"Monica was trying to protect him," Claire realized.

Lawson continued through Ray's file, finding recordings of conversations with witnesses, photos of evidence lockers, financial analysis of the money trail. "He was clean. Just like Bram Kowalski. Another honest cop who got too close to the truth."

At the bottom of the folder lay a sealed envelope marked "URGENT - CHIEF WALLACE." Inside, Lawson found a handwritten memo from Drummond to Wallace dated three days after the podcast interview revealed Ray's "relationship" with Monica.

Hutchinson interview compromised operational security. Subject has documentation linking warehouse storage to evidence tampering. Recommend immediate containment. Suicide scenario provides closure for Landry case while eliminating threat. Your authority to execute and control scene investigation.

"Drummond ordered Ray's death," Lawson said, her voice hollow. "Gave Wallace the blueprint to stage it as suicide."

Claire read the memo over her shoulder. "And Wallace had the authority to ensure the investigation would be superficial."

They found more documents detailing the plan. Wallace's access to

Ray's apartment. Instructions for staging the scene. Even contingency plans if the initial investigation revealed inconsistencies.

"The fake confession note served dual purposes," Lawson said. "Closed Monica's case while eliminating another threat to their operation."

Lawson connected the portable hard drive to Claire's laptop. Password protection appeared on screen. She entered Monica's badge number as Richardson had instructed. The drive unlocked, revealing hundreds of audio files organized by date.

"Richardson recorded everything," Lawson said, scanning the files. "Every conversation with the Bureau. Every meeting with Monica. Every interaction with Byrd after Monica's death."

She selected a file dated three days before Monica died. Richardson's voice emerged from the laptop speakers.

"The asset is moving too quickly. Timeline compression threatens operational security."

Another voice responded. Deeper. East Coast accent. "How much does she have?"

"Enough to connect Byrd directly to Hutchinson. Financial records. Meeting documentation. Witness statements from court personnel."

"That's not sufficient for full network exposure. We need the entire organization, not just two principals."

"She's planning to take everything to the federal prosecutor next week. Says she can't wait any longer."

A pause on the recording. "Contain the situation, Tom. By any means necessary."

"Charles, are you authorizing what I think you are?"

"I'm authorizing operational security measures appropriate to the threat level. How you implement those measures remains at your discretion as field handler."

"That's Bureau double-talk, and you know it."

"It's protection for both of us, Tom. The operation cannot be compromised. Asset control falls under your direct authority. Handle it."

The recording ended. Lawson and Claire sat in silence, absorbing the implications.

"That's Drummond authorizing Monica's murder," Lawson said finally.

"In carefully ambiguous language that maintains plausible deniability," Claire noted.

Lawson selected another file, dated the day after Monica's death.

"It's done." Richardson's voice, flat and empty. "Asset neutralized. Operation compromised."

"Any witnesses?" Drummond asked.

"Her partner arrived early. Saw nothing clearly. Intoxicated and emotionally compromised due to previous personal conflict with the asset."

"Perfect. Local investigation will handle cleanup. Bureau involvement remains confidential under national security protocols."

"What about the evidence she collected?"

"Secure it. All of it. Nothing goes to the prosecutor. Nothing enters official channels."

"She died for this case, Charles."

"She died because she refused to follow operational timeline parameters. Asset loss is unfortunate but ultimately self-inflicted through protocol violation."

"Jesus, that's cold."

"It's realistic, Tom. The Bureau cannot afford public exposure of an agent's death during unauthorized investigative acceleration. Secure the evidence. Sanitize the scene. Maintain cover going forward."

Lawson selected another file, dated two weeks before Monica's death. Richardson's voice, strained and reluctant.

"The financial irregularities are in place. Regular deposits to her account that match the pattern we use for documenting bribes from criminal informants."

"Good," Drummond's voice replied. *"If the operation goes sideways, she'll look like any other dirty cop taking money from dealers."*

"Charles, she's clean. She's never taken a dime from anyone."

"That's the point, Tom. Clean cops who get too close to the truth need to look dirty when they die. Creates reasonable doubt about their credibility. Makes their evidence questionable."

"You want me to destroy her reputation posthumously?"

"I want you to protect the operation. If Monica Landry dies looking like a corrupt detective, no one will take her investigation seriously. Her evidence becomes the desperate accusations of a dirty cop trying to save herself."

Richardson's long pause before responding. "The deposits are already showing on her statements. She hasn't noticed yet, but her partner will when they investigate her death."

"Perfect. Let Detective Lawson discover that her beloved partner was just another corrupt cop. It'll destroy her credibility if she tries to continue Monica's work."

Lawson stopped the recording. The confirmation of everything Richardson had confessed at the hospital was now preserved in digital clarity.

"This demolishes Drummond's career," Claire said. "Authorizing the murder of a federal agent, then covering it up. Criminal conspiracy at the highest levels of the FBI."

"And it vindicates both Monica and Ray. Proves they were honest cops who died trying to expose corruption."

They continued through the remaining evidence. More recordings documenting Richardson's careful accumulation of evidence against both Byrd and Drummond over the five years following Monica's death. His own confession to the murder, recorded six months ago and stored alongside the other files. Medical records showing his recent cancer diagnosis, explaining his accelerated timeline for exposing the truth before natural death claimed him.

"What are you going to do with all this?" Claire asked as they returned the materials to the container.

Lawson closed the lid, sealing five years of deception and betrayal inside. "I'm resigning from the force. Effective immediately."

"And the evidence?"

"I need time. Time to process everything. Get my life together. Five months sober before this all exploded. Need to maintain that while I figure out what comes next."

"This evidence could collapse half the legal system in Savannah." Claire gestured toward the container. "Federal investigation into Bureau corruption. Criminal prosecution of high-ranking FBI personnel. Civil suits from everyone convicted through Byrd's court."

"I know." Lawson stood, lifting the container from the table. "That's why I'm giving it to someone better equipped to handle it than me."

"Who?"

"Someone who knows how to tell this story the right way. Someone who almost died trying to expose the truth."

Claire nodded in understanding. "Blackwell."

"She's already got an audience of millions. Public platform that can't be easily silenced or buried in bureaucracy."

"What about Drummond? He'll come after this evidence the moment he realizes it exists."

"Let him try." Lawson's eyes hardened. "Monica and Ray both deserve justice. Real justice, not the kind Byrd claimed to deliver. Not the kind the Bureau buried to protect careers."

They left the viewing room, signed the necessary documentation confirming their access to the box, and walked through the bank's marble lobby toward the entrance. Morning sunlight streamed through the glass doors ahead, illuminating their path forward.

Truth no longer needed vaults or whispers. It needed sunlight, and Lawson knew exactly who could provide it.

dead air episode 7:

"Final Transmission"

[Somber electronic theme music fades in, then quiets]

LEAH BLACKWELL: This is Dead Air. I'm Leah Blackwell. Today's episode marks the conclusion of our investigation into Detective Monica Landry's murder.

Five years ago, a dedicated officer died pursuing truth. Her investigation into judicial corruption cost her life. For five years, that truth remained buried beneath fabricated evidence, redirected investigations, and institutional silence.

No more.

[Brief pause]

I've spent the past week recovering from my own encounter with the forces that silenced Detective Landry. Many of you witnessed my abduction during our live broadcast. That experience gave me firsthand insight into how far certain individuals would go to maintain their secrets.

Today, I can reveal the complete truth about what happened to Monica Landry and the systematic corruption she uncovered. This account is supported by evidence secured in multiple locations, now in the hands of federal prosecutors.

[Sound of shuffling papers]

Let's start with the most recent development. Thomas Hutchinson, senior partner at Hutchinson & Associates, is currently in federal custody. Contrary to reports that he fled the country with me as his hostage, Hutchinson boarded his private jet with a hired decoy—a young woman of similar build wearing my clothing and kept sedated during transport.

This deception was orchestrated by Judge Elizabeth Byrd to create the impression I had been taken out of the country, diverting attention from my actual location in her pool house, where I was held under sedation until rescued by federal agents.

[Brief pause]

The federal warrant for Thomas Hutchinson's arrest details his role in orchestrating his brother Ray's murder, staging it as a suicide after Ray threatened to expose their criminal enterprise. Ray, contrary to his statements, never had a romantic relationship with Monica. Rather, he used it as a cover so that he could assist her in her investigation into the Rafferty case. If they were having a romantic relationship, it made sense for them to spend time together, at least that's what he figured.

So, who killed Ray Hutchinson? Who falsified the suicide note claiming responsibility for Monica Landry's death?

Because Ray Hutchinson didn't kill Monica Landry.

[Music intensifies]

The truth is far more disturbing. Monica Landry and Ray Hutchinson were both killed by former Captain Thomas Richardson under orders from his FBI handler.

This revelation comes directly from Richardson's deathbed confession to Detective Erin Lawson, recorded in its entirety and verified by federal investigators. Richardson admitted to recruiting Monica Landry for an FBI operation investigating judicial corruption. What she discovered threatened not just local officials but reached into the federal agencies themselves.

[Audio clip plays] **RICHARDSON:** "Monica was supposed to gather evidence slowly. Build comprehensive documentation over years. But she discovered Thomas Hutchinson's connection to Byrd. Couldn't resist moving quickly once she understood the scope."

[Brief pause]

When Monica accelerated her timeline without authorization, Richardson received containment orders from FBI Special Agent

Charles Drummond. Under the guise of protecting operational security, Drummond authorized lethal action against a federal asset.

Richardson executed those orders personally. He arrived at the warehouse before Detective Lawson, set up the floodlight to create momentary blindness, and took the shot when Monica stepped into the illumination.

[Music shifts to more somber tone]

For five years, Richardson protected Detective Lawson from suspicion while concealing his own guilt. He removed evidence that might have revealed the truth. Redirected investigations away from judicial corruption. Maintained the appearance of pursuing justice while actively obstructing it.

This deception extended beyond Richardson to Judge Elizabeth Byrd, who used her judicial authority to manipulate cases and protect Thomas Hutchinson's criminal network. The evidence Monica Landry discovered before her death revealed a systematic corruption operation that reached from street-level enforcement through the highest levels of Savannah's judicial system.

[Music intensifies briefly]

Judge Byrd died during the federal raid that secured my release. Thomas Hutchinson faces multiple federal charges for racketeering, conspiracy, and his role in his brother's murder. FBI Assistant Director Charles Drummond has been suspended pending investigation into his authorization of lethal action against Monica Landry.

[Brief pause]

Detective Erin Lawson has resigned from the Savannah Police Department. Her statement, which she's permitted me to share, reads in part:

[Reading from document] "I can no longer serve within a system I no longer trust. Monica died seeking truth about corruption that reached into the highest levels of our justice system. Her courage deserves more than resignation, but it's what I can offer while I rebuild my life and honor her memory."

[Brief pause]

For listeners wondering about my own connection to this case—why I pursued it with such determination—I can finally acknowledge what some have suspected. Monica Landry was my cousin. We grew up together before our paths diverged—she to law enforcement, me to law. When the official investigation stalled, I used the tools available to me to seek the truth she died for.

[Music shifts to resolution theme]

The evidence Monica gathered five years ago has now resulted in twenty-seven indictments across Savannah's justice system. Officers who facilitated evidence tampering. Court personnel who manipulated case assignments. Judges who dismissed cases in exchange for financial considerations.

The system that failed Monica Landry is being dismantled and rebuilt. The corruption she discovered is being excised through federal intervention and legislative reform. The truth she died for has finally emerged.

[Brief pause]

I want to thank the sources who risked careers and personal safety to help expose this corruption. Detective Lawson, whose persistence despite personal cost kept this case alive. Rachel Banks, who never stopped asking questions about her sister's death. And the federal agents who ultimately secured justice when local institutions failed.

[Music builds toward conclusion]

Most importantly, I want to acknowledge Detective Monica Landry. She recognized corruption others missed. Pursued truth when easier paths existed. Maintained her integrity in a system designed to compromise it. Her sacrifice ultimately forced accountability upon those who considered themselves beyond the reach of justice.

[Final pause]

This is Leah Blackwell. This has been Dead Air. The truth doesn't stay buried forever.

[Theme music plays out completely]

chapter
thirty-seven

CARDBOARD BOXES COVERED every surface in Lawson's apartment. Each labeled in black marker: KITCHEN, BOOKS, CLOTHES, DONATE. The place she'd called home for eight years now lay dismantled into categorized containers waiting for their next destination. Florida, probably. Her mother had been suggesting it for years. Warm weather. Fresh start. No ghosts.

Lawson taped another box closed, the ripping sound echoing in the half-empty living room. The walls looked strange with picture hooks but no frames. Bare patches where furniture had protected the paint from years of sunlight. Evidence of a life being erased.

The kitchen counter looked bare without her badge and gun. She'd turned them in yesterday during a brief, awkward meeting with the interim chief. Her resignation letter had been concise. No dramatic explanations or accusations. Just the simple truth that she could no longer serve within a system she no longer trusted. The knock at her door came right on time.

Claire stood in the hallway, having traded her suit for more casual attire. She balanced two coffee cups on top of a bakery box.

"Breakfast," she announced, sweeping past Lawson into the apartment. "You can't pack on an empty stomach."

Lawson cleared space on the counter, moving aside the mail she hadn't bothered opening all week. "You didn't have to bring food."

"Yes, I did. Your refrigerator's empty. I checked yesterday."

The pastry box revealed cinnamon rolls topped with thick frosting. Claire had remembered her weakness for sugar, another detail that made their friendship both comforting and occasionally annoying. The woman noticed everything.

"How's Leah's podcast doing?" Lawson asked, accepting the coffee cup Claire offered.

"Five million downloads of the Richardson confession episode." Claire placed a roll on a paper towel and handed it to Lawson. "FBI Director issued a formal statement this morning announcing Drummond's suspension pending internal investigation."

"Suspension. Not arrest."

"Give it time. Federal bureaucracy moves slowly, but the evidence is overwhelming."

The evidence. Richardson's meticulous documentation now in Blackwell's possession, released through carefully structured podcast episodes. Each revelation more damaging than the last. The Bureau's authorized execution of its own agent. The subsequent cover-up. The systematic corruption of Savannah's justice system.

"Chief Wallace's arraignment is Tuesday," Claire continued. "Federal charges for conspiracy and obstruction. Prosecutors expect him to start naming names in exchange for leniency."

Lawson bit into the cinnamon roll without answering. Sweet food that tasted like nothing. Another side effect of grief she'd never quite shaken.

"Let's finish Monica's boxes," she said after swallowing. "I promised her sister the last of her things by tonight."

Monica's belongings occupied the bedroom that had functioned as Lawson's home office. Boxes Rachel had stored after the funeral, retrieved from the storage unit a week ago. Clothing Lawson couldn't bring herself to donate. Books with Monica's notes in the margins.

They worked in companionable silence, with Claire sorting through paperwork, and Lawson handling the more personal items. A jewelry box containing the simple silver pieces Monica had favored. Photo albums from her academy days. Birthday cards from her family.

Lawson picked up a framed photograph from Monica's dresser—

the two of them at Forsyth Park fountain, arms around each other's shoulders, both grinning at the camera. It had been taken during their first month as partners, before everything became complicated by feelings neither wanted to acknowledge.

As she lifted it to place in the box, the frame felt heavier than expected. She turned it over and noticed the backing was slightly loose. Working her fingernail under the edge, she pried it open.

A folded paper slipped out from behind the photograph. Lawson opened it to find a letter on department letterhead. Dated one week before Monica died. Addressed to Lawson but never delivered.

Erin,

I'm writing this knowing I might never find the courage to give it to you. We haven't spoken in two weeks. The silence between us has become its own presence, something living and growing with each day we avoid each other.

I need to tell you the truth. Not about us—you already know how I feel there. The truth about my work. About what I've been doing these past two years.

I'm not just a detective. I've been working with the FBI, gathering evidence of corruption within our justice system. Judges. Prosecutors. Fellow officers. It started as something small, a favor for Richardson, who recruited me. It's grown into something that consumes every part of my life.

I've discovered things that change everything we thought we knew about Savannah's legal system. Evidence that will shatter careers and rewrite everything we've built our lives around.

I'm turning everything over to federal prosecutors next week. After that, nothing will be the same. My career here will be over.

I want you to come with me. Leave Savannah. Start somewhere new together. Somewhere we don't have to hide what we are to each other. Somewhere without the weight of badges and departmental politics and corruption that seeps into everything.

I know it's asking too much. I know your career matters. I know we left things broken between us. But I can't do this alone anymore.

I'll explain everything. If you still want nothing to do with me afterward, I'll understand.

I love you. I've never stopped.
Monica

The letter trembled in Lawson's hands. She sat heavily on a nearby box, legs suddenly unable to support her weight.

"Erin?" Claire looked up from the book she'd been examining. "What is it?"

"She was going to leave." The words scraped Lawson's throat. "She wanted us to go together."

Claire moved beside her, reading the letter over Lawson's shoulder. She placed a gentle hand on Lawson's back but said nothing. There were no words adequate for this moment.

"I never knew." Lawson's voice cracked. "All this time, I thought our fight was the end. That she died angry with me."

"She loved you," Claire said simply. "That's clear."

Lawson looked down at the photograph still in her lap—the fountain where she'd searched futilely for Monica's "insurance policy" weeks ago. The realization hit her like a physical blow.

"Our place," she whispered. "The insurance policy she mentioned in her journal. She didn't mean evidence about the case. She meant this—us. Our relationship. Our future together."

She held up the letter, her voice strengthening with understanding. "She hid this behind our photo because she knew if something happened to her, I'd eventually find it. The real insurance policy wasn't about Rafferty or corruption. It was about giving me permission to leave. To start over somewhere new, just like she wanted us to do together."

The tears came without warning. Five years of compartmentalized grief finally breaking through. Lawson bent forward, the letter clutched against her chest, body shaking with sobs she could no longer contain.

Claire kept her hand on Lawson's back. Silent support without attempting to fix what couldn't be fixed. Understanding that some wounds required acknowledgment rather than comfort.

When the worst of the storm passed, Lawson straightened and wiped her face with her sleeve. "Sorry."

"Don't apologize for grieving."

"Five years late."

"Grief doesn't follow schedules." Claire took the letter gently and refolded it. "You needed to find the truth first. Now you can finally mourn."

A knock interrupted their conversation. Lawson checked her watch—1:15 p.m. Leah Blackwell stood in the hallway, laptop bag slung over one shoulder. Her bruises had faded to yellow shadows across her cheekbones. She'd cut her hair shorter since leaving the hospital.

"Come in," Lawson said, stepping back to allow her entry. "We're just sorting through the last of Monica's things."

Blackwell entered cautiously. Despite multiple meetings since Byrd's death, tension remained between them. Professional respect mixed with mutual wariness. Too much had happened for immediate trust, despite their shared purpose.

"Claire." Blackwell nodded. "Good to see you."

"How's the podcast?" Claire asked.

"Breaking download records." Blackwell set her laptop bag on the counter. "FBI Director issued a formal statement this morning. Drummond's suspended pending investigation."

"So we heard."

Blackwell surveyed the boxes stacked around the apartment. "Moving?"

"Florida," Lawson admitted. "Mom's been after me to move closer for years."

"Fresh start." Blackwell nodded. "Can't blame you. Savannah carries too many ghosts now."

An awkward silence settled between them. Blackwell shifted her weight, eyes darting toward Monica's photograph still hanging on the wall.

Lawson studied her face, the weight of that final podcast episode still fresh in her mind—the raw edge in Blackwell's voice when she'd finally laid it bare. "I listened to the episode last night. Hearing you say it out loud ... about Monica being family. That she wasn't just a case to you. Why wait so long to put that on the table? All those months digging, and you kept it locked down like it was just another source."

Blackwell's fingers tightened around the handle of her laptop bag, her jaw working for a beat before she met Lawson's gaze head-on. "Journalism 101—don't let the personal bleed into the story until the facts demand it. But yeah ... it was her. Second cousin. Our mothers were first cousins. We grew up thick as thieves, summers at the same lake house until we were teenagers and life pulled us different ways."

"Monica never mentioned a cousin gunning for law school, let alone one who'd turn podcaster." Lawson's tone softened the edge, curiosity edging out the old wariness.

"I wasn't that yet when she died. Still buried in casebooks and caffeine." Blackwell reached into her bag and pulled out a worn photograph, the edges soft from handling. "This was us, summer before she joined the academy. Proof she wasn't always the one with the badge."

The image showed younger versions of both women, arms around each other's shoulders at a lakeside cookout. The family resemblance obvious now that Lawson knew to look for it—the same jawline, similar eyes.

"You hid this connection during your investigation."

"I had to. A journalist investigating family murders becomes a human-interest story, not serious reporting." Blackwell tucked the photo away. "The evidence needed to stand on its own merits, not filtered through emotional family connections."

"Understandable." Lawson's response came easier than expected. "I probably wouldn't have trusted you if I'd known."

"Still. I misrepresented myself. Used you as content when you were grieving."

"You got justice when the system failed. That's what matters in the end."

Blackwell reached into her bag and extracted a manila folder. "I brought something. From my mother's collection. Family photos Monica might not have shared with you."

The folder contained photographs Lawson had never seen. Monica as a teenager, laughing at a family picnic. Monica in a graduation cap, standing beside a younger version of Blackwell. Monica at a family wedding, radiant in a bridesmaid dress.

"Thank you," Lawson said simply.

"My mother wanted you to have them. She said Monica talked about you. Said you made her happy."

The statement opened fresh wounds just beginning to scab over. Lawson nodded, unable to formulate an adequate response.

"Erin found this," Claire said, breaking the moment. She handed Blackwell the letter.

Blackwell read it, expression softening as she absorbed Monica's final words to Lawson. "She was planning to leave law enforcement."

"Like me. Too late."

"Not too late to honor what she wanted." Blackwell returned the letter. "A fresh start somewhere. Living honestly."

"After your story concludes."

"I don't think I'll be airing another episode of Silence in Savannah, actually. Drummond wouldn't return my request for comment, and the Bureau's going to take some time to make structural changes to prevent similar corruption."

"Where do you think you'll head next, then?" Lawson asked.

"D.C. for a new series. Maybe they won't volunteer the statements I asked for, but that doesn't mean I should stop pushing on what we as Americans deserve."

"Which is?" Claire chimed in.

"Transparency. Honesty from our public officials." She turned to Lawson. "Would you consider a brief statement? For the opening episode?"

Lawson hesitated. "What kind of statement?"

"Your perspective on justice. On Monica's legacy. On moving forward after learning the system failed both of you."

The request shouldn't have surprised her. Blackwell remained a journalist despite their newfound understanding.

"I'll think about it."

Claire glanced at her watch. "I should go. Court prep waiting at home."

Blackwell nodded. "I should leave too. Just wanted to drop off those photos."

"Stay," Lawson said, surprising herself. "Both of you. There's something I want to show you."

She retrieved a bottle from the kitchen cabinet. Sparkling water, not the bourbon that would have occupied that space six months ago. Three glasses joined it on the counter.

"A toast," she explained at their questioning looks. "To Monica. To justice finally delivered. To what comes next."

They raised their glasses.

"To Monica," they said together.

epilogue

SUNLIGHT GLINTED off the Gulf of Mexico, painting the water in shimmering gold as Lawson drove along the coastal highway. Palm trees swayed in the gentle breeze, their fronds casting dappled shadows across her windshield. The radio played quietly, background noise until the news bulletin caught her attention.

"...final vote on the Judicial Accountability Act passed the Senate today. The bill, inspired by the Savannah corruption scandal exposed last year, creates independent oversight for judicial conduct and sentencing patterns. Senator Michaels called it 'the most significant reform to our justice system in decades.'"

Lawson turned up the volume.

"In related news, former FBI Assistant Director Charles Drummond received a twenty-year sentence for his role in the murder of federal agent Monica Landry. Prosecutors credited podcast journalist Leah Blackwell's investigation with providing key evidence that led to the conviction."

The announcer continued: "Lieutenant Eli Parks has been appointed to head Savannah PD's newly reformed Internal Affairs division, tasked with implementing the transparency measures recommended by federal investigators. Parks, who played a crucial role in exposing the corruption network, will oversee the department's restructuring under federal oversight."

Lawson smiled at that news. Parks had earned the promotion through his principled investigation when others looked the other way. The reformed department would be in good hands.

"The new protocols include mandatory body cameras, independent review boards for officer-involved incidents, and civilian oversight of internal investigations. Chief Martinez called it 'a new era of accountability and community trust.'"

The small coastal town of Cedar Key appeared around the bend. Population 702 according to the weathered welcome sign. Main Street consisted of a handful of businesses—seafood restaurant, bait shop, small grocery, sheriff's office. No traffic lights. No department stores. Nothing resembling the urban chaos of Savannah.

Lawson parked in front of the sheriff's office, a single-story building with white clapboard siding and blue trim. The American flag hung limp in the still morning air. She checked her reflection in the rearview mirror. The past year had softened the lines around her eyes. Florida sunshine had added freckles across her nose.

Sheriff Martinez waited inside, boots propped on his desk, reading glasses perched on his nose as he reviewed paperwork. He looked up at her entrance, a smile crinkling the corners of his eyes.

"Morning, Erin. Right on time."

"Morning, Joe." She settled into the chair across from him. "Got those case files you mentioned?"

He pushed a thin folder across the desk. "Just petty theft and vandalism. Nothing like your Savannah days, but we could use your insight."

"Perfect." She accepted the folder, already scanning the first page. "The quiet is exactly what I signed up for."

"Part-time consultant position's still yours if you want it." Martinez leaned back in his chair. "Three days a week. No badge, no gun, no pressure. Just that detective brain of yours helping us connect dots."

"I'll take it." The decision had already been made during her three-month trial period. Cedar Key felt right—small enough to know neighbors by name, large enough to offer privacy when needed.

Martinez extended his hand. "Welcome aboard permanently, then."

She shook it, feeling the calluses of a man who split his time between law enforcement and fishing. Honest work, both of them.

"I'll review these and have notes for you tomorrow." She stood, tucking the folder under her arm.

"No rush. Fish aren't going anywhere. Neither are small-town criminals."

Outside, the morning had fully bloomed. Shopkeepers swept sidewalks. Fishermen unloaded the day's early catch. Children pedaled bicycles toward the small public beach. Life continued in its steady, predictable rhythm.

Lawson climbed back into her car, setting the folder on the passenger seat. The photograph on her dashboard caught the sunlight—her and Monica at the academy graduation, arms around each other's shoulders, futures bright with possibility. She'd kept it in a drawer for years. Now it rode with her daily, memory without pain.

The changes Monica died trying to make were finally happening. Judicial oversight. Law enforcement accountability. Systemic reforms triggered by one woman's determination to expose corruption, carried forward by those who survived to tell her story.

Parks would ensure those changes took root in Savannah. A good man rebuilding a broken system from within.

Lawson started the engine, glancing once more at the photograph before pulling away from the curb. "We did it, Mon," she murmured.

She drove toward her small beachfront cottage, windows down to catch the salt breeze. New case. New town. New beginning.

The dead could rest. The living must continue.

Join the LT Ryan reader family & receive a free copy of the Alex Hayes story, *Trial by Fire*. Click the link below to get started:
https://ltryan.com/alex-hayes-newsletter-signup-1

savannah shadows series

Echos of Guilt
The Silence Before
Dead Air

also by l.t. ryan

Find All of L.T. Ryan's Books on Amazon Today!

The Jack Noble Series
The Recruit (free)
The First Deception (Prequel 1)
Noble Beginnings
A Deadly Distance
Ripple Effect (Bear Logan)
Thin Line
Noble Intentions
When Dead in Greece
Noble Retribution
Noble Betrayal
Never Go Home
Beyond Betrayal (Clarissa Abbot)
Noble Judgment
Never Cry Mercy

Deadline

End Game

Noble Ultimatum

Noble Legend

Noble Revenge

Never Look Back

Bear Logan Series

Ripple Effect

Blowback

Take Down

Deep State

Bear & Mandy Logan Series

Close to Home

Under the Surface

The Last Stop

Over the Edge

Between the Lies

Caught in the Web

The Marked Daughter

Beneath the Frozen Sky

Rachel Hatch Series

Drift

Downburst

Fever Burn

Smoke Signal

Firewalk

Whitewater

Aftershock

Whirlwind

Tsunami

Fastrope

Sidewinder

Redaction

Mirage

Faultline

Switchback

Mitch Tanner Series

The Depth of Darkness

Into The Darkness

Deliver Us From Darkness

Cassie Quinn Series

Path of Bones

Whisper of Bones

Symphony of Bones

Etched in Shadow

Concealed in Shadow

Betrayed in Shadow

Born from Ashes

Return to Ashes

Risen from Ashes

Into the Light

Blake Brier Series

Unmasked

Unleashed

Uncharted

Drawpoint

Contrail

Detachment

Clear

Quarry

Dalton Savage Series

Savage Grounds

Scorched Earth

Cold Sky

The Frost Killer

Crimson Moon

Dust Devil

Savage Season

Maddie Castle Series

The Handler

Tracking Justice

Hunting Grounds

Vanished Trails

Smoldering Lies

Field of Bones

Beneath the Grove

Disappearing Act

Affliction Z Series

Affliction Z: Patient Zero

Affliction Z: Abandoned Hope

Affliction Z: Descended in Blood

Affliction Z : Fractured Part 1

Affliction Z: Fractured Part 2 (Coming Soon)

Alex Hayes Series

Trial By Fire (Prequel)

Fractured Verdict

11th Hour Witness

Buried Testimony

The Bishop's Recusal

The Silent Gavel

Stella LaRosa Series

Black Rose

Red Ink

Black Gold

White Lies

Silver Bullet

Avril Dahl Series

Cold Reckoning

Cold Legacy

Cold Mercy

Savannah Shadows Series

Echoes of Guilt

The Silence Before

Dead Air

Receive a free copy of The Recruit. Visit:

https://ltryan.com/jack-noble-newsletter-signup-1

about the authors

L.T. RYAN is a *Wall Street Journal* and *USA Today* bestselling author, renowned for crafting pulse-pounding thrillers that keep readers on the edge of their seats. Known for creating gripping, character-driven stories, Ryan is the author of the *Jack Noble* series, the *Rachel Hatch* series, and more. With a knack for blending action, intrigue, and emotional depth, Ryan's books have captivated millions of fans worldwide.

Whether it's the shadowy world of covert operatives or the relentless pursuit of justice, Ryan's stories feature unforgettable characters and high-stakes plots that resonate with fans of Lee Child, Robert Ludlum, and Michael Connelly.

When not writing, Ryan enjoys crafting new ideas with coauthors, running a thriving publishing company, and connecting with readers. Discover the next story that will keep you turning pages late into the night.

Connect with L.T. Ryan
Sign up for his newsletter to hear the latest goings on and receive some free content
➜ https://ltryan.com/jack-noble-newsletter-signup-1

Join the private readers' group
➜ https://www.facebook.com/groups/1727449564174357

Instagram ➜ @ltryanauthor

Visit the website ➜ https://ltryan.com
Send an email ➜ contact@ltryan.com

LAURA CHASE is a corporate attorney-turned-author who brings her courtroom experience to the page in her gripping legal and psychological thrillers. Chase draws on her real-life experience to draw readers into the high-stakes world of courtroom drama and moral ambiguity.

After earning her JD, Chase clerked for a federal judge and thereafter transitioned to big law, where she honed her skills in high-pressure legal environments. Her passion for exploring the darker side of human nature and the gray areas of justice fuels her writing.

Chase lives with her husband, their two sons, a dog and a cat in Northern Florida. When she's not writing or working, she enjoys spending time with her family, traveling, and bingeing true crime shows.

Connect with Laura:

Sign up for her newsletter: www.laurachaseauthor.com/

Follow her on tiktok: @lawyerlaura

Send an email: info@laurachase.com

Made in United States
Orlando, FL
13 November 2025